They fled for their lives as the great Hell-hounds caught their scent and bayed in savage glee. A howl showed that the dogs were close. The cool night air burned in Corbett's straining lungs.

"Ranulf!" he gasped. "You go for some tree. Climb and hide!"

"If I am to die, Master, I prefer to be with you."

Corbett nodded and they staggered on, bodies soaked in sweat, eyes blinded with panic, legs and feet threatening to turn into the heaviest lead. Corbett could have sworn that momentarily he glimpsed another figure, shadow-like, but fled on. Behind him the dogs bayed in triumph, then suddenly there came a terrible scream which clutched Corbett's heart.

———————— ★ ————————

"The pace is excellent..."

—*Mystery News*

"Doherty brings a sense of humanity to all his characters..."

—*Publishers Weekly*

P.C. DOHERTY

The Prince of Darkness

WORLDWIDE.

TORONTO • NEW YORK • LONDON
AMSTERDAM • PARIS • SYDNEY • HAMBURG
STOCKHOLM • ATHENS • TOKYO • MILAN
MADRID • WARSAW • BUDAPEST • AUCKLAND

To Aunt Doreen and Uncle Tom Murphy of Bishop Auckland, Co. Durham

THE PRINCE OF DARKNESS

A Worldwide Mystery/March 1995

First published by St. Martin's Press, Incorporated.

ISBN 0-373-26164-0

Printed in U.S.A.

The
Prince
of
Darkness

ONE

A HEAVY RIVER MIST, boiled in the heat of the day, had rolled in from the Seine making the night more dreadful, shrouding the buildings and palaces of Paris in its grey, wraith-like tendrils. The curfew had sounded, the streets and alleyways were now silent except for scavenging cats and the dregs of the Paris underworld snouting like rats for easy prey. Eudo Tailler, ostensibly a wine merchant from Bordeaux in Gascony, in fact an agent of Edward I of England and his master spy, Hugh Corbett, slipped quietly along an alleyway, dagger half-drawn as he edged towards the dark, decaying house which stood on the corner.

It had been a glorious summer day, the weather proving the prophets of doom wrong, those Jeremiahs who had proclaimed that the first year of the new century would see fire from heaven and blood spurting up to stain the sky. Nothing had happened. Eudo had arrived in Paris at mid-summer 1300 and found little amiss. Of course, his masters in England thought there was; Philip IV, King of France, they insisted, was secretly plotting to seize the English Duchy of Gascony by fair means or foul. The French King's master spy, Seigneur Amaury de Craon, was already in England, poking about in the dark corners of the English court, looking for juicy morsels of scandal.

Eudo suddenly stepped into a darkened doorway as the night watch, four soldiers carrying spears and lanterns, marched past the mouth of the alleyway. The spy

leaned against the door. Oh, there was scandal enough
in England, he thought, and most of it centred round
the Prince of Wales and his former mistress, Lady
Eleanor Belmont, who had been locked up in Godstowe Priory. Yet a bad situation had grown worse because the young prince had recently found the real love
of his life—not the daughter of some nobleman but a
man: the young Gascon catamite, Piers Gaveston. De
Craon would use that, Eudo reflected, to fan the sparks
of gossip into a fiery scandal. In order to seize Gascony, the French would destroy the prince's reputation
and, if that failed, like the hypocrites they were insist
that the heir to the English throne be betrothed to the
French king's daughter, Isabella, in accordance with a
peace treaty forced on England some years earlier.

Oh, the French had been cunning! Either way King
Edward of England was trapped. No wonder Eudo's
master, Hugh Corbett, senior clerk in the English
Chancery, had sent him a stream of instructions begging him to find out the secret counsels of the French.
Eudo smiled. He had been successful and surely he
would reap his well-deserved reward? First, he had
found there was an assassin in England, a member of
the accursed de Montfort family, stalking the King and
plotting his death. Eudo had sent this information directly to King Edward some months earlier but nothing
had come of it so he had mentioned it again in his most
recent despatch to Corbett.

He lifted his hand and wiped the sweat from his brow.
He had done what had been asked, it was up to the King
and Corbett how they used the information he sent. Yet
he had learnt more: the French were not only plotting
mischief around the Prince of Wales' former mistress,

the Lady Eleanor Belmont, they even had a spy at Godstowe where the woman had been immured...

Eudo heard the footfalls of the night watch fade away. He adjusted his cloak, grasped his dagger and continued on his way.

The leprous beggar was crouched as usual in the corner of the alleyway opposite the house.

'Is everything all right?' Eudo whispered.

He could barely make out the huddled outline of the beggar, shrouded in his robe, but he saw the silvery head nod gently and the skeletal hand thrust out for its usual payment. Eudo swallowed, hid his distaste, threw a coin at the man and padded toward the door of the house. As arranged, it was unlocked. He lifted the latch, slipped quietly in and looked around. The flagstoned passageway was dark and empty. A candle flickered weakly in its brass holder fixed high in the wall, affording some light as he climbed the rickety wooden staircase. Eudo was pleased. How fortunate he had been to find Mistress Céleste, a plump young doxy, rosy-cheeked and fresh from the Norman countryside. Eudo had used her charms to bait and trap one of Philip's clerks from the Royal Chancery at the Louvre Palace: the wench proved to be intelligent, sweetly protesting her innocence, promising all sorts of delights as she wheedled one secret after another from the gullible French clerk.

Eudo reached the top of the stairs and gently pushed open the chamber door. The room was dark and he tensed. Something was wrong. Surely Céleste would leave a candle burning? He stood like a dog, sniffing the darkness, his eyes strained against the gloom. He caught the heavy fragrance of Céleste's perfume and made out the sleeping form of the young prostitute on her pallet bed underneath the small, half-open window. Eudo relaxed and grinned. Perhaps the girl was tired after a busy night? Perhaps he could savour some of the joys the young French clerk had experienced?

'Céleste!' he whispered. 'Céleste, it is me, Eudo!'

Silence greeted his words.

'Is there anything wrong?' he asked softly.

Alarmed now, he paused, ears straining for a sound.

He heard the house creak and groan but it was old and the beggar on the corner would surely have alerted him to any approach. Eudo drew his dagger and walked over to the bed.

'Céleste!' he hissed, and gave the girl a vigorous shake.

Her body flopped over and Eudo opened his mouth in a silent scream. Céleste's throat had been slashed from ear to ear and the viscous red blood soaked the bodice of her dress and coagulated in dark pools on the blanket. Eudo felt something warm and sticky on his fingers. Breathing deeply, he stepped back, loosening his cloak as his hand went to his long dagger. He took another step back, then another, turned and dashed for the door. A shadowy figured loomed up but Eudo sank to one knee even as his dagger hissed out, slitting the man's belly. He sprang up and pushed the man aside, clattering down the stairs. Another figure was waiting for him, hooded and menacing. Eudo did not stop but jumped the final few stairs and crashed into his assailant, sending him flying against the hard wall. Eudo was then through, out into the dark, fetid alleyway. He glared across at the beggar.

'You bastard!' he screamed. 'You lying bastard!'

The wretch retreated deeper into his corner. Eudo scrabbled at the ground, picked up a loose cobblestone and sent it crashing into the beggar's skull, knocking him backwards into a moaning, huddled heap. Eudo turned the corner of the alleyway, running down towards the crossroads. He sobbed and groaned as his chest heaved for air and his heart beat like a drum. He knew it was all futile. So far he had been lucky, but where could he go?

He saw a line of men-at-arms suddenly appear at the far side of the square. Eudo stopped and screamed defiance. He would not be taken alive. He was still screaming abuse when the crossbow bolt hit him full in the thigh and sent him crashing to the cobbles, mouthing curses and groans. He grasped the quarrel embedded deep in his flesh and moaned at the sheer agony of it. No rewards now, no journey back to Bordeaux! No more cups of wine! He heard the thud of boots on the cobbled square and felt a mailed foot against his shoulder, pushing him over to sprawl flat on his back. The captain of the French guard took off his helmet and knelt down beside him.

'Well, well, Monsieur,' he murmured. 'Your days of wine and song are over.'

He brought his mailed fist back and gave the English spy a sickening blow across the mouth.

'That's just the beginning of your troubles, Monsieur!' he hissed. 'I lost two good men tonight because of you.' He seized Eudo by the jerkin and dragged him upright. 'But come, the dungeons in the Louvre are only a short walk and there are others who want a few words with you.'

LADY ELEANOR BELMONT sat on the edge of the bed, her heart-shaped face pale and drawn except for the red flush on her cheeks. She wove her fingers together, turning and twisting them as if to vent the excitement which flooded through her. She rose and walked over to the diamond-shaped window. A beautiful August day; the sun was now beginning to set, the stillness of the priory broken only by the clear birdsong from the trees beyond the nunnery walls. Eleanor stopped, straining her eyes as she peered through the casement window. She was sure she had seen men-at-arms—horsemen amongst the trees—her attention drawn by the flash of steel from their weapons. She leaned against the glass, her hot cheek welcoming its coolness. Was someone there? Had they come? No, she could hear nothing except the clatter of the nuns as they filed through the cloisters before Compline. Eleanor sighed, dismissing what must have been another phantasm of her fevered imagination.

She looked around the chamber. All was ready. She drew herself up, gulping in air. Her friend, whoever he was, would surely send help. Soon she would be out of this benighted place, be reunited with her lover and working hard to recapture his affection. Edward might be Prince of Wales and heir to the English crown, but Lady Eleanor had decided she was made of sterner stuff. Hadn't her father reminded her on many occasions that the Belmonts were of noble stock, sturdy and sure?

She would ignore the rumours. Eleanor laughed abruptly to herself then froze as she heard a sound, a slither of footsteps in the corridor outside. She shook her head.

'Surely,' she whispered to herself, 'the Lord Edward means me no harm?'

They were evil people who claimed he wanted her dead but she could not believe that of him. Oh, of course, others might wish it, members of the Prince's secret council—Eleanor would believe anything of *them*, especially the ubiquitous silken-tongued Piers Gaveston, who had ensnared the Prince's heart. Eleanor stamped her foot at the thought of him.

'Gaveston the demon-worshipper!' she hissed. 'Gaveston the limb of Satan! Gaveston the sodomite!'

She calmed herself. And the rest of the coven? Lady Amelia Proudfoot, Prioress, in whose nunnery she was now staying, and Proudfoot's silent shadows, Dames Frances and Catherine? They would do anything to keep her here; poison, the dagger, the garrotte, or the sudden fall...

Eleanor smiled and hugged herself. Oh, she had been so careful, so cautious, watching what she had eaten and drunk, where she had walked, politely refusing any offer to go hunting. After all, the Lady Eleanor smiled sourly to herself, hunting accidents were common. True, she had been sick but this was due to evil humours of the mind caused by loneliness and anxiety. Indeed she had begun to despair, but at last help had come. Some weeks ago, she had found a message here in her chamber, hidden in a small leather wallet. The writer had told her to be of good heart, not to worry, and to look for further messages in the hollowed oak tree near the Galilee Walk on the far side of the chapel. Her well-wisher, whoever he was, had promised to deliver her today so she had told her companions to leave her and go to Compline. Only the ancient ones, Dame Elizabeth and Dame Martha, had remained whilst Lady Amelia and her henchwomen would soon be enthroned in the chapel glorying in their power. Lady Eleanor turned as she heard the old building creak beneath her. A haunted place, people said, apparently ghosts walked here. It was certainly no abode for a young lady, mistress to one of the greatest men in the land.

Eleanor sat back on the bed, chewing her lip, then got up agitatedly, putting her cloak on and playing with the ring on her finger, the Prince's last gift to her, a huge blue sapphire which always shimmered in the light. She turned her head, straining to hear. Surely there was another sound, not just the creaking of the stairs? Someone was outside. She heard the slither of footsteps along the gallery. Surely they were approaching? Lady Eleanor looked at the door. Good, the key was turned in the lock. She patted her hair and pulled up her hood. She wished Dame Agatha was here. Perhaps it had been foolish to dismiss her. Again the sound. Lady Eleanor stood transfixed. She watched the latch of the door go down. Suddenly she panicked, but too late! She heard the soft knock and knew she would have to answer.

LADY ELEANOR WAS in the minds of other people that day. Edward, Prince of Wales, and his favourite, Piers Gaveston, had once again quarrelled violently about her and then become reconciled, swearing they would divert themselves by a hunt. They had left Woodstock Palace with their soldiers, grooms, huntsmen and retainers. A gaudy, colourful masque, their horses sleek and well fed, resplendent in their scarlet and blue dressings and silver-gilt saddles and housings. Amidst shouts, the bray of silver trumpets and the glorious fluttering of gold-encrusted banners, the royal hunting party made its way down the dusty tracks of Oxfordshire which wound around the great, unfenced cornfields where the stooks were piled high as farmers laboured to bring the harvest in.

The sun was still brilliant in a light blue sky. The grass on either side of the track was alive with the sound of crickets and the scurrying of mice and voles fleeing from the harvesters. Above them a lark soared, singing for sheer pleasure, whilst in the distant trees, blackbird and thrush trilled their hearts out. Suddenly, a darkened scarecrow of a man seemed to step from nowhere on to the track, his long hair black as night, flapping like raven's wings around his gaunt face, his clothes more like bandages around his emaciated body. Prince Edward lifted a hand and the cavalcade stopped.

The Lord Edward had immediately recognised the man: a mad prophet who had been stalking round the walls of the palace for the last few days. The fellow claimed he came from the Devil's Anvil, the hot burning sands which lay to the south of the Middle Sea; his dirty and rag-attired figure now stood motionless though his eyes flamed like burning coals.

'I bring a warning!' the prophet boomed. 'A warning of death and disgrace. A warning against the soft perfumed flesh of the whores who lounge on feathered beds and bawl of their lust!' The fiery eyes flashed again; one sinewy arm was raised in quivering anger. 'You bawds who gulp wine from deep-bowled cups, be warned! This age will be cleansed by Death himself! Mark my words, he lurks in the sombre forests. He mounts his pale horse and soon he will be here. Be warned, you strumpets and whores!'

The group of silk-clad couriers behind the Prince simpered, laughed softly, and turned away. The mad prophet searched out the tall, blond figure of the Prince as he slouched on his horse under the blue and gold banner of England. The prophet's eyes narrowed.

'Repent!' he hissed. 'You young men who lust after each other's flesh and seek comfort in forbidden love!'

The Prince grinned and, raising one purple-gloved hand, touched his smaller, darker companion.

'He talks of us, Piers.''

The young Gascon's expression grew harsher though it was nonetheless a girlish face with its smooth olive cheeks, perfect features, and neatly cropped, dark red hair. Girlish, innocent, except for the eyes—a surprisingly light blue like a spring sky fresh washed by the rain. These were hard and empty.

'I do not think so, My Lord,' Gaveston rasped.

Prince Edward shook his head and took a silver coin out of his purse.

'A wager, Piers. The fellow is bound to be speaking about me.' He stroked his moustache. 'Let's be frank. I am the only one here worth talking about.'

The prophet must have heard him.

'You, Edward, Prince of Wales!' he roared. 'Son of a greater father, bearer of his name but not his majesty. Yes, I warn you, you and your grasping catamite, Gaveston, son of a whore!' The prophet's voice fell to a hiss. 'Son of a witch, you come from the Devil and to the Devil you will go. Be sure, Prince Edward, you do not go with him, for all of Satan's army bays for Gaveston's sin-drenched soul!'

Prince Edward nodded solemnly.

'Most interesting,' he commented. He smiled and stretched out a hand. 'Your silver, Piers.'

The Gascon, grumbling with rage, handed it over.

'Your Grace,' Gaveston muttered, 'let me kill the bastard!'

''No, Piers, not now. You will only alarm the hawks and spoil the hunt.' He stroked the Gascon's dark hair.

'Don't be a scold, Piers,' he whispered. 'You are becoming more like Father and the Lady Eleanor every day.'

The Lord Edward urged his horse forward as the prophet slipped off the road. Gaveston turned and, crooking a finger, summoned closer the captain of the guard.

'Kill the bastard!' he muttered. 'No, not now. But before he's a day older.'

The sun had hardly moved in the heavens when the mad prophet's body, his throat slashed from ear to ear, was dumped in a scum-rimmed marsh deep in the forest and sank without trace. An hour later the mercenary captain rejoined the royal party as they sat on their horses amongst the thick, rich weeds of a slow moving river. The soldier nodded at Gaveston, who winked back, smiled, and slipped the hood off the falcon which stirred restlessly on his wrist, the bells of its jesses tinkling a warning of the death it would bring to this soft, green darkness.

'Now I have drawn blood,' Gaveston muttered to himself, 'I can enjoy the hunt.'

He waited until the beaters roused a huge heron which broke cover and soared up above the trees. Gaveston lifted his wrist, stroked his favourite bird with the finger of his gauntlet and let it loose. The falcon, its dark wings spread like the angel of death, flew in pursuit; it rose high in the sky, paused, drifting on the late summer breeze, and then, wings back, plunged like an arrow. The falcon struck the heron with a high-pitched scream and a burst of feathers. The courtiers 'oohed' and clapped their hands but gasped as the old heron turned its long neck and, drawing back its head, plunged its daggered beak deep into the falcon's body.

Gaveston watched, speechless, as the falcon fell in a bundle of blood-soaked feathers, whilst the heron swooped low to hide in the reeds.

'Quite extraordinary,' the Prince murmured. 'I have heard of it, but that's the first time I have seen it.' He nudged his favourite playfully, 'A warning, Piers,' he whispered. 'You aim too high! The Earldom of Cornwall *and* the premier place on my council—but not now!' He raised a finger to his lips. 'Not yet, Piers. Whatever would my father, not to mention the Lady Eleanor, say to that?'

Gaveston glared back, wondering once again if he had truly broken the hold of that bitch, Eleanor Belmont. Prince Edward looked away. Would Gaveston heed the warning? he wondered. Edward loved Piers more than life itself but dared not prefer him any higher. The Prince glanced sideways at his favourite: Gaveston had his ways but Edward knew his dark side. He had seen the small, yellow wax figures his paramour kept; one with a crown representing the king, the other with a little scarlet skirt, the colour of a whore, Gaveston's description of the Lady Eleanor Belmont. The prince stared into the darkness of the trees. So many secrets, so much tension! When would his father die? And, above all, when would the bitch Eleanor?

FROM A WINDOW HIGH in Woodstock Palace Sir Amaury de Craon, spy, assassin and special envoy of his most sacred majesty, Philip IV of France, watched the Prince's hunting party return up the winding gravelled path of the palace. De Craon thought fleetingly of the Lady Eleanor as he studied the two figures riding so close together, ahead of everyone else, the Lord Edward and Gaveston, chatting like David and Jonathan

coming home from a day's hunt. De Craon glared
down. Lady Eleanor he had not liked but Gaveston he
could gladly murder.

De Craon sucked in his breath, trying to calm his
rage, and stared up at the sky. The day was now drawing to a close. A slight chilly wind snapped and flut-
tered the banners carried in front of the Prince. De
Craon shivered and pulled his cloak tightly about him:
with his sharp, pointed features, russet hair and goatee
beard, the Frenchman looked like some inquisitive fox
watching his prey approach. Great God, he fumed, how
he hated Gaveston! The Gascon was no more than the
son of a jumped up yeoman farmer and a witch from
the English province of Gascony; indeed, a convicted
witch who had been burnt alive, chained to a barrel in
the middle of Bordeaux marketplace. What should he
do about Gaveston? de Craon wondered for the ump-
teenth time. Before he had left Paris his master, Philip
IV, had taken de Craon into his velvet-draped, secret
chamber in the Louvre Palace and explained his mis-
sion. They'd sat at a table, bare except for the candle
flickering in its stand.

'Always remember, de Craon,' the French King had
remarked, 'the Duchy of Gascony is in the hands of
Edward of England. By rights it should be in mine!'
Philip had grasped the candlestick. 'It nearly was,' he
continued, 'but His Holiness the Pope intervened. Now
Edward has Gascony and I have a peace treaty.'

De Craon had watched Philip closely.

'However,' his master hissed, 'I intend to have Gascony, the peace treaty, and much more. According to
the Holy Father's dictate, Edward I of England was to
marry my sister and he is welcome to her, but his feckless Prince of Wales is to wed my beloved daughter,

once she is old enough for this marriage to take place. Now, if that happens, one day my grandson will sit on the throne of England whilst another becomes Duke of Gascony. So, in time, that province and perhaps England itself will be absorbed under the French crown.' Philip had paused, licking his bloodless lips.

'However,' he continued, 'all that is in the future and there is a more immediate path I could follow. You are to go to England and confirm my daughter's betrothal, but you must insist that the Prince of Wales has no scandal attached to him. He is to remove from his person his favourite whore, Eleanor Belmont. Otherwise,' Philip gave one of his rare smiles, 'in the light of such scandal, I shall appeal to the Holy Father, the treaty will be null and void, and my troops will be all over Gascony within a week. Now the Prince may well agree to that—I hear he tires of the woman—in which case, a third path is open to me.'

Philip had risen, come round the table and whispered the most secret instructions in de Craon's ear. The French envoy remembered these now and smiled. Perhaps he should follow that path. He clenched his fists in excitement: if he did, he might settle scores, not only with Edward of England, the benighted Prince of Wales and his male bawd, Gaveston, but also with Master Hugh Corbett, de Craon's old rival and enemy.

TWO

HUGH CORBETT, senior clerk and master spy of Edward of England, was dreaming a dreadful dream. He was standing beneath the spreading branches of one of the elm trees which stood along the boundaries of Godstowe Priory in Oxfordshire. A late summer sun was shining but the air was silent, eerie, devoid of birdsong. Alongside him, from the branch of a nearby tree, hung a body, its neck broken, head to one side; it hung there like some ancient sacrifice or the Figure of Death from the Tarot. Corbett felt compelled to turn but found he could not. His gaze was fixed on the windows, like empty eye-sockets, of Godstowe Priory. He stirred. No sound broke the chill silence except the hollow screeching of cruel-eyed peacocks and, in faint cadence, the ghostly chanting of the nuns.

In his nightmare Corbett walked across a lush green lawn, the shadows behind forcing him on. No sign of life was apparent as he crossed the gravel path up to the great door of the nunnery; unlatched, half-open, he pushed this aside and entered the cold, dark house. A guttering row of candles, their flickering flames filling the silent hall with dancing shadows, formed a path leading to the bottom of steep stone stairs. There, as if sleeping, lay the body of a young woman, her face half-averted, one pale ivory cheek peeping out from under the hood pulled over her head. Corbett walked softly across, knelt and turned the body over; the young woman's arms flapped like the wings of a fallen bird.

He pushed back the hood, expecting to see the face of
Eleanor Belmont, former mistress of the Lord Edward, but silently screamed in horror: the dead, ice-cold
features belonged to his wife, Maeve. Above him, in the
far darkness of the house, a low mocking laugh greeted
his discovery but, as he jumped up, Corbett awoke,
soaked in sweat, in his own bed chamber in the Manor
of Leighton.

Chest heaving, Corbett sat up beneath the blue and
gold canopy stretched across the carved uprights of his
huge four-poster bed. The window casement rattled
under the persistent batterings of a sobbing wind and
Corbett wondered if he had been merely dreaming or
else visited by some dark phantasm of the night. He
looked quickly to his right side but Maeve, his wife, was
lost in gentle sleep, her silver-blonde hair spread out like
a halo across the huge bolster. He leaned over and
gently kissed her on the brow. Outside, the lonely call
of a hunting owl and the death shrieks of some animal
in the shadowy darkness of the trees re-kindled his
sombre mood.

Corbett got up, dressed in his robe and, with tinder
and taper, lit a candle. He walked to the heavy, thick
arras which hung on the far wall of his bed chamber and
pulled this aside, the light of his flickering candle making embroidered figures spring to ghostly life. Corbett
grasped the cunningly contrived lever, pressed it, and
the wooden panelling gently swung back on its oiled
hinges, giving him access to his secret chamber. This
perfectly square, white-washed room was the centre of
his work, the one place Corbett could be alone to think,
to plot, and take every measure against the King's enemies, both at home and abroad.

He stretched and felt his shoulder twinge with pain where, months previously, the mad priest, de Luce, had plunged his dagger. Corbett had survived, nursed by Maeve, now his wife of six months and already two months gone with child. He smiled; a source for happiness there but not here, in this darkened chamber. Edward I of England had given him Leighton Manor on the borders of Essex in recognition for services rendered but also in return for his continued efforts in building up a network of spies in England, Scotland, France and the Low Countries. Corbett had been happy to accept the charge but the information he gathered carried further problems: he felt he had sown dragons' teeth and was about to reap the whirlwind.

The clerk lit the cresset torches fixed in their iron brackets on the wall and walked over to his intricately carved oak desk; the secrets he had locked away in its hidden drawers and compartments were the source of his present cares and anxiety. From a stone beneath the desk, Corbett removed some keys, lit the two candelabra which stood on either side of the desk, sat down and unlocked the secret compartment.

He plucked out the King's letter, the one he had received the previous evening as he and Maeve ate their dinner in the great darkened hall below. It had been sent in secret cipher which Corbett had already decoded. He picked up a quill from the writing tray, smoothed a piece of parchment and began to draft his own reply. A memorandum to clear his own thoughts rather than to inform the King.

Item—King Edward is old, locked in combat against Scottish rebels whilst trying to defend his possessions in France. The English Exchequer and Treasury are bankrupt. The King's only way forward is the peace treaty laid down by the Papacy, which stipulates the betrothal of the Prince of Wales to the infant daughter of the French King, Philip IV.

Item—the Prince of Wales is feckless, pleasure-loving, a possible sodomite. He is dominated by the Warlock, Gaveston, and hates his father. The breach between father and son is permanent. The King would like to banish Gaveston but this may well lead to civil war which would only assist the Scots and certainly draw in the French.

Item—Philip IV of France had demanded the removal of Eleanor Belmont, and the Lord Edward had been only too pleased to agree with this. Eleanor had been placed under virtual house arrest in Godstowe Priory, a place the Prince could control from his nearby palace of Woodstock.

Item—were the rumours true that the Lady Eleanor had been ill of a malady of the breast and did the Prince send medicines to her? If so, were they really medicines, or poisons?

Item—on Sunday last Lady Eleanor Belmont had not joined the nuns at Compline or the evening meal afterwards in the refectory. Indeed, she had told her companions amongst them to leave her alone. The convent building where Lady Eleanor had her chambers had been empty during the evening service except for two aged nuns, Dame Elizabeth and Dame Matilda. After Compline all the nuns had gone to the refectory as was customary. Once the meal was over (again as was customary), the Lady Prioress with the two Sub-prioresses, Dame Frances and Dame Catherine, had walked around the main building, gone through the open door and found Lady Eleanor Belmont cloaked and hooded at the bottom of the stairs. They claimed her neck had been broken from the fall, yet the hood over her head had not been disturbed.

Item—did the Lady Eleanor Belmont fall? If so, why was her clothing not disturbed? And why had the old nuns not heard the crash of her fall and her cries? If she had fallen, where was she going to or returning from? Was it suicide? Reports said that the Lady Eleanor had been melancholic, the victim of malignant humours.

Corbett stroked his cheek with the quill of the pen, half listening to the wind moaning like some wandering spirit amongst the trees: their branches rustled, one of them tapping insistently against the window. He dipped the quill into the blue-green ink. Had the Lady Eleanor been murdered? And if so, by whom? The Lord Edward? He had been at the nearby palace of Woodstock. By the Lord Gaveston, who had also been present there? Or by both in complicity? Or was it murder by someone in the priory? Either because of jealousy or on the orders of someone else. The French perhaps? There was a delegation from Philip now in England led by Corbett's old adversary, Amaury de Craon.

Corbett bit the knuckles of his hand. De Craon, his counterpart on the French council, was a skilful, devious man who bore no love for Edward of England, or, indeed, Edward's chief clerk. The French would love a scandal involving the English crown. Belmont had been the Prince of Wales' paramour but she had been removed from the court and so they had no grievance there. Of course, Gaveston could have taken her place but the French had no proof that this relationship with the young Prince was anything but an honourable friendship. However, if de Craon started insinuating that the Prince or Gaveston were involved in murder, Philip might well decide the betrothal was off, the peace treaty be null and void, and the English would find themselves in a costly and bloody war. The clerk grasped his quill and began to write.

Item—they had information from a spy in Essex that the Prince of Wales had been secretly married to the Lady Eleanor Belmont. Was this another reason for the Prince to murder the poor girl?

Corbett suddenly went cold. The Prince, or his father? Corbett had no illusions about either the King or his son; both were equally ruthless and self-seeking.

Item—another piece of information from Eudo Tailler, an English spy busy in the shadows of the Louvre Palace. Eudo had sent it weeks ago but had since disappeared. His message was cryptic enough: a member of the de Montfort family was loose in England.

Corbett's anxiety increased. Forty years ago, eight years before Corbett had been born, Edward I had crushed a savage revolt led by Earl Simon de Montfort. The King, who had so nearly lost his crown, defeated the Earl's army outside Evesham. De Montfort had been killed and Edward had told his soldiers to hack his body and feed it to the royal dogs. The remnants of de Montfort's family had fled abroad and, whenever possible, sent assassins into England against the King and the royal family. The feud had lasted decades. A few years previously the King had used Corbett himself to uncover one of these secret covens. Corbett rubbed his face as he remembered the dark passion of Alice, the coven leader. Who was this new assassin, he pondered, and where was he now?

'Hugh! Hugh!'

Corbett looked up. Maeve stood in the doorway, one of his cloaks wrapped about her. Despite his anxieties, he was struck by her beauty: the silver hair, the skin which glowed like burnished gold in the candle light, and those blue-violet eyes now heavy with sleep.

'What are you staring at, man?' she asked.

'You know what I am looking at,' he murmured.

He rose and snuffed out the candles and led her back into the bed chamber.

'Hugh, what are you doing?' Maeve struggled free and faced him gravely. 'For God's sake, it's the middle of the night! I awake and find my bed cold and you gone.' She smiled, letting her cloak drop to the floor, and put her arms around his waist. 'The King's letter, isn't it? The business at Godstowe?'

He took a deep breath.

'Yes, and tomorrow I must go there. As soon as Ranulf returns.'

She made him sit down on the edge of the bed beside her.

'The woman was murdered, wasn't she?'

Corbett nodded. 'Yes, I fear so.'

'And the King will be held responsible?'

Corbett rubbed his face in his hands.

'Yes, I think he will. If a scandal breaks, God knows what will happen.'

He took her hand in his.

'For forty years, Maeve, there has been no civil war in England. Yet the Lady Eleanor's death could cause one.'

She shivered and rolled under the thick coverlets.

'Hugh,' she murmured, 'you will not solve it now, in the middle of the night!'

He smiled bleakly.

'Perhaps there will never be a solution, not even in the full light of day.'

RANULF-ATTE-NEWGATE, body servant to Hugh Corbett, turned his horse on to the sun-baked track which led round to Leighton Manor just as the bell of the village church tolled the Angelus. He turned and watched the labourers bent low in the fields gathering the stooks of corn and placing them in great two-wheeled carts. He heard the sound of their laughter; a woman singing a lullaby to a child held at her breast; now and again, carried on the breeze, the shouts of children playing on the banks of a brook as their busy parents gathered in the harvest.

Ranulf had been up to London on his master's business in the Chancery as well as calling on certain goldsmiths in the Poultry. He had also visited his son, the glorious offspring of one of his affairs. Ranulf was pleased that the boy was looking more like him as every day passed: the same, spiked reddish hair, generous mouth, freckled face, snub nose and cheeky green eyes, sharp as a cat's. The child had been born months earlier in the depths of winter and Corbett had persuaded Ranulf to give him to some foster-parents in Threadneedle Street. Ranulf had agreed but then changed his mind, taken him back, and promptly lost his son in a tavern. A saucy, heavy-bosomed wench had caught his eye, Ranulf had put the baby down, went to take his pleasure then walked home, forgetting about the little bundle he had entrusted to the tavern-keeper's wife. On Corbett's advice he had subsequently returned the child to his heart-broken foster-parents.

'A good decision,' Ranulf murmured to himself.

He loved the boy but never could remember where he had left him last. A squirrel chattered, a bird flew out of a gorse bush. Ranulf's hand went towards his dag-

ger. He felt uneasy in the countryside, missed the city
and wished that Corbett would return to their house in
Bread Street, but his master's new wife, Maeve, had
changed all that. Ranulf groaned to himself. He lusted
after most women. In fact, Ranulf found any women of
whatever degree or age attractive, if not for seducing,
then as a useful target for his good-natured bantering or
teasing.

Maeve-app-Llewellyn was different. Ranulf feared
her. Those chilling blue eyes which seemed to be able to
read his every thought; her shrewd management of his
master's affairs, be it buying a field or placating that old
grey granite-faced King. When Maeve was there Hugh
seemed to relax, even smile. Ranulf stirred, easing his
aching backside as he urged his horse through the
manor gates. She had changed Corbett. Oh, his master
was still secretive and withdrawn, but more even-
tempered, cooler and more calculating. On previous
occasions Corbett had worked in the Chancery, accept-
ing individual assignments for the old King. Now all
that had changed. Corbett acted as if he loved the intrigue, building up a system of spies which stretched like
some huge net from Rome to Avignon, Paris, Lille,
Edinburgh and Dublin.

Ranulf reigned in his horse and listened to the sound
of the woodland as Maeve had urged him to. He shook
his head. He would give a gold piece to hear the sound
of the hucksters and coster-mongers of London, the
lusty shouts of the apprentices and the raucous bawl-
ing of stall-holders. He looked around him. There was
too much space here, the air was too fresh and the
prospect of hard work imminent. There were no soldiers for Ranulf to draw into a game with his loaded
dice or crooked chequer-board. No pretty girls to make

eyes at and, above all, no Mistress Sempler, the volup-
tuous young wife of an ageing woolsmith.

Ranulf smiled like the cat who had drunk the cream.
He had spent a pleasant time the previous evening con-
soling the good lady during her husband's absence. He
thought of her white, soft as satin body, nubile and
generous as she stood dressed in nothing but her head-
dress and gartered hose. He groaned again, cursed
softly, and urged his horse up into the grassy area before the manor door, scattering the lazy sheep grazing
there.

Ranulf, however, could never be despondent for long:
after all, his master was now the landlord of well-
stocked barns, granaries, and lush meadows, and Ranulf could always pretend he had been very busy in London and so earn some reward. He licked his lips as he
dismounted and assumed a doleful expression. He had
rehearsed his speech. He would present matters in their
worst light, depicting the toils and tribulations he had
endured in pursuing his master's business...yet he had
scarcely prepared himself for what happened. Corbett
was waiting just inside the oak-panelled hall, cloaked,
booted and spurred; his saddle bags, packed and
strapped down, were being taken out by a servant.
Ranulf expected the worst when he saw the grin on
Corbett's face.

'*Benedicte*, Ranulf!' he exclaimed. 'I have been
waiting. We are off to Godstowe Priory in Oxfordshire. Your son, how is the little cherub?'

Ranulf caught the sarcasm in his master's voice and
grinned. His master loved little Hugh, or Hugolino, but
often described him as a monster, a true son of his father, from his spiked hair to his innate ability to fall into
mischief.

'Well, Master, as well as can be expected,' Ranulf replied, glimpsing Maeve coming out through the chancery door. She looked resplendent in a simple white wimple and a long, dark maroon dress clasped at the neck with silver-white bows, rather spoilt by the heavy belt she wore around her swelling waist, which bore most of the keys to the manor chambers. As usual Maeve looked solemn though Ranulf saw the mischief dancing in her eyes.

'You had a pleasant time, Ranulf, in London?'

The servant was going to lie but Maeve caught his glance.

'Yes, Mistress.'

'No excitement or frivolity?'

'Of course not,' Ranulf muttered. 'Just hard work.'

He glanced away but Maeve continued her inquisition. She would find out about Mistress Sempler whether he liked it or not, so Ranulf mumbled some excuse and fled to his own chamber. He washed his face in the lavarium, packed a new set of saddle bags, plucking whatever possessions he could find from his customarily chaotic chamber, and went down the side stairs out to the front of the manor where a groom had brought fresh horses and a sumpter pony. In the hall Maeve was growing truculent at Corbett's strictures against baiting Ranulf.

'You will miss me?' he asked, changing the conversation abruptly, grabbing her by the hands and pulling her close.

'No,' she teased.

'You'll look after the fencing in the long meadow?'

'No, I'll break it down.'

'And the grange with loose slats?'

Maeve shook her head.

'I'll burn that as well, together with the tithe barn. And I'll tell Father Martin, with his usual litany of complaints about his congregation using the graveyard as a playground, to go hang himself. After that,' she shook her head, 'God knows what I'll do!'

Corbett grabbed her, kissing her passionately.

'Then I'll bid you adieu, wife.'

He winked at her, smiled, and slipped through the door to the waiting horse.

CORBETT AND RANULF travelled north, passing through small villages, little more than a cluster of rickety, thatched cottages clustered around some church or manor house. Soon harvest time would be over. Corbett remembered such days from his youth as he saw the crops standing high and yellow, next to fields of fallow green and the narrow ribs of turf which separated one village's strip from another. The cottages themselves were no more grand than that owned by his father with their walls of wattle and daub and the small patch of garden to grow onions, cabbages, garlic and shallots.

His horse stumbled and Corbett cursed, Ranulf quietly admiring his master's grasp of some of the filthiest oaths he had ever heard. The roads were ruined by huge potholes filled with makeshift clumps of brushwood or mounds of earth which would be washed away in the first heavy shower. They stopped at a village inn for a dish of spiced eels and a few gulps of heady local ale. The place was packed with men and women, country folk, falconers, huntsmen, lackeys from the stables, bakers, brewers, cooks and kitchen scullions. They all crowded in for their pottle of ale, rubbing shoulders with shepherd and hog-herds, teasing and slapping the laundresses and dairy maids who came to exchange gossip or catch the eye of their favourite swain.

Corbett sat in a corner and listened to Ranulf's description of affairs in London before quietly informing him of what awaited them at Godstowe Priory. Ranulf's face paled. Gaveston and the Lord Edward were twice as dangerous as the old King; Gaveston in particular, a spiteful, powerful lord who had made his presence felt in both court and city. For the first time since attending Mass at Christmas, Ranulf closed his eyes and really prayed that his master would not fail or slip from royal favour. Corbett was truly caught in the raging animosity between Edward and his truculent heir. If he failed the King, Corbett would certainly feel the royal displeasure, but the Prince of Wales was irrational, veering like a bird on the wing, one moment the cheerful companion, the common man; the next standing on every inch of his authority. Gaveston was worse; he was just downright dangerous. Ranulf loved his master, even though he might quietly cheat him of the odd coin or two and silently mock his solemn ways but, if Corbett fell, so would he. Ranulf stood up and ordered another black-jack of ale from the greasy aproned slattern to drown the panic curdling in his stomach.

'All of us know about Eleanor Belmont!' he exclaimed. 'They were talking about her death at the Guildhall and in St. Paul's Walk.' He looked enquiringly at his master.

Corbett sat up and dragged his eyes away from the relic-seller who had now moved into the tavern with his bag of goods.

'Who do they say is responsible?'

'They blame the Prince, or even the old King.'

'What else do they say, Ranulf?'

'How the Prince loves Gaveston more than any man does his wife. The old ones talk about the return of civil war, and the armourers and fletchers are doing brisk business.'

Corbett nodded and sat back on the bench. His spies had told him the same; up and down the country the great lords were seeing to the repair of their castles, laying in provisions and arms against possible siege. Would war come? Godstowe might hold the answer.

Corbett looked out of the door and saw the daylight was beginning to fade so they continued their journey, keeping a wary eye as the sun began to sink and they followed the old Roman Road north into Oxfordshire. Earlier it had been busy with merchants, students in their tattered gowns, mountebanks, or the occasional friar wheeling his portable altar from village to village. Now, as evening fell, despite the warm summer closeness, Corbett knew the road was a dangerous place. The woods and desolate moorlands were inhabited by landless and lawless men, filthy verminous beings dressed in tattered, weather-stained garments, disfigured by every sore and disease under the sun. Such men plagued this highway, even boasting of their deeds, telling their bruised and wounded victims how they had been robbed and beaten by 'Rawhead', 'Bloody Bones' or 'Robin Badfellow', or whatever such name the outlaws assumed. Corbett touched the sword and dagger strapped to his belt and, feeling more comfortable, urged his tired horse into another canter.

They arrived late at night at the village of Woodstock, which lay between the palace and the priory. They lodged in a chamber of The Bull tavern, which stood at the far edge of the town on the forest fringes. Corbett, ever prudent, spent his money carefully; the room they obtained was really a garret, furnished with a trestle straw bed which he and Ranulf would share, together with a woollen coverlet, chest, table and two stools. They were promised a pot of watered ale in the morning, a mess of oats and a meal at night. The poxy-faced landlord also agreed to provide stabling and fodder for their horses.

After his master had retired, Ranulf went down to the taproom, taking with him a small bag of goods he always carried in such rural areas; a few jars filled with coloured water and crushed flower petals, hair from a boiled red dog, crushed skin from a dead man's head, mixed with grease. These and other delicacies Ranulf sold to the landlord and his customers as cures for every known ailment under the sun. Satisfied that he had at least recouped some of his master's losses, he pocketed their money, stole back upstairs and, lying on one edge of the trestle bed, slept the sleep of the just.

AT GODSTOWE PRIORY, however, murder had once more taken up camp. The aged Dame Martha was busy arranging an unaccustomed bath in her large spacious chamber. A screen had been set up around it and cooks from the kitchen had brought up great earthenware jugs, filling the wooden tub with scalding hot water. Dame Martha wanted to look her best. She was sure the Lady Prioress would be very interested in what she knew.

Dame Martha had taken off her brown serge robe lined with blue, the habit of her Order, the Daughters of Syon, and was busy, dressed only in her white linen shift, placing the screen more closely round the bath. She made sure the chamber door was locked and bolted, picked up the wine goblet and sipped it greedily.

She would have liked some soap, the perfumed type, fragrant and sweet-smelling which the priory had imported from Castille. She had used some three months previously when she had last bathed just before the Easter celebrations.

Dame Martha touched her hair, noticing how greasy the grey locks were. She stood, sucking on her gums, and her little black eyes hardened. Yes, she had to look her best when the Lady Amelia saw her: Dame Martha wanted to impress her as being perceptive and clever and not be dismissed as some garrulous old nun lost in stupid daydreams. She didn't want one of those bitches, Dame Frances or Dame Catherine, pooh-poohing her information as some fevered phantasm of an ageing mind. No, Dame Martha had seen something the night the royal whore had died, something which just didn't fit into place, and she would use her knowledge to get more for herself: some sweetmeats, perhaps linen sheets or bigger portions from the refectory. After all, she deserved them; she had given long years of service to the Order.

Dame Martha doffed the linen shift and climbed into the bath, allowing her vein-streaked, decaying body to sink into the hot, relaxing water. She leaned her head back, then sat up as Murder tapped on her door.

THREE

CORBETT AND RANULF arrived at Godstowe late in the morning, just after Dame Martha's drowned cadaver was sheeted and moved to the death house, a small brick building which stood behind the priory church. The two riders studied the convent buildings which nestled at the foot of a shallow, wooded valley. Facing them was a high, double-gated entrance and further along the steep curtain wall, the postern door or Galilee Gate leading to the forest.

Corbett patted his horse as it stirred restlessly at the faint tolling of the priory bell calling the lay workers in from the fields beyond the walls for their mid-day meal. The priory was a grand building built from the yellow stone carved from local quarries. The main house, a two-storeyed building, was built in a square around the cloister garth. Beyond this was the church with its red-tiled roof and soaring towers. Corbett identified the other buildings: the infirmary, the novitiate, the chapter house built above the refectory, the Prioress' house at the far side of the church, and then, huddled up against the walls, the maltings, kiln room and other outbuildings. A place of ostensible serenity, contemplation and prayer, Corbett thought. Still, he must force himself to see it as a place soaked in blood and intrigue.

'Ranulf.' He turned in the saddle and looked across at his servant. 'Godstowe is a nunnery, the women reputedly consecrated to God. Be prudent and remember my advice—nothing will be what it appears. Oh, by the way, what was in that bag you took down to the tap-room last night?'

'Nothing, Master.' Ranulf gazed back in round-eyed innocence.

Corbett grunted and they cantered down the hill following the path up to the main gate. Ranulf pulled at the bell cord hanging there and kicked his boot against the small postern door. A tall, thin pole of a man with a face as white as snow, bleary eyes, and a nose so red it flared like a beacon, opened the small door and stepped out, half-closing it behind him.

'What do you want?' he snapped. He studied the dark face of the clerk, noting the expensive quilted cote hardie, woollen hose and costly Spanish riding boots. 'I mean,' he added more politely, 'what business brings you here?'

He was joined by two men-at-arms dressed in the blue and gold livery of the Prince of Wales, well armed with sword and dagger, their faces hidden by the nose-guards of their conical helmets.

'Bugger off!' one of them shouted.

He swayed slightly and, behind Corbett, even Ranulf could smell the stench of ale.

Corbett urged his horse forward, freed his foot from the stirrup and pushed the guard up against the gate, pressing his boot firmly into the man's chest.

'My name is Corbett,' he announced quietly. 'Hugh Corbett, senior clerk in the Chancery of the King and his special envoy to Godstowe Priory. I treat you courteously so I resent your bad manners. Now,' he turned to the porter, 'you will either open that gate or I will kill one of you!'

He smiled. 'After all, it is treason to interfere with a royal envoy.'

Corbett withdrew his foot and both soldiers scuttled away like rabbits whilst Red Nose hastily unlocked one of the great gates and led them in. He didn't even stop to lock it behind him, so eager was he to show them to the stables. After that one of the soldiers, mumbling a profuse apology, led them across to the Prioress' lodgings. Word of the débâcle at the gate must have preceded them for Lady Amelia was already awaiting their arrival in her cool upper chamber with its painted blue walls, polished wooden floor and oval-shaped windows filled with precious coloured glass. The Lady Prioress sat in the centre of the chamber on her favourite throne-like chair. She rose as Corbett entered, extending one elegant hand for him to kiss.

'You are most welcome, Master Corbett. We heard you were coming. I must apologise for the greeting.' She smiled falsely. 'But we have so many curiosity seekers. Lady Eleanor's death draws constant visitors here. Anyway you are most welcome, Master Corbett. I did think His Grace would send . . .' Her voice trailed off.

'Someone more important than a clerk, My Lady?'

She nodded her head.

'Then, My Lady, you are disappointed!'

Corbett looked at the haughty face framed by its white starched wimple: the gimlet eyes, imperious nose, and a mouth no more than a line. Lady Amelia smelt of perfume, crushed herbs, and something deeper, more cloying. This lady, Corbett thought, would kill if her honour or pride were at stake. Lady Amelia, however, disregarded his answer and graciously introduced her two companions, the Sub-prioresses, who had been sitting on either side of her like two fire dogs: Dame

Frances, tall, thin and dry, hard-eyed, and sour-faced
with twisted lips; Dame Catherine, comely, plump and
pert, cheery-faced and with a generous mouth though
her eyes were like two black pebbles in her rosy face.
Lady Amelia indicated a chair for Corbett. She clapped
her hands and a servant brought in cups of malmsey
and a plate of sweetmeats. Ranulf she ignored and left
to stand behind his master. He swallowed his pride as he
studied the nuns. Hell's teeth, a most unholy trinity!
Dame Catherine, however, drew his glance; she was
studying Corbett intently, her small pink tongue constantly wetting her lips. Ranulf grinned to himself. A
wanton one there, he thought, and began to daydream
quietly of what would happen if he and the good dame
were alone in some small, cosy chamber. The Prioress
settled herself, allowing a faint smile to grace her face.
She nibbled at the doucettes.

'What does His Grace the King command?' she began.

'His Grace requires nothing save a full explanation of
the Lady Eleanor's death.'

Lady Amelia made a face.

'We regret Lady Eleanor's death, as we do that of the
unfortunate Dame Martha. One of our sisters,' she
added quickly, noting the puzzlement in Corbett's face.
'She was found drowned in her bath this morning. Remember, Master Clerk, in the midst of life we are in
death.'

'Yes, but it makes a difference how Death comes.'

'In Lady Eleanor's case, by accident.'

Corbett adjusted his belt and settled himself more
comfortably.

'Was she melancholic?' he asked.

'A little. She was often heard praying to be delivered from her sickness. She had a malady of the breast. Dame Catherine?' She turned to her cheery-faced companion.

The fat nun shrugged as if freeing herself from a daydream.

'Lady Eleanor,' she piped up, 'had a malignancy in her breast. The Prince sent her medicines.'

'Did he bring them himself?' Corbett asked.

'Oh, no.'

'Did any visitors come?'

'Of course not!' Lady Amelia snapped. 'We are a convent, not a guest house.'

'These medicines—why should the Prince be so concerned?'

'The Prince is a caring man.'

'How do you know that?'

'My father was a steward in his household.'

'Which is why you got preferment here?'

'Naturally.' Lady Amelia's smile faded. 'Though one approved by both the bishop and the community.'

Corbett noticed how Dame Frances pursed her lips in silent but eloquent repudiation of her mistress' claims to merit.

'These medicines?'

'Oh,' Dame Catherine spoke up, 'brought from a physician in London, distilled by the best apothecary.'

Lady Amelia saw the flicker of doubt in the clerk's eyes and forced a more gracious smile. She must be wary of these quick answers. She had been warned about this inquisitive clerk with his abrupt questions and reputation for honesty. She scrutinised him more carefully. Yes, more than some petty official, with his hair black as night, that sardonic face and those clever eyes which didn't seem to accept a single thing she said. Perhaps attack was the best form of defense. She could be as abrupt as he.

'Be careful, Master Corbett,' she retorted. 'The Prince may have ended his relationship with the Lady Eleanor but he wished her well. The medicines were potions not poisons.'

The Prioress snapped her fingers and Dame Catherine got up and crossed to a small, iron-bound chest. She lifted the lid, took out a cachet and handed it to Lady Amelia. The Prioress, her eyes fixed on Corbett, opened the pouch and poured some of the white powder into the palm of her hand, then scooped it up with the tip of her tongue, cleansing her mouth afterward with a sip of wine.

'See, Master Corbett, I have taken the same potions the Prince sent to Lady Eleanor and I do not die!'

Corbett grimaced.

'Very well. It was you who found the body?'

'Yes, after Compline. The community and I went over to the refectory for the usual collation before we retired. As was customary, I and my two Sub-prioresses went into the convent building through the main door. The hall was dark and only one torch burnt. We found the Lady Eleanor lying at the foot of the stairs.' The Prioress stared directly at Ranulf as if acknowledging him for the first time. 'She looked as if she slept,' she murmured.

'But how could a woman fall downstairs and not disturb the hood on her head?' Corbett asked.

'Oh, I have heard a lot of useless speculation about that,' Lady Amelia replied briskly. 'The hood was tied tight.'

'And no one heard her fall?'

'There was no one there to do so.'

'Except Dames Martha and Elizabeth? And one of them is now dead?'

'Both of them were very deaf!' Lady Amelia snapped.

'Then what happened?'

'We sent our porter to Woodstock to inform the Prince.'

'And he did what?'

'My Lord Galveston came down to ensure all was well as could be in the circumstances. He left some silver for the funeral and the Prince's instructions that the Lady Eleanor be buried here.' She shrugged. 'That was all.'

'Did a physician look at the body?'

'No, why should he? The Lady Eleanor was dead.'

'And who was the dead woman's closest companion?'

Lady Amelia smiled triumphantly as if she had caught the clerk out.

'I wondered when you would ask me that.'

She nodded at Dame Frances who rose, went out, and immediately returned accompanied by another sister. The new arrival stood in the doorway so Corbett could only make out her height, her face and figure being concealed by veil and habit.

'Master Corbett, may I introduce our sacristan and cellarer, Dame Agatha?'

The nun came forward and Corbett remembered his manners and rose. He heard Ranulf gasp behind him. Dame Agatha was beautiful. Her face had a full fresh colour, the eyes were well spaced, calm, serene, full of laughter and good humour. She was honey-mouthed, sweet and wholesome. Her hand felt cool and dry, and as Corbett kissed it, he smelt the perfume of her body—

fresh, pleasant, and fragrant as a spring rose. Lady Amelia seemed to enjoy Corbett's consternation.

'What did you expect, Master Clerk?'

'I expected nothing, My Lady.'

Dame Agatha studied him carefully. Was she laughing at him? Corbett wondered. Dame Frances seemed to have produced a stool from nowhere and, at Lady Amelia's insistence, Dame Agatha sat down, indicating that Corbett should resume his seat.

'You wished to question me, Monsieur?' Her voice was low, tinged with a French accent.

'Yes, My Lady. You were a companion of Lady Eleanor?'

'Yes, I was.'

'You shared chambers?'

'No, the Lady Eleanor occupied one corridor of the convent building. She had the use of all the chambers there. Lady Amelia appointed me to be her companion but I slept with the sisters in the dorter.'

'You were appointed companion?'

'The Lady Eleanor asked for Dame Agatha,' the Prioress interrupted.

'And how was the Lady Eleanor the day before she died?' Corbett asked the young nun.

'Oh, quite happy but rather secretive. She insisted I go to Compline and refused to accompany me.'

'She usually went?'

'Oh, yes.'

'And, when you left her, she was still alive?'

The young nun looked sideways, warning Corbett with her eyes that she wished to say something but dare not here.

'Of course,' she replied. 'As sacristan I went to church early to prepare the altar. Dame Frances, you saw me there before Compline began?'

The tall, ascetic nun nodded. Corbett realised the implication of her question.

'Lady Amelia, when was Eleanor Belmont last seen alive?'

The Prioress paused, fingers to her lips.

'She was seen just before Compline. Yes, by the ancient ones—that is, Dame Elizabeth and Dame Martha. They were gossiping in one of their chambers which overlooks the passage to the chapel. They saw Lady Eleanor walking down the path as if she was going towards the Galilee Gate.'

Corbett raised his hand for her to pause as he tried to remember the lay-out of the nunnery. There was the convent building, to its right the priory church, behind that some trees and outbuildings, then the wall and the Galilee Gate. He smiled.

'I am just remembering what I have seen. Please continue. The two old sisters who saw Lady Eleanor?'

The Prioress shrugged.

'Dame Agatha, what do you think happened?' Corbett asked.

She made a face, lifting her shoulders prettily, but again warned Corbett with her eyes.

'I think she went for a walk, returned during Compline, went up the stairs, tripped, fell back and broke her neck. Poor thing!'

'But should such a fall mean immediate death?'

Corbett heard Ranulf stir restlessly behind him and suddenly realised his servant was edging slowly across the room towards some small silver figurines arranged on a gold tray on top of a chest. Oh, God! Corbett prayed quietly. Please, Ranulf, not here, not now!

'It's quite possible.' Dame Frances spoke for the first time, her voice harsh and decisive. 'I have some knowledge of physic. When a woman suffers from a malignancy in her breast, her bones become dry as the humours of her body become juiceless. In such a state, a fall could be most grievous.'

Corbett now moved to the most important question, like a good archer leaving his most lethal arrow to the last.

'So,' he said, 'the Lady Eleanor was last seen walking near the church on Sunday before Compline. Dame Agatha, you left her in good spirits?' The young nun nodded her head. 'She was seen by Dames Elizabeth and Martha?'

'Oh, yes,' Lady Amelia interrupted. 'And by the porter. He, too, saw her walking near the church before Compline, as he passed the Galilee Gate.'

Corbett cleared his throat.

'Lady Amelia, I must ask you this and I ask you with the full force of the King's law, did you or any of your sisters leave the church during Compline, after Compline, or excuse themselves from the refectory?'

'No!'

'Dame Agatha, did you?'

'She certainly did not!' Dame Frances spoke up promptly. 'She was in the sacristy before Compline. I was with her.' She glanced spitefully at the young nun. 'I always have to keep an eye on Sister Agatha. I am responsible for the stores and the plates, and—' Corbett noticed the young nun blushed '—Dame Agatha can be forgetful, can't you, my dear?'

The young nun averted her gaze.

'May I see the corpse?' Corbett asked, brusquely rising to his feet. 'Lady Prioress, I need to see the body. The King insists on that.'

Lady Amelia drew back her head, shocked.

'Lady Eleanor, for all she might once have been, was when she died a member of our Order,' she answered.

'My Lady—' Corbett realised that Ranulf was by now very close to the silver figurines '—she was also a subject of the King's and died in mysterious circumstances. Do you wish me to produce warrants and writs?'

The Lady Prioress sighed.

'Her corpse lies in the death house,' she replied quietly. 'The mortuary near the church. Dame Frances, Sister Agatha, take our guests across.'

Behind Corbett, Ranulf sighed with relief. He had acted just in time and two of the silver figurines were now carefully hidden beneath his jerkin. He trailed behind his master as Corbett, nodding politely to the Lady Prioress, followed Dame Frances and Sister Agatha out of the chamber. They walked out into the blinding sunlight, Ranulf kicking the hard turf, Frances and Agatha moving softly and silently as shadows.

The nuns led the two men round beautiful, sandstone buildings, across the grass, up to the church, and behind that to the small, red-brick death house which stood near the wall at the end of a dusty path.

Now and again Corbett stopped to ask Dame Frances some questions about Godstowe. She would politely mumble a reply and try to move on but the clerk stood his ground, idly making conversation as he gazed around. Priory servants scurried past and nearby some lay sisters were busy hoeing the garden beds, purifying

the dark soil round the rose bushes and the neat, square
herb plots.

Corbett breathed in deeply, relaxing in the warmth of
the sunshine, half-listening to the wood pigeons cooing
in the forest. Behind him, under the eaves of the church,
the swallows chattered musically against the walls.
Dame Frances, however, proved to be equally contained and stood her ground, quite prepared to answer
anything he asked. All the time she watched the silent
Dame Agatha. Corbett caught a warning look in the old
woman's eyes, indicating the young nun should say
nothing or offer any information beyond what polite-
ness demanded. Corbett looked up once more at the
blue sky and took two steps closer to Dame Frances.

'That was a pack of lies, wasn't it?' he asked
abruptly. 'Back there. Something's wrong. What is it,
woman?' He ignored Dame Agatha's gasp, quietly enjoying Dame Frances' flustered air at such an abrupt
challenge. 'I am the King's Justiciar in these matters.
Lady Eleanor did not fall, did she?'

Dame Frances stepped back, her face sour as a dried
fig, eyelids fluttering as she gathered her wits.

'Perhaps you are right, sir,' she muttered. 'I believe
the Lady Eleanor may have committed suicide. The
Prioress is trying to hide that. Something was preying
on Lady Eleanor's mind, but Lady Amelia will not accept it was suicide. She might be held responsible.
Moreover,' she muttered, 'the Lady Eleanor...you
know what could happen if suicide was proved?'

Corbett just gazed stonily back.

Dame Frances' voice rose. 'The Lady Eleanor would
be denied burial in hallowed ground. Do you want that,
Clerk? Her body tossed in some shallow grave at the
crossroads with a stake driven through her heart so her

poor soul will never rest? That's what church law decrees!'

Corbett pointed down the path.

'And that is the death house?'

'Yes,' she snapped. 'Do what you have to do.'

Corbett told Ranulf to stay and went down and opened the unlocked door. Inside it was cool, moist, reeking of the soil and something more corrupt. The clerk closed the door behind him. He felt the menace of death pressing against his own spirit. He jumped as a bat, startled by the noise, spread its dark wings above the rafters and screeched in annoyance. One small window high in the wall afforded some light. Curiously enough two candles had been lit, slender beeswax ones, and placed at the head of the two plain elm-wood coffins, each resting on its own trestles. Corbett went over to the nearest, lifted the gauze veil and stepped back at the sight of the wrinkled old face which stared up at him. The eyes were half-open, the lips parted, showing a red-black mouth. In the flickering candlelight it looked as if the old woman lying there was on the point of rising. Corbett remembered the Prioress telling him about the old nun who had died early that morning. He took a deep breath, replaced the veil and moved across to the other coffin.

As was customary, the lid had not yet been put in place; this would be done just before the funeral service. The veil had already been drawn back and Corbett caught his breath at the ice-cold beauty of the young woman lying there. She had Maeve's silvery-gold hair and flawless features. Corbett reflected that, as Lady Eleanor had been dead for six days, the priory must have spared no expense in hiring the best embalmers to preserve her body for burial. He said a short prayer to the Madonna, hoping the dead woman's shade would accept he meant no blasphemy. He pulled the veil further down, picked up the candle and examined the dead woman's throat. At the base of the throat, on each side, was a small yellow bruise. Corbett then removed the veil completely and almost screamed with terror as a voice suddenly boomed out.

'Man, what are you doing?'

Corbett turned. At the foot of the coffin, a friar, who had been kneeling there all of the time, was now standing, his hands clenched tightly on the rim of Lady Eleanor's coffin. The friar's face, a mask of anger, looked ghastly in the flickering light. His head was tonsured, his eyes deep-set under furrowed brows. His mouth and chin were fixed in a determined expression. He glared at Corbett.

'I asked, man, what you were doing?'

Corbett's hand went to the knife as the priest came round the coffin.

'Leave your dagger alone!' he rasped. 'Or I'll give you a rap across the head you'll never forget.'

Corbett kept his hand on the knife hilt.

'I am on the King's business here. My name is Hugh Corbett.'

'I couldn't give a devil's fart who you are and why you are here!' The friar pointed down to the corpse. 'A whore she may have been, and her sins as scarlet as those of the Great Whore of Babylon, but you'll treat her with respect.'

The friar paused as Corbett drew his knife. Behind them the door was flung open and a breathless Ranulf burst into the room.

'Rest easy, Ranulf!' Corbett shouted as the friar spun round. 'Father and I have business here.'

His man reluctantly closed the door.

'Father,' Corbett continued quietly, 'I mean no disrespect. I am here on official business to examine the corpse. Who are you?'

The friar drew a deep breath.

'Father Reynard, parson of the local church, and by episcopal authority, Chaplain to this benighted place.' He nodded, his eyes never leaving Corbett. 'I suppose you had better finish.'

Corbett returned to the head of the coffin and lifted the veil, pulling it down again, paying special notice to the bruises on either side of the woman's neck. He noticed the marks on the finger of the right hand where a ring had been pulled off. He went to the bottom of the casket, lifted the veil there and pushed back the dark gown in which the corpse had been dressed, noticing the yellowing bruise on the right leg mid-way up the calf. Behind Corbett the friar breathed heavily. The clerk, as tactfully as possible, examined the rest of the body and, for the first time, despite the oils and unguents of the embalmers, caught a whiff of corruption. The clerk softly said the Requiem and moved back to the corpse of the old nun. He stood looking down, the friar still watching, before carefully replacing the veil and walking wordlessly to the door. Behind him the friar snuffed the candles and followed him out. Despite the golden sunshine, Corbett felt a cold shiver run down his spine at what he had seen.

'Aye, it's the Valley of Death,' Father Reynard intoned, watching him intently.

Corbett stared at him. Reynard did not look so fierce now. Of medium height, he gave an impression of strength, as if drawn from oak and the dark rich soil. A man of the Commons, blunt and honest in speech and action. His face was ascetic, though Corbett noted the humour lines which offset the fanaticism in the brooding eyes.

'You knew the Lady Eleanor?' Corbett asked.

'Aye, a fine lady even though she was a whore.'

The priest gazed about, his eyes narrowing when he saw Dame Frances standing with Ranulf at the top of the path.

'A place of evil,' he muttered out of the corner of his mouth, 'make no mistake of that, Clerk. Satan walks and devours souls whose bodies will burn in his belly for all eternity.'

'And the Lady Eleanor?'

'A poor blighted toy of princes. Now she is dead, Christ have mercy on her soul!'

'How do you think she died?'

'By her own hand, of course!'

The friar wiped his own and continued speaking.

'The dark forces present here may have unsettled her mind.' He gestured toward the far convent wall and a polished plinth of stone which rose five feet from the ground. 'Look at that, Clerk—the sign of Priapus. They say in ancient times it was a shrine, an altar to some ancient, bloody-mouthed god.'

Corbett followed his gaze. The stone was polished smooth and glinted in the sunlight. He smiled to himself. There was no mistaking its shape and he wondered how the nuns could allow such a pagan object within their grounds. He looked back at the friar.

'You still haven't told me, Father, what you were doing in the death house?'

'Praying, man. I was praying for Christ to have mercy on the souls of those two unfortunate women. As I will pray for you.' He looked darkly at the clerk. 'Believe me, before you have finished here, you may have need of my prayers!'

FOUR

CORBETT REJOINED RANULF and Dame Agatha.

'So you met Father Reynard?' she said. 'A good man though rather extreme. I suppose he ranted about our plinth?'

Corbett nodded.

'The sisters regard it as nothing more than a piece of harmless magic but, like all men, Father Reynard thinks women are feckless creatures, easily swayed by a piece of rock.'

'Where's Dame Frances gone?' Corbett asked more abruptly than he intended.

The young nun smiled mischievously.

'She said she had better things to do than dance from one foot to another waiting for clerks.' She became more serious. 'The Sub-prioress means no harm. She has invited you to stay and has gone to prepare a guest chamber. You will stay, won't you?'

Corbett looked at Ranulf.

'Talking of dancing from one foot to another, Ranulf, if you go back round the convent building, over near the stables, you will find the necessary house.'

His servant flushed with embarrassment.

'I thought you had never been to Godstowe before, Master?'

'I hadn't but, as we entered, I noticed a groom hurrying in that direction and, a short while later, emerge with a look of relief on his face. So go! After that, see to our baggage.'

He waited until Ranulf was out of earshot.

'Dame Agatha,' he said, 'I do not wish to stand on my authority but I would like to question the other nun, Dame Elizabeth.' He pointed back to the death house. 'I have just seen the corpse of her friend.'

'Of course.' Dame Agatha smiled. 'I am sure the Lady Prioress would agree.'

She led him back round past the Prioress' lodgings to the front of the main convent building, up the broad steps and into the hall—a large, forbidding place dominated by the great wooden staircase with dark-shadowed recesses on either side.

'The Lady Eleanor died here,' Dame Agatha murmured, pointing to a spot at the foot of the stairs.

'How was she found?' Corbett asked. 'I mean, the position of her body?'

'I don't really know. The Lady Prioress discovered her and sent Dame Catherine to get me from the refectory. When I arrived Lady Eleanor's corpse had been arranged more decently.'

'What did you think when you first saw it?'

'I thought she had fainted.'

Corbett noticed the young nun look away, raising her white, lace-edged cuff to her eyes. The clerk placed his hand gently on her shoulder.

'I am sorry,' he murmured. 'If I could only help...'

Dame Agatha turned, her eyes like two dark butterflies swooping up to meet his. She murmured her thanks and, raising the hem of her gown, led Corbett upstairs, allowing him full view of her seductive, swaying hips and elegant, trim ankles. She turned left at the top of the stairs, entering a long sombre gallery, and stopped at a huge metal-studded door on the right.

'Dame Elizabeth!' she called, knocking urgently.
'You have a visitor, a Master Corbett.'

'Come in, come in.'

The voice was strident and harsh. Dame Agatha
pushed open the door and Corbett walked into a spacious but gloomy chamber, lit only by the weak sunlight filtering through the mullion glass window on the
far side which overlooked the priory grounds. Corbett
could hear the faint sounds of the community; labourers returning from the fields and gardens, the neigh of
horses from the stables and the chatter of nuns as they
took advantage of the sunlight before Plainsong.

The room was luxuriously furnished and, though the
weather was still warm, charcoal braziers full of sput-
tering coals had been wheeled in. Around the walls
stood cupboards openly displaying silver and gold fili-
greed goblets and plates. Corbett thanked God that
Ranulf wasn't here: his servant's fingers would have
positively itched at being close to so much wealth. A
press for clothes stood in one corner, its cunningly de-
vised doors half-open to reveal gowns, cloaks, and other
garments, indicating Dame Elizabeth was a woman
dedicated as much to this world as she was to the next.
In the other corner stood a bed, a huge four-poster, its
fur-edged curtains pulled back to show a carved head-
rest, large white bolsters and a tawny and silver bed-
spread. Corbett had heard of the luxury of some
religious houses but never witnessed it first hand. So
intent was he upon assessing the wealth of the room that
the clerk failed to see the diminutive figure sitting in a
coffer next to one of the braziers.

'Sir, who are you?' The small, white, podgy face under its brown head-dress was both angry and alarmed.

Corbett walked across and stared down at Dame Elizabeth. She glared back, her tiny eyes like two black currants in a plate of dough, her face tight and sour as if she perpetually smelt something offensive. Corbett smiled, and in a dazzling show of courtesy gave a bow which would have been the envy of the most professional courtier.

'Madam,' he began softly, 'the chamber, your august self... unless I'd known differently, I would have thought myself in the presence of the queen.'

Dame Elizabeth positively beamed with pleasure, putting down her piece of embroidery and gesturing Corbett to sit on a small quilted footstool beside her. In the face of such flattery, Dame Elizabeth was as pliable as a piece of soft clay in Corbett's hands. The clerk sketched the barest details of his life, lying that a distant relative always spoke so highly of Godstowe and was considering applying to the Prioress for admission. Dame Elizabeth, in truth an old and garrulous woman, drank this in like a thirsty man would the purest water. They conversed about the past, Corbett's nimble wits leading the conversation in the direction he wanted.

Naturally, Dame Elizabeth was interested above all in her health, with a litany of her aches and pains as long as a psalm, so they discussed the different elixirs: how the blood of a horse mixed with weasel hair was a sure cure for the rheum, and that elk's hoof, if obtainable, could cure the most severe agues. At last Corbett steered the conversation on to the fate of the Lady Eleanor. Dame Elizabeth pursed her lips as if she was the fount of all knowledge and gradually divulged her self-important view.

'Oh, yes,' she exclaimed. 'The Lady Eleanor had been so ill with an inflammation of the chest that the Lord Edward had sent her special powders.'

'Rumour has it,' Corbett interrupted, 'these powders were poisons.'

'Nonsense!' the old nun replied in her quivering voice. 'The Lady Prioress, as well as Dame Agatha, tasted them. No harm befell them,' she added wistfully, as if she would have liked that to have happened.

'But the lady's mind,' Corbett persisted. 'She was melancholic?'

'Oh, yes, poor thing. Deserted by her lover, she pined for him.'

'You think her death was an accident?'

'It may well have been. The hall was dark, and you have seen how steep the stairs are. I am always complaining about them.'

'You saw the lady's body?'

'Yes, yes. She looked as if she was asleep except for the bruise on her neck and the savage twist to her head.'

'But you don't think it was an accident, do you? How could a lady fall downstairs? Even in the dark, she must have known them well.'

The old nun wetted her lips and leaned closer.

'You are correct. There can only be one conclusion,' she whispered. She leaned so close their heads almost touched. 'Suicide,' she hissed.

Corbett's heart sank in despair. Not the same old theory!

'Then why was she cloaked and hooded?' he asked. 'Surely someone else would have heard her cry or the noise of her fall? After all, both you and the late Sister Martha were here.'

'Oh, yes.' The nun leaned back triumphantly. 'But we went for our sleep. We always do. One of the lay sisters brings us some food. Anyway, this building's old, it groans and creaks all the time.'

Corbett bit his lip in despair. If they were unable to hear Lady Eleanor fall, how could they be so sure no one entered the convent building? But did that matter? Lady Eleanor would hardly let anyone slip into her room.

'Yet the hood on her head was not disturbed?' he asked despairingly.

The nun's eyes narrowed and Corbett sensed any closer questioning would arouse suspicion.

'Oh,' Dame Elizabeth snapped, 'I don't know why people keep gossiping about that. This place is dank and cold. On an autumn evening it's quite customary for a lady to dress against the chill.'

'And you saw her?' he asked smilingly. 'You and Sister Martha, God rest her soul.'

'That's right. Dame Martha was here in this room. She always was, God rest her. We used to sit and watch the sisters getting ready for Compline.' She pointed to the window. 'Over there. Now—' Dame Elizabeth squirmed in her chair and popped a sugared sweetmeat into her mouth so fast Corbett hardly saw it '—we were sitting there and we saw Lady Eleanor pass. She was dressed in a cloak and hood, walking as if to go behind the church. We called out and she turned, shouting she was going for a walk, and waved at us.'

'You're sure of that?'

'Of course. She turned and waved her hand.'

'And Dame Martha saw that?'

'Oh, yes.'

'And Dame Martha was your friend?'

'Well, I helped the poor thing. She was a yeoman's daughter, you know,' she added patronisingly.

'Who?'

'Dame Martha: her education was incomplete so I would often help her. She still had a great deal to learn about the spiritual life and I was only too willing to assist.' The old nun shook her head. 'I was always telling her she needed to mortify herself, pray more.'

'And now she is dead?'

'Yes, God rest her. I found her body.'

Corbett leaned forward.

'How did it happen?'

'Well, the old dear's mind had turned. She wanted to see the Prioress, said she knew something about Lady Eleanor's death. I told her she should bathe, prepare herself well.' She smiled thinly. 'Dame Martha was not particular in her personal habits.'

'What did she know about Lady Eleanor's death?'

'Oh, she talked about something she had seen. "*Sinistra non dextra*", she kept chanting. "The left not the right!" Silly old thing! I don't know what she meant so don't ask me. Anyway, I thought she was a long time bathing so I went over. The chamber door was unlocked and I went in.' The old nun paused in mock sorrow. 'Dame Martha was in the bath, her legs sticking out like two thin sticks, her face under the water.'

'Did you notice anything untoward?'

'No, nothing, except I nearly slipped when running out of the room. There was a trail of water right to the door.'

'Anything else?'

'No,' she snapped. 'Why should there be?'

Corbett shook his head sympathetically and neatly turned the conversation back to the hoof of an elk and the blood of the weasel before rising, bidding farewell, and making the most solemn assurances that if Dame Elizabeth would be so gracious as to welcome him, he would definitely call again.

Closing the door on the old nun's grateful acceptance of his offer, Corbett strode back to the top of the stairs and with one look dismissed her vapid outpourings. If the Lady Eleanor had committed suicide there was no need to throw herself downstairs. A fall from a window or even over the balustrade of this gallery would have been just as effective. Corbett went along the darkened galleries to Lady Eleanor's chamber: these were large rooms next to each other, occupying one side of the convent house. They were unlocked but he found nothing of interest as they had already been stripped of all furniture and hangings. He sighed and tiptoed downstairs. He'd hoped Dame Agatha was waiting but glimpsed only a grey-garbed lay sister scurrying past the foot of the stairs. Corbett walked slowly towards the main door.

'Master Clerk!'

Corbett allowed himself a half smile before he turned.

'What is it, Dame Agatha?'

'You found Dame Elizabeth well?'

'I did.'

'Good.'

Corbett noticed the colour high in the woman's cheeks.

'It's just that we have so few visitors,' she flustered.

Corbett walked back.

'I feel sorry for you, Madam, locked up in the presence of death. I can only imagine your grief and loneliness.'

'There are celebrations tomorrow,' she boldly interrupted. 'At the local church. It's harvest time. I have to visit Father Reynard for altar breads—he always insists that we use the unleavened wafers he bakes himself. The roads are—'

'Madam,' Corbett smoothly intervened, 'I would consider it an honour to accompany you.'

Dame Agatha led him silently back to the guest house which stood on the other side of the nunnery and showed him into a pleasant, comfortable chamber with a few sticks of furniture. Ranulf was already unpacking their saddle bags. Dame Agatha left them there saying a kitchener would bring across food as their rules forbade visitors in the refectory. Corbett sat on his cot and pulled off his boots. He waited to speak until he heard the nun's soft footsteps fade into the distance.

'So, Ranulf, what do you think?'

His servant slumped on the bed opposite him.

'For ladies concerned about the next world,' Ranulf tartly answered, 'they seem very interested in this one. Hell's teeth, Master! They live as grandly as any princess.'

'And the Lady Eleanor's death?'

'I think they are all lying, and they know it. The Lady Prioress may be an arrogant cow but she is also a very frightened one.'

'Anything else?'

'Those two Sub-prioresses—Dames Frances and Catherine—they detest each other. Did you notice they hardly exchanged a glance?' Ranulf grimaced. 'And you, Master?'

'I believe the Lady Eleanor did not fall downstairs. If she had, her body would have been a mass of bruises whereas, apart from on her neck, I noticed only one contusion on her leg. She was killed elsewhere and her corpse dumped at the bottom of the stairs to make it appear an accident. I also think,' he added softly, 'the old nun was murdered in her bath because she knew something, though God knows how I am going to prove what really happened.'

Corbett lay on the bed trying to sort out the jumble of facts in his head. A servant brought them up bowls of hot broth, small white loaves and a dish of cold pheasant garnished with spices and a mess of vegetables. After they had eaten, Ranulf went for a walk, coming back still praising the wealth and luxury he had seen. Corbett stared up at the ceiling. He wondered how Maeve was doing. Would she look after herself? Could she manage the reeve and bailiff? Tomorrow the manor court would meet: John the Heywood was petitioning for leave to marry his daughter to a man from the next village. William Attwood wanted to send his son to school. Hik the warrener had broken the ordinance about using the manor mill and had ground his own corn at home. Robert Arundel had stolen a yard of land from his neighbor. Could Maeve deal with all these problems? Outside it fell dark. Corbett's eyes grew heavy. He heard the yip-yip of a hunting fox, together with the sounds of Ranulf preparing for bed.

'Ranulf!' he murmured.

'Yes, Master?'

'Somehow, please return the silver figurines to the Lady Prioress!'

'Yes, Master.'

The next morning Corbett rose early, woken by the tolling of the priory bell. He washed, cleansing his face and hands in a deep brass bowl placed in the wooden lavarium, dressed and roused Ranulf for early morning

Mass. The air was heavy with mist as Corbett made his way towards a small farm within the priory grounds. He heard the gulping noise of greedy sows; a peasant called to his sons across the dawn-dark grass to put away their mattocks and hoes and prepare for Mass. One of the nuns, her face pale as cheese and heavy with sleep, was talking to one of the lay sisters who was yoked with clanking buckets, returning from milking the cows. Another lay sister, her gown rucked up, sleeves pushed high above her elbows displaying lean, brown, muscular arms, was walking slowly up from the well, a brimming bucket in either hand; beside her a barefooted, dusty girl drove a flock of hissing geese back into their pen.

Corbett walked right round, through the now open Galilee Gate and on the dry, dusty track which wound past the priory. He took a deep breath, enjoying the sweet-scented smells. In the woods across the track, dew still dripped from the branches; cuckoos, wood pigeons and thrushes sang their morning chorus in the deep green darkness. The priory bell tolled again, calling him back from the part of the day he loved most. The clerk drew deep breaths, sucking in the fresh morning air. A beautiful morning which brought memories of Leighton Manor and other older images flooding back into his mind. He closed his eyes, revelling in the peace as he braced himself against the troubles of the day: he must remember that the calm serenity of Godstowe hid murky, murderous secrets which threatened the crown itself.

Corbett opened his eyes, fingered the stubble on his chin, and promising himself he would shave as soon as possible, went back to collect a sleepy-eyed Ranulf.

If the priory was luxurious, the church would have done justice to any great earl or nobleman. The walls were covered by a brilliantly coloured painting of Christ harrowing Hell, freeing souls from the grip of black-faced demons who looked all the more horrible for their scarlet bodies covered in dark blotches of fur. The church was divided by a heavy wooden chancel screen, every inch of it covered with the most intricate carvings of angels, saints, and scenes from the Old and New Testaments. As they went through it into the sanctuary, the Lady Prioress swept majestically as a bishop towards her stall, indicating the bench where they should sit. Corbett bowed, muttering at Ranulf to hush his mumbled observations about the arrogance of some women.

The clerk sat and looked around: on either side of the chancery were the nuns' stalls, each with their own carved oak recess with bench and prie dieu. Beyond these the altar rail and the marble white purity of the sanctuary: the great ivory-coloured altar now covered in costly clothes, with pure beeswax candles fixed in heavy silver holders standing on either side. The sunlight pouring through the small rose window made the precious cups and chalices placed there glitter and shimmer with an almost blinding light. Corbett heard a sound and turned, looking round the chancel screen. The peasants from the nunnery farm were now filing in. According to custom they would not be allowed any further than the nave, so they squatted in their dusty green, brown or russet smocks upon the flagstoned floor.

Corbett studied them, travelling back in time, as if they were ghosts from his own past. His father and mother had once sat like that, no more than peasants and so, by King's law and divine decree, not worthy to sit beyond the chancel screen. Instead they could look at the priest from afar, listen to his sermon, and study the paintings put there for their spiritual improvement.

A bell tinkled and Father Reynard, dressed in fiery red and gold vestments, swept out of the sacristy and up to the altar. He stood at the foot of the steps, making the sign of the cross, his great voice intoning the introductory psalm:

'I will go unto the altar of God, to God who gives glory to my youth!'

Corbett studied the nuns on either side, watching each face intently. In the main they were fat, well fed and smug, Dame Elizabeth being a notable exception in her austerity. Lady Amelia in her silk habit and lace-edged wimple, gazed round with all the hauteur of a noblewoman; Dame Agatha's face looked serene and composed in prayer, though Corbett watched her dark sloe eyes glance quickly across at him. He caught the hint of mischief in her face. Now Father Reynard had gone up the altar steps, standing beneath the blue and gold canopy which swung on velvet cords from the costly hammerbeam roof. The spiritual magic was being worked, Christ called down under the likeness of bread and wine, but Corbett stirred at the end of the Mass as Father Reynard mounted the wooden pulpit to give the sermon, his hands resting on the great eagle with its carved, outstretched wings.

'Woe to you!' the Franciscan began. 'You rich and pampered ones who ignore the needy, the poor folk, prisoners in dungeons created by your wealth. What they scrimp by spinning, they pay out to you in rents and tithes so they have only watered porridge to satisfy their young ones who groan aloud for food.' He drew back the sleeves of his gown, exposing his strong brown wrists. Eyes half-closed, he rocked to and fro. 'Woe to you rich, you pampered ones who ignore the peasants, too ashamed to beg, who wake at night to rock the cradle, to patch and wash!'

Corbett looked along the line of nuns. Even the most somnolent had now stirred themselves.

'Woe to you, the pampered ones with your secret lusts, who do not revere the Madonna but pine after the secret mysteries of Queen Mab and the harlotries offered by hobgoblins, be they human or demoniac. Can you not read the signs? Satan walks and has already made his mark!'

Corbett now sat up, seeing the fury in Lady Amelia's face so apparent, he thought the Lady Prioress would rise and walk out of the church whilst Father Reynard's litany of woes only grew stronger. The priest's eyes now gleamed with fanaticism; his tongue lashed the rich, a veil for his warnings against the Priory of Godstowe. Behind him Corbett heard the peasants stir and murmur their approval. Ranulf was openly grinning. A self-confessed sinner from the gutters of Southwark, he had one virtue: he was totally devoid of hypocrisy. Corbett hoped the sermon would benefit him as well, something to take back to London with him.

At last Father Reynard finished, gave his final benediction and swept into the sanctuary. Lady Amelia rose, genuflected before the altar step and led her sisters out, their hauteur and arrogance now dimmed. None dared raise her eyes as they filed down the nave. Only Dame Agatha, with an impish wink to Ranulf, indicated her approval of what the Franciscan had said. Corbett remained seated. The friar's words had affected him also. Was he, so eager for royal justice, ready to show the same to his tenants or had he forgotten his own roots? He remembered the words of his old comrade, de Couville, who now worked in the royal records office at Westminster.

'What does it profit a man, Hugh,' his aged mentor had cackled, 'if a clerk pleases his King but loses his soul?'

Corbett smiled and shifted on the bench. So far his King would hardly be pleased with him. The clerk's sharp, suspicious mind probed at what lay underneath Father Reynard's sermon. Did the Franciscan believe Lady Eleanor had been struck down by God? If so, was Reynard the type of man who passionately believed that Divine Justice should be given a helping hand? He thought of the friar's strong hands and wrists. If Lady Eleanor had been murdered, her neck expertly broken and the body dumped at the bottom of those stairs, a man like Father Reynard was well suited to be her assassin.

'What do you know about the friar, Ranulf?' Corbett asked.

His manservant, half-dozing now, shook himself, stood up and stretched.

'Not much,' he whispered, aware how his words would echo in the cavernous sanctuary. 'But have you seen the way he walks, Master? Shoulders back, head up. I believe our Franciscan has seen some military service. And his little finger—I glimpsed it when he was leaning on the pulpit—it's been hacked off, there's only a stump. And there are purple welts on his wrists.' Ranulf smiled, basking in his master's approval. 'Father Reynard undoubtedly wielded a sword. I would wager he was as good with that as he is with his tongue. It's a long time since I heard a sermon like that.'

'Your eyes are sharp, Ranulf. Listen, saddle our horses and seek out Dame Agatha. Tell her I'll meet her and you at the Galilee Gate. We are going down to the village of Woodstock.'

Ranulf threw one last hungry glance round the richness of the sanctuary and swaggered off.

Corbett stared at the light pouring through the multicoloured windows. What do we have here? he wondered...A priory full of every luxury and home to a once powerful courtesan, now discarded by the Prince of Wales. The woman perished in mysterious circumstances. She had not fallen downstairs but died elsewhere and her body been put there. Rumour had it that she had a malady of the breast.

Corbett reflected on what he had seen when he had examined the corpse. True, it was only a cursory examination, but he had seen no tumour or abscess or any other sign of malignancy. He knew little about medicine but Maeve had informed him that such an illness was usually fatal and made its effect felt in the drying of the skin and its victim turned from any nourishment, yet Eleanor had been a well-formed and proportioned woman. Moreover, she had been imprisoned in Godstowe for the last two years. Again, Maeve had assured him how a malady of the breast usually killed its victim within a few months, yet Lady Eleanor had been able to eat, drink, and go for walks. There had been no reports or suggestions that she had been seriously ill or near death's door.

Corbett rubbed his face wearily. So how had she died? Not from suicide. The body would have been more severely marked, and surely a woman like Lady Eleanor would have chosen some swifter road to oblivion.

Corbett looked up, staring hard at the great wooden crucifix which hung above the altar. So it had to be murder. If so, by whom? Lady Eleanor had been last seen walking in the grounds of the priory before Compline. All the sisters, including the Lady Prioress, her two deputies and Sister Agatha, had been in church. No one had left half-way through the service or made an excuse to return to the convent building before the sisters went over to the refectory. Of course, the Lady Prioress might be lying but Dame Elizabeth had remarked that she had heard no one come up the stairs, certainly not whilst Compline was being sung. Nevertheless, even if the old lady was deaf, Corbett concluded, the assassin or assassins must be someone outside the priory.

He gnawed his lip. And who would want her dead? The King would be only too willing to be rid of an embarrassment whilst involved in delicate negotiations over his son's betrothal to a French princess. The royal favourite, Gaveston, detested Lady Eleanor and saw her as a potential rival. He had the malice as well as the means to hire soft-footed assassins. And the Prince of Wales? A feckless youth, had he too tired of his former paramour? Corbett sighed and blew out his cheeks. Did the Prince want to be rid of the Lady Eleanor because of some secret she held, such as a clandestine marriage ceremony between them? Only three years ago the court had been fascinated by the delicious scandal of the young Prince's infatuation with Lady Eleanor.

Corbett stood up and went to sit in one of the nun's stalls. If it could be proved, he thought, that either the King or his son had been involved in murder, the scandal would rock the English throne, cause distress abroad and put Edward of England firmly in the hands of

Philip of France. Corbett smiled mirthlessly. He knew Philip, with his public morality and private evil. He would not be above stirring the muddy waters of the English court, and his envoy and master assassin, Amaury de Craon, was now in England. But could de Craon get an assassin in here or did he have an agent in place already? Or was the murderer someone totally unconnected with the murky world of the English court? Such as Father Reynard, a priest who might see himself as the embodiment of Divine Wrath...

'Master Corbett, you wish to join our Order?'

The clerk looked up. Lady Amelia stood in the door of the chancel screen.

'My Lady.' Corbett rose. 'Accept my apologies,' he looked around, 'but this is a quiet and beautiful place to think.'

The Prioress walked slowly across, toying with the silver tasselled cord round her waist.

'Sit down, man,' she said wearily.

Corbett looked sharply at her as she slumped in the stall beside him.

'What did you think of Father Reynard's sermon?'

Corbett shrugged.

'I took it for what it was—a harsh warning to the rich.'

'He meant us, Corbett,' Lady Amelia retorted. 'And he was a trifle unfair.'

'What do you mean?'

'We are not an order dedicated to poverty. We are a refuge for women who cannot survive in the harsh world of men. Do you know what it's like, Clerk, to be a woman, married off to some man you hate, or else left alone to fend for yourself? You know the King's court. There we are, like pheasants allowed to play just under a nest of falcons. The church is controlled by men; men go to war, build ships and ply the seas.' She sighed. 'The Daughters of Syon are a refuge, that is why the Lady Eleanor was sent to us.'

'Did you like her?'

'She kept to herself, borrowed books, went for walks—fitted into our normal order and routine. A sad young woman who never came to terms with the sudden shock of her fall from grace. I did not want her here but the King's writ was quite explicit. At first she protested, but in the two years here,' the Lady Prioress made a face, 'she became one of us.'

'So why don't you tell me the truth about her death?'

The Lady Prioress looked quickly at Corbett. The clerk realised how attractive she was without the air of hauteur and arrogance. Lady Amelia stretched over and wiped a thin film of dust from the top of the prie dieu in front of her.

'You're sharp, Corbett. I wondered when you'd return to challenge me.'

'My Lady, I am the King's clerk. The questions I ask are His Grace's. You must answer.'

'You'd best come with me.'

She took a surprised Corbett delicately by the wrist and led him out of the stalls up to the high altar. The red and gold Gospel Book still lay in the centre. She placed her long slender fingers against the cover of the book.

'Ask me your questions, Clerk. I wish to help. I have nothing to hide and, hand on the gospels, swear to tell the truth. When this matter is finished, I don't want to be removed because the King was dissatisfied—though he may well not be pleased with the answers I am going to give.'

Corbett rested against the altar.

'Was the Lady Eleanor suffering from a malady of the breast?'

'She said she was.'

'Did the Prince send potions to her?'

'Yes, he did. And we tasted them and suffered no ill effects.'

'Did the Lady Eleanor receive visitors?'

'No, the Prince never came, though of course he sent messengers with letters and gifts. The letters Lady Eleanor always burnt, the gifts she gave to the community.'

'Why did she not go to Compline the night she died?'

'I don't know. She had been very secretive during the previous week but we thought it was due to some evil humour.'

'You are sure that, apart from Dame Elizabeth and Dame Martha, all the community were in Compline and went to refectory afterwards?'

'Yes, you saw me this morning. I check each stall personally. Some of the sisters, such as Dame Agatha and Dame Frances, were here just before Compline. After the ceremony we processed to the refectory. Again, there were no absentees. I particularly noticed Dame Agatha because she was reading that evening from the homilies of Saint Jerome whilst the other sisters were eating.'

'And afterwards? You and the two Sub-prioresses returned to the priory and found Lady Eleanor?'

'Yes and no.'

Corbett looked up sharply.

The Lady Prioress gazed evenly back, her hands still on the Gospel Book.

'I mean,' she replied slowly, 'we went back to the convent building. I was very concerned about Lady

Eleanor's prolonged absence. The hall was dark and deserted. We went upstairs. Dames Martha and Elizabeth, as usual, were fast asleep. We hurried to Lady Eleanor's room. The door was unlocked, the chamber dark. Lady Eleanor was lying on the floor. She wore a cloak, its hood pulled well over her head. I thought she had fainted but Sister Frances pronounced her dead.'

The Lady Prioress looked away.

'I panicked. The King had entrusted me with Lady Eleanor's safety and security and I had failed. So we took her corpse downstairs and placed it at the foot of the steps to look as if she had fallen or committed suicide. I sent for Dame Agatha and a messenger to Father Reynard. That is all,' she whispered.

Corbett sensed the woman was not telling lies but what she said was not the full truth.

'So Lady Eleanor was murdered?'

The Prioress nodded.

'By whom?'

'I don't know,' she muttered. 'Anyone could have sent assassins to climb over the wall and await their chance.'

Corbett reflected on what she had told him: the murder would explain the bruises on each side of the neck and on the leg when Lady Eleanor probably lashed out in her death throes. Corbett had no doubt that a professional assassin had killed the wretched woman.

'Do you know what the ancient one, Dame Martha, wanted to see you about?' he asked.

Lady Amelia shook her head.

'Or the meaning of her phrase—"*Sinistra non dextra*"?'

'No,' she muttered. 'But Dame Martha was senile. She often gabbled nonsense.'

'And afterwards?'

'Father Reynard anointed Lady Eleanor's body, the Prince sent his servants to take away all the jewellery. He was quite insistent: it was rather pathetic to see the corpse stripped of its finery, particularly the great sapphire ring he had given her. A symbol,' she added tartly, 'of his supposedly undying love! I can tell you no more, Clerk.'

She walked around the altar.

'My Lady,' Corbett asked softly, 'did anything strange happen in Godstowe or its neighbourhood during the two years Lady Eleanor was with you?'

Lady Amelia frowned and looked down the church.

'Yes, two things.' She turned quickly. 'First, about eighteen months ago, two corpses were found—a young man and woman. Both had their throats cut; their naked bodies were discovered dumped in a shallow marsh deep in the forest. Nobody recognised them as being from the area or came forward to claim their bodies. No clothes or possessions were found. I believe they were given a pauper's funeral in the village churchyard. It caused some stir at the time.'

'So no one ever found out who they were? Or why they had been murdered?'

'That's correct.'

'And the other matter?'

'A Frenchman,' Lady Amelia replied. 'An envoy from the King in Paris. He wished to come here to pay his respects but he had no licence or permission to do so. King Edward was most insistent on that so I turned him away from the gates.'

'When was that?'

'Why?' she asked. 'Do you know him?'

Corbett just shook his head and watched the Prioress turn and walk out of the sanctuary in stately fashion. Only then did he smile. Of course he knew who it was. His old enemy, that bastard Seigneur Amaury de Craon, had been pushing his snout into a matter which did not concern him.

'Oh, Master Clerk?'

Corbett looked up. The Lady Prioress had walked back under the entrance of the chancel screen.

'Yes, Lady Amelia?'

'Father Reynard,' she replied. 'He was near the Priory the night Lady Eleanor died. Every Sunday evening, as a penance, he walks barefoot from the village to the Galilee Gate.' She smiled. 'Ask him if he saw anything suspicious as he mumbled his psalms.'

And before Corbett could answer, she spun on her heel and flounced out of the church.

FIVE

RANULF AND DAME AGATHA were waiting for him near the Galilee Gate, the young nun apparently enjoying an account of one of his manservant's many escapades in London.

'Ranulf, we are ready? Dame Agatha?'

His man nodded and scowled. Solicitously he helped the young nun to mount, muttering under his breath about how certain clerks seemed to turn up when they were least expected or wanted. Corbett just grinned over his shoulder and led them out on to the beaten track down to the village of Woodstock. He felt tempted to continue through the village to visit the young Prince at Woodstock Palace but, considering what he had just learnt, thought he had better wait for a while.

The day proved to be a pleasant one and Corbett, with Ranulf in tow, humming some filthy ditty, enjoyed the quiet ride down the winding country lane, the trees on either side forming a green canopy above their heads. The countryside was peaceful under a late autumn sun, the silence broken only by the liquid song of a bird, the chatter of insects and the loud buzz of honey-hunting bees. Dame Agatha, elegant in her light brown riding habit, sat sidesaddle on a small gentle cob from the priory stables. Corbett allowed their conversation to be as desultory as possible, wanting his companion to relax and feel safe in his presence.

At last they reached the village and joined the rest of the crowd as they thronged toward the green in front of the parish church. They paused to watch the rustics, bedecked with scarves, ribbons and laces, dance and carouse around their makeshift hobby horses to the raucous noise of pipers, drummers and other musicians. Corbett assisted Dame Agatha to dismount. She pointed toward a large, two-storey building on the other side of the green.

'I have business with the merchant who imports our wine,' she remarked. 'Afterwards I'll go to the church and meet you there.'

Corbett agreed, telling Ranulf to accompany her whilst he stabled their horses at The Bull. For a while he sat on one of the benches, ordering a pot of ale and relaxing in the sunshine. He looked again at the church and remembered Father Reynard's sermon. He went up through the wicket gate and into the cemetery, a quiet, surprisingly well-kept plot. The grass was scythed, the elm trees well-pruned and vigorous in their growth. Corbett went past the church towards the priest's house and knocked gently on the half-open door. He heard voices and Father Reynard suddenly appeared.

'Come in! Come in!'

The friar's smile was welcoming and genuine. He told Corbett to sit on a bench and went back to where he and a young man, a villein from the village, were poring over a great leatherbound book open on the table. Corbett stared around. An unpretentious place: two rooms downstairs with possibly two small chambers above. The floor was of beaten earth, the walls washed white with lime to keep off the flies. A crude stone hearth, a few sticks of furniture, chests and coffers and a shelf full of kitchen implements were all the friar's apparent possessions. Corbett was impressed. Many village priests insisted on living in luxury, dressing in the best garb, jerkins and multi-coloured hose, and making every effort to palliate the hardships of their lives. A few were downright criminal: Corbett had seen cases in King's Bench of priests who used their churches to brew beer, as gambling dens, or even worse.

At the table the young man murmured his pleasure at something Father Reynard had pointed out, shook the priest's hand and quickly left. Father Reynard closed the leather-bound book and placed it reverently back inside a huge ironbound chest.

'The Blood Book,' he observed, straightening up. 'It says who marries whom in the village. The young man's betrothed is related to him but only in the seventh degree.' He smiled. 'I am glad I have made someone happy. Now, can I do the same for you?'

'A powerful sermon, Father. The sisters were uncomfortable.'

The priest frowned.

'They need to be reminded,' he replied sharply. 'What will they say when Christ comes and shows his red, wounded body to them? We are Christ's wounds,' he continued, 'the poor and the dispossessed, while the rich luxuriate in their comfortable sties.'

'Did you think Lady Eleanor was one of these rich?'

'I have told you already.'

'You were a soldier, Father?'

The priest sat down on the bench next to him.

'Aye,' he replied wearily. 'A master bowman, a royal serjeant-at-arms. I have spilt my fair share of blood in Scotland, Wales and Gascony.' He looked up. 'I have pursued the King's enemies by land and sea but now I understand, killing's no answer.'

'Surely, Father, sometimes it is?'

The priest rested his elbows on his knees and looked down at the floor.

'Perhaps,' he murmured. 'If God wills it, perhaps. He told David to kill the Philistines and raised up heroes to defend his people.'

'Did you think the Lady Eleanor deserved to die?'

'Perhaps. Her sins pursued her but I was not her judge.'

'You were near Godstowe when she died. I understand as a penance, you walk barefoot from your church here to the Galilee Gate, saying your beads and go back chanting the psalms. A strange practice, Father.'

The priest rubbed his face.

'My sins,' he murmured, 'are always before me. My lusts, my drinking, my killing. How shall I answer to Christ for that, Clerk?'

He turned and stared at Corbett and the clerk glimpsed madness dancing in his eyes. A tormented man, Corbett concluded, struggling to break free from his own powerful emotions.

'You were at Godstowe, Father? When on that Sunday?'

'The nuns were in Compline.' Father Reynard edged closer and Corbett smelt his wine-drenched breath. 'But I did not go into the priory, if that is what you are asking, Clerk. I would not lay hands on the Lady Eleanor, even though my eyes . . .' His voice trailed off.

'Even though your eyes what, Father? You, a priest, found the Lady Eleanor attractive?'

The priest smiled, stretching out his great body and flexing his fingers.

'Beautiful,' he murmured. 'Of all God's women . . .'
He shook his head, lost in his own thoughts. 'One of the
most comely I have seen.'

Corbett watched those hands. Powerful, calloused,
sunburnt, they could have twisted the white swan neck
of Lady Eleanor as easily as a twig. The friar took a
deep breath.

'Do you know, Corbett, if you had insinuated what
you are doing now before I became a friar, I would have
killed you. I went as far as the Galilee Gate, I turned
and came back to my church. I stayed in my house until Lady Arrogance, the Prioress, sent for me. I went to
Godstowe, said a prayer for that poor woman's soul,
gave her Christ's unction and left. But come, you can
ask your other questions elsewhere. I have business in
church.'

Corbett followed him out of the house. The friar's
threats didn't unnerve him. Father Reynard was a man
striving for sanctity, though he sensed the priest was
hiding something, as if he wanted him out of the house
before Corbett noticed anything amiss.

The church was a hive of activity; some villagers had
wheeled a huge cart into the nave. This was sur-
mounted by a gilded griffin and bore a crudely painted
canvas of hell's mouth. The other two sides were draped
with coloured buckram to provide a makeshift stage for
a miracle play. The villagers working there greeted Father Reynard warmly and Corbett recognised that they
admired, even loved, their priest. The clerk stared
around the simple church which was freshly decorated.
An artist was finishing a vigorous painting of the Angel in the Apocalypse coming from the rising sun. Some
of the pews were new and both the chancery screen and
the choir loft had been refurbished. Corbett waited un-

til Father Reynard had finished his business with the villagers.

'You admire our church, Clerk?' he asked proudly.

'Yes, a great deal of work has been done. You must have a generous benefactor.'

The priest looked away.

'God has been good,' he murmured. 'And works in mysterious ways.'

'Except for the two unfortunates buried in your churchyard.'

The friar narrowed his eyes.

'What do you mean?'

'About eighteen months ago,' Corbett explained, 'two corpses were found—a young man and woman, strangers. They were discovered in the woods completely stripped of all clothing and possessions.'

'Ah, yes.' Father Reynard gazed at a point above Corbett's head. 'That's right,' he murmured. 'They are buried in paupers' graves beneath the old elm tree in the corner of the churchyard. Why do you ask?'

'No reason. I wondered if you knew anything about them?'

'If I did, I would have told the King's Justices, but nothing was ever discovered about them or their dreadful deaths.'

Father Reynard turned away to speak to one of his villagers and Dame Agatha and Ranulf came through the church door. Ranulf's face was flushed and Corbett surmised he had been sampling some of the tavern's heady ale. He glowered at his servant but Ranulf grinned back as he swayed slightly on his feet and looked around, admiring the church. Dame Agatha took Father Reynard by the sleeve and they walked away, the young sister apologising loudly for being late and asking if Father would give her the altar breads as she must return to the priory. Corbett marched Ranulf out into the porch.

'A good day's drinking, Ranulf?'

He slyly tapped the side of his nose.

'I have been renewing my acquaintance with the wench at The Bull. I have learnt a lot, Master, and not just in the carnal sense.' He licked his lips. 'Nothing is what it appears to be around here.'

'I have gathered that,' Corbett replied drily. 'What do you know?'

Ranulf was about to reply when Dame Agatha suddenly emerged, carrying a small wooden box of altar breads, so they went across the green to reclaim their horses. The autumn sun was beginning to set. The villagers, tired now, were bringing their festivities to an end and streaming back across the green to the tavern or to their homes in search of other pleasures. Corbett allowed Ranulf to slouch sleepily in the saddle and waited for Dame Agatha to draw alongside him.

'I understand Lady Eleanor's funeral is tomorrow?'

The young nun stared soulfully at him, making Corbett catch his breath. Apart from Maeve's, he had never seen such a beautiful face. The autumn sunlight seemed to lend it a glow; her eyes were larger, darker; the half-open lips full and sweet as honey. He coughed and cleared his throat.

'A sad day for you.'

'Yes.' She smiled wanly. 'A sad day for me and for the community.'

Corbett looked over his shoulder. Ranulf was now fast asleep and the clerk breathed a prayer that his servant would not fall out of the saddle and break his neck.

He also hoped Dame Agatha would shed some light on the murder at Godstowe.

'Do you blame yourself?' he began softly. 'For leaving Lady Eleanor like that? I mean,' he stammered, 'when I asked about the funeral, you looked shocked and grieved. It's such a mystery,' he continued hurriedly. 'I believe Lady Eleanor liked you?'

Dame Agatha nodded.

'Yet that day she dismissed you. Was she so melancholic?'

Dame Agatha gathered her reins, pushing her mount closer to Corbett.

'Everyone says that,' she whispered. 'You know the Lady Prioress was lying when you talked to her on your first day at Godstowe?'

'Yes, I gathered that from your face.'

Dame Agatha smiled to herself.

'Yes, the Lady Prioress is a bad liar. I mean, would a melancholic woman order everyone to leave her? I tell you this, Master Corbett, in the weeks prior to her death, Lady Eleanor's humour had improved. She was happy, more alert. If she had been really melancholic, I would never have left her alone.'

'What caused this change, do you think?'

Dame Agatha laughed mockingly.

'I don't know. Sometimes I think she had a secret lover.'

'What makes you think that?'

Dame Agatha chewed her lip, carefully measuring her words.

'A week before her death,' she began slowly, 'she wrote one of her rare letters to the Prince. A short one. I glimpsed what she had written—nothing extraordinary except that she hoped she would soon find deliverance from her troubles. I think Lady Eleanor was nursing some secret but she would tell no one.'

'Do you think she had a lover?' Corbett persisted. 'I mean, apart from the Prince?'

'Perhaps. But I would not say that in public. The Prince is a dangerous man. I wouldn't want to be the one responsible for proclaiming him a cuckold for the world to laugh at.'

'On that Sunday evening,' Corbett asked, 'do you think Lady Eleanor was waiting for this lover? She was seen walking near the church. Perhaps she had a secret assignation?'

Dame Agatha looked at him archly and Corbett panicked. Was the nun going to refuse to answer?

'You swear to tell no one?' she asked.

Corbett had one hand high.

'I swear!'

'I believe,' Dame Agatha said in a hushed whisper as if eavesdroppers lurked in the very trees, 'that Lady Eleanor was preparing to flee Godstowe Priory.'

'What makes you say that?'

'She was receiving messages. There's a hollow oak tree behind the church. Lady Eleanor took me into her confidence and told me how every day, late in the evening, she went down there to see if another letter had been left.'

'How often did these messages come?'

'In the month before she died, about two or three arrived. They were delivered in a small leather pouch.'

'You were never curious and opened them?'

'No, the pouch was sealed and the Lady Eleanor would soon have realised if I'd tampered with it. But I do know the messages pleased her. She became happier, more settled. On one or two occasions she even hinted she would be leaving.'

'But who would send her messages?'

The young nun shrugged.

'I don't know, but on the night she died the Lady Prioress asked me to help take the corpse back to her own chamber. It was dark and in our haste we only lit one candle. I helped her rearrange Lady Eleanor's body on the bed, drawing the curtains around it. Only then did I notice, lying in the far corner, two sets of packed saddle bags full of clothes and small caskets of personal jewellery. I later unpacked these. I've told no one until today.'

'Why not?'

'Would you be the person responsible for insinuating that Lady Belmont was preparing to flee Godstowe and the Prince? You see,' Dame Agatha continued excitedly, 'I believe that Lady Eleanor, in her haste to leave, stumbled on the stairs and fell to her death.'

Corbett shook his head.

'But she left her chamber without her saddle bags?' he asked, not revealing that the Lady Prioress had already refuted any allegation that Lady Eleanor had fallen downstairs.

Dame Agatha pursed her lips.

'I cannot answer that.'

'You discovered nothing else?'

Dame Agatha smiled and shook her head.

'And the old sister, the one who drowned in her own tub of water? Do you know what she meant by "*Sinistra non dextra*"?'

'Right not left,' Dame Agatha murmured. 'No, I do not.'

'How long were you Lady Eleanor's companion?'

'My name is Savigny,' the nun replied. 'I was born of a Gascon father and an English mother in the town of Béarn near the village of Bordeaux. I was left an orphan at an early age and became a ward of the court. I expressed a desire to enter the religious life and decided to come to England.' She narrowed her eyes. 'That was about eighteen months ago. Lady Eleanor was already at Godstowe. I began to talk to her, and she asked the Lady Prioress if I could become her companion.'

Corbett settled his horse as it fidgeted nervously at the rustling of some animal in the undergrowth at the side of the track. Both he and Dame Agatha laughed as the commotion roused Ranulf, who woke with a muttered oath, smacking his lips, apparently quite refreshed after his short slumber. He brought his horse alongside theirs as they rounded the corner and the dark green spire of Godstowe Priory came into sight.

Corbett fell silent as Ranulf began his bantering teasing of Dame Agatha. Once inside the Galilee Gate Corbett bade the nun goodnight, asking Ranulf to take the horses round to the stables. He watched his manservant lead the horses off, still continuing his good-natured teasing, innocently asking the nun if she had heard the story about the naughty friar of Ludlow. Corbett shook his head and went back to the house. He asked the Guest Mistress if any letters had arrived for him.

'Oh, no,' she cried. 'Lettuce? This year's crop has not been good.'

Corbett groaned and went up to his chamber, throwing himself down on the small cot and reflecting on what he had learnt. First, Father Reynard had secretly admired Lady Eleanor and had been near the Galilee Gate the night she had died. Secondly, Lady Eleanor had been murdered in her own chamber on the night she intended to flee to a secret lover or friend. But who was this? Corbett let his mind drift, feeling guilty because when he thought about Maeve he also kept remembering Dame Agatha's angelic face.

He got up and went back down the stairs, going out into the gathering darkness, across the priory grounds behind the chapel from where he could hear the sweet, melodious chant of the nuns as they sang the first psalm of Compline. The old ruined oak tree beckoned him like some great finger thrust up from the green grass. He went and inspected the cavernous interior carefully. There was nothing except a handful of dried leaves and mildewed wood.

'Whoever brought the message must have come across the wall,' Corbett murmured to himself.

He measured out thirty paces and stared up at the crenellated boundary wall which was about twenty feet high. The mysterious messenger, Corbett surmised, must have been a very nimble young man to scale that, leave a message and depart. There was no other way in except to walk through the priory, but a stranger would have been stopped by the porter and seen by any of the community, be it nun or one of the lay workers. Corbett rubbed his face. There was something wrong but he was too tired to reach any conclusion so he went back to his chamber where Ranulf, a fresh cup of wine in his hand, was waiting for him.

'The horses are stabled, and Dame Agatha safely returned to the bosom of her community?'

Ranulf grinned.

'And what did you learn in the village?'

'Well,' Ranulf answered, scratching his head, 'as I have said, nothing is what it appears to be. Father Reynard may be a fierce preacher but he is a source of spiritual and material comforts to his parishioners.'

'What do you mean?'

'Well, he not only refuses his tithes but seems to have a source of wealth which enables him to distribute alms, to mend the church as well as have it painted and refurbished.'

'And no obvious benefactor?'

Ranulf shook his head.

'What else?'

'The tavern wench says she saw the young man and woman who were later found murdered in the forest. She glimpsed them as they passed the tavern. They were taking the road to Godstowe.'

'And were never seen alive again?' Corbett asked.

'The tavern wench also believes the landlord of The Bull is a poacher.'

'So?'

Ranulf grinned.

'She says he met someone from the convent on the night that Lady Eleanor died, and that Father Reynard did go to Godstowe but then disappeared until the next morning.'

Corbett leaned back against the bolster and stared up at the ceiling.

'One person we haven't questioned,' he said, 'is our drunken porter. Perhaps he could shed further light on our mystery?' He looked across at Ranulf. 'Do you wish to carouse late tonight?'

Ranulf nodded, put the wine cup down, took his cloak and went downstairs. He breathed a sigh of relief as he heard Corbett begin to play gently on the lute he always carried, a sign his master was content, reflecting on his own secret thoughts and not keeping a wary eye on him. Ranulf, too, was content. The tavern wench seemed a promising young lady and he was making a tidy pile of silver out of selling his exotic cures to the villagers and visitors to The Bull.

Outside it had turned dark and rather cold as Ranulf trotted along, following the curtain wall to the porter's lodge near the gate. He tapped gently on the door which was pulled open by Red Nose. Ranulf peeped over his shoulder. Inside the two guards of the Prince's retinue sat at a table, much the worse for drink. Ranulf saw the dice and smiled.

'Good evening, sirs!' he cried. 'I am bored and cannot sleep.' He jingled the coins in his purse. 'I'd pay for a cup of wine and I have dice, though I would love to know the finer points of the game!'

Both the porter and the guards welcomed him like a long-lost brother. Ranulf slumped on to the bench and pushed across a silver piece.

'My donation for the wine.' He smiled. 'And here are my dice. I bought them in London but my master...'

His voice trailed off as his hosts rushed to reassure him. So Ranulf's 'education' began. He acted the fool, losing at first to whet their appetites, but in an hour emptied his three victims' purses. The guards were so drunk they hardly realised they had been outcheated and slunk off to their pallet beds. The porter, however, had a harder head and Ranulf did not like the suspicious look in his bleary eyes.

'Look, man,' he said. 'I'll divide with you on this. It's only fair. I had beginner's luck!'

The porter stretched out his hand.

'Not now! A little information about the Lady Eleanor's death first.'

The porter drew back his hand and rubbed his mouth with the back of his wrist. Ranulf refilled their cups. Outside a wind had sprung up, gently moaning through the trees, carrying the distant shrieks of the night creatures from the dark forest beyond the walls. The thatched roof of the lodge creaked as if mourning over the dreadful secrets of the priory. Ranulf let his own eyes droop. He sighed, rose, and began to scoop his winnings into a small leather purse.

'Wait!' The porter staggered drunkenly to his feet. 'I will tell you my secret. You must come with me!'

Ranulf agreed and, with the inebriated porter on one hand and a lantern horn in the other, went out into the darkness. The door slammed behind them like a thunder clap. Ranulf looked up and groaned. It was obvious a storm was coming in. The clouds were beginning to gather, hiding the hunter's moon, and Ranulf shivered as he heard an owl hoot and the ominous chatter of other night birds. The wind blew in a low hum, making the trees shift and rustle eerily as if there were shadows waiting in the darkness. Ranulf pulled his cloak tighter, stopped, and looked back at Godstowe Priory, a huge pile of masonry dark against the sky. No lights burned now. He let the fresh air clear the wine fumes from his head and, dropping all pretence, began to question the porter on what he had hinted earlier. The fellow fenced for a while but Ranulf persisted. Eventually the porter broke away from him.

'I'm going to tell you,' he slurred drunkenly.

Ranulf allowed the fellow to walk ahead of him, round the priory to the Galilee Gate. For a while the man stood muttering and cursing as he clanked his heavy ring of keys, but at last he found the right one and they stepped on to the moonlit track which ran down like a strip of silver through the overhanging trees. They walked along until suddenly the porter turned, following a track into the thick, dark wood. A lonely place, though the porter caused some light comedy with his staggering and drunken curses, stopping every so often to wave Ranulf on, urging him to hold the lantern horn higher. They must have walked for at least three miles and eventually came out of the wood and on to a pathway which led to a crossroads.

Ranulf lifted the lantern horn and his blood ran cold as he glimpsed a gibbet standing there. On it a body, half-decayed, still turned and twisted in its iron jacket. The porter gestured him over.

'You want to know my secrets?' he slurred.

'Yes,' Ranulf hissed.

'Then swear you will keep them.'

Ranulf raised his right hand.

'No,' the porter growled. 'Here!'

He took Ranulf's hand, led him over to the gibbet and pushed his hands between the iron bars until the tips of his fingers touched the decaying flesh of the hanged man, just above where his heart had been. Ranulf felt his stomach lurch as all the wine he had drunk threatened to spew out. The porter, staggering beside him, made the iron gibbet creak and groan until it appeared that all three were partners in a deadly dance. Ranulf was sworn to secrecy, but there was worse to come. The porter pulled out his knife, slashed the corpse, and then gave Ranulf's arm a small nick on the wrist. He then forced Ranulf's hand close to that of the corpse. Ranulf felt the wet scaliness against his skin as if some dreadful snake was slithering along his arm. Oblivious to the words he spoke, cursing Corbett and near fainting with terror, he swore he would never divulge the secret in this life or the next. Once the macabre masque was over, Ranulf stepped back. His usual good humour had vanished and his hand dropped to the dagger pushed in his belt. The porter stood swaying drunkenly before him.

'Listen, man!' Ranulf snapped. 'I have sworn the oath—now what is it you wish to tell me? What is so dreadful and so secret about the Lady Eleanor's death?'

'I didn't say Lady Eleanor!' he chanted. 'I didn't say Lady Eleanor! I said my secret. You promised to take the oath and divide your winnings with me for a secret!'

He stood still, his drunken face sagging as Ranulf's dagger pricked him under the chin.

'Now, now,' he slurred.

'The secret, you bastard.'

The porter fell to his knees and began to scrabble at the soft soil next to the wooden scaffold pole. Rocks and loose dirt were pulled away and eventually he dragged out a tattered leather bag.

'That's my secret!'

Ranulf knelt beside him, cut open the neck of the bag and shook out the contents into the small pool of lantern light. Nothing much. A collection of thin yellowing bones and a small leather collar.

'What is this?' Ranulf muttered.

'Well, you've heard about the murder?' the porter replied. 'The young man and woman whose naked bodies were found in the marsh? A week afterwards, I was out poaching very near the place and I found the body of a small lap dog. The poor creature had died, probably from neglect, or else pined away for its mistress. Only a lady would have a lap dog. There was no one in the village who would own such a pet and the

Lady Prioress is quite strict with her community on that, so I knew it must belong to the young woman who had been murdered.'

The fellow grinned, his yellow stumps of teeth shining garishly in the poor light. He pointed to the tattered piece of leather.

'That's the only thing which gave any clue about her.'

'Why didn't you hand it to the Sheriff or the Justices?'

'Because there was a gold clasp on it,' the fellow muttered. 'I sold it to a tinker. So I thought I'd better bury the poor thing.' He glimpsed the look of anger in Ranulf's eyes. 'Take the collar!' he urged. 'There's a motto inscribed inside. Examine it carefully. Now, that's my secret,' he whined. 'I know nothing about Lady Eleanor. I was drunk as a bishop the night she died. The Lady Prioress had to sober me up to send me to Woodstock. God knows how I got there. I gave the message to some chamberlain and staggered back.'

'You went by horse?'

'No, there's a quicker route across the fields. In daylight it's quite clear. Go out the other side of the priory, beyond the farm. You will see the track. It's not an hour's walk.'

Ranulf sighed, pocketed the leather strap, waited for the porter to re-bury the bones and half-carried him back to the priory, listening to the fellow's litany of self-congratulation.

'Nobody would ever think,' he slurred, 'of looking beneath a gibbet!'

Ranulf humoured him and, once they were through the Galilee Gate, handed over the promised coins and went back to the guest house.

Corbett was still up, seated on the floor, pieces of parchment strewn around him. Ranulf knew his master had been scribbling his own memoranda, trying to make sense of the mystery which confronted them. Ranulf gave a brief account of what had happened. Corbett grunted, impatiently hurrying him on, and seized the tattered leather strap. He asked Ranulf to hold up a candle and carefully examined the inscription on the faded, leather collar: '*Noli me tangere*'. Do not touch me.

'What do you think, Ranulf?'

'A family motto?'

'Perhaps.'

Corbett rubbed the strap between his fingers and went to stare out of the window, half-listening to the sounds of the night outside. In his heart Corbett knew that the murder of Lady Eleanor and the dreadful silent slaying of that mysterious young woman and her male companion in the nearby woods were inextricably linked.

THE DUNGEONS of the Louvre Palace were the antechambers of hell though very few of those who went down the dark stony steps ever emerged to recount their experiences. Philip IV's master torturers, a motley gang of Italians and strange wild creatures from Wallachia, were expert in breaking the bodies and souls of their prisoners. Eudo Tailler, however, had proved to be one of their strongest victims. Despite the crossbow bolt in his thigh, Eudo had survived the rack, the boot and the strappado: every limb was broken but he clung tenaciously to life. He had seen the young French clerk whom Céleste had seduced, be broken in a matter of days and confess to whatever question had been put to him. Eudo was different. He was not frightened for he hated the French more than he feared death. Fifteen years earlier Philip's troops had attacked his father's village and razed it to the ground, wiping out in one night Eudo's brothers and sisters, as well as his young wife and child.

Eudo refused to say anything. Oh, he had told lies and they had trapped him by asking for the names of other English agents in Paris. He had told them many a fairy story and when they checked, they returned more furious than before, dragging him out of his dirty, fetid pit back into the great vaulted torture chamber to be questioned once again. Sometimes Eudo had glimpsed the French King, his blond hair glinting in the guttering torchlight. Philip would stand behind the black-masked torturers waiting for Eudo to speak. Now it was all over. Eudo knew he was going to die. He had also realised what the French wanted from him: the truth about the Prince of Wales' former mistress, now immured at Godstowe.

What had Corbett told him about her? they asked. Had she been married to the Prince? Were any of the nuns royal agents? Did the name de Courcy mean anything to them?

Eudo had replied through swollen, bloody lips that he knew nothing, so the questioners changed tack.

Who was the de Montfort assassin now stalking Edward of England? Was he at Godstowe or in London?

He could not have told them. All he knew was a conversation heard second-hand at a hostelry in Bordeaux, although Eudo, a Gascon, had a shrewd idea of the true identity of the assassin. Now, on this last day of his life, he showed he could stand the pain no more. The torturers had chained him to a wall, applying searing hot pokers to the softest and most tender parts of his body. Eudo opened his bloody lips in a soundless scream.

'The assassin, Master Tailler?'

Eudo shook his head. Again the hot searing pain.

'The assassin, Master Eudo? Give us his name, then you can sleep.'

Eudo felt his life seeping from him. He felt detached, as if he was floating high up above them and the executioners were only playing with the useless bundle of flesh that had once been his body. He began softly to mutter the final act of contrition to himself. Surely God would remember he had been loyal to his king? The torturers were waved back by a senior clerk who had accompanied the French King to the dungeon. He hid his distaste as he pressed his ear up against the dying man's lips.

'What did you say, Monsieur Tailler? The name of the assassin?'

Eudo summoned all his strength, as if he could stand the pain no longer, and whispered a name. The clerk stood back, smiling triumphantly over his shoulder at his royal master.

'He has told us, Your Grace. We have our man.'

Philip remained impassive.

'Ask him again!' he snapped.

The clerk moved forward, took one look at Eudo and hastily stepped back.

'He is dead, Your Grace.'

Philip nodded.

'Cut him down!' he ordered. He turned to the clerk. 'Send the following despatch in cipher to Seigneur de Craon. He must have it as soon as possible.'

SIX

THE NEXT MORNING Corbett roused Ranulf, who awoke bleary-eyed.

'For the love of God, Master!'

'You've been too long in the service of the Devil,' Corbett joked. 'You drink too late and rise too late.'

'I have been too long in your service,' Ranulf grumbled. He rose, scrubbed his teeth by dipping his finger in some salt, washed his face in a bowl of rosewater, put on his boots and, led by a still joking Corbett, went downstairs to break his fast in the small buttery.

'What's the business of the day, Master?'

Corbett chewed thoughtfully on a small manchet loaf from a basket covered by a white linen cloth.

'Do you believe in Hell, Ranulf?' he asked suddenly.

'Of course, Master. Why?'

Corbett pointed to the one stained glass window in the room where the artist had painted a graphic vision of demons, their eyes glaring fiercely, their mouths and nostrils poured forth fetid breath as they tore the flesh of sinners with red hot pincers and pierced their bodies with glowing iron nails, whilst others beat the unfortunates with spikes and scourges. Ranulf studied the painting curiously and felt a shiver of apprehension as he saw how the sinners were thrust into hot ovens, cauldrons of boiling oil, or broken on huge revolving cartwheels. At the bottom of the picture serpents, dragons, adders, ferrets, loathsome toads and horrible worms, gathered to prey upon the damned.

'If you look at that picture long enough, Master, you'd believe you were in Hell itself,' Ranulf murmured. 'Why do you ask?'

Corbett sipped thoughtfully from his goblet. 'A quiet place, Godstowe,' he replied. 'Just listen.'

His manservant turned, stared out of the doorway and caught the sounds of the priory community as it went about its daily tasks; the clang of milk pails, the rumble of cartwheels, and beneath the liquid song of the birds, the gentle chanting of the nuns from the priory church.

'Peaceful,' Corbett continued shortly. 'Yet I believe that Satan himself, the Prince of Darkness, has risen from his cauldron in Hell and now stalks this sun-dappled place.'

The servant shivered.

'Do you know, Ranulf,' Corbett continued, wiping his mouth on a napkin, 'when I was a boy, my mother took me to hear a famous preacher. He talked about Hell being a boiling hot lake full of venomous serpents. In it backbiters stood up to their knees. Fornicators,' Corbett threw a sly glance at Ranulf, 'up to their necks, adulterers and traitors up to their eyes.' Corbett smiled. 'I remember this sermon because my father, who never laughed but always kept a straight face when he joked, leaned over and murmured that this preacher spoke so eloquently of Hell, he must have been there himself.'

Ranulf grinned and relaxed.

'However,' Corbett continued, clasping his sword belt around his waist, 'one thing I do remember is that the preacher was really a gentle man; he told my mother that Holy Mother Church merely wished to frighten its children except—' Corbett narrowed his eyes and looked through the doorway '—for murderers, those who slay, especially the sons of Cain who plot with ice-cold malice the destruction of someone they hate.' Corbett paused. 'This is what happened at Godstowe, Ranulf. First,' he ticked the points off on his finger, 'Lady Eleanor Belmont was murdered. Believe me, it was no accident but coolly planned and carefully calculated. Secondly, the aged nun, Dame Martha, was also murdered for what she knew. And somehow or other, I believe these murders are linked to the two corpses found in the forest nearby.' He stared seriously at Ranulf. 'I think it's time we had further words with our porter friend.'

'Master!'

'Yes?'

'I haven't finished my wine.' Ranulf glared balefully.

Corbett smiled and leaned against the doorpost. 'I'll wait, Ranulf. But that's not your real problem, is it?'

Ranulf gulped from the goblet. 'No, Master Corbett, it isn't. Who is the murderer?'

'God knows, Ranulf. The King? The Prince? Gaveston? That royal catamite would do anything.' Corbett sighed. 'Or the assassin could be one of the nuns, or even our good parish priest.' He paused. 'You are ready?'

'As always, Master.'

Corbett smiled and they went across to the porter's lodge near the main gate. Surprisingly, the fellow was already up, squatting on a bench outside the door, sunning himself, a jack of ale cradled in his hands.

'Good morrow, Master Clerk.' The fellow squinted up and grinned conspiratorially at Ranulf. 'You wish to leave?'

'Good morrow to you too.' Corbett tapped the fellow's boot with his own. 'Yes, I wish to leave, and I want you to come and show us the place where those two corpses were found.'

'Which corpses?' The fellow glared at Ranulf.

Corbett leaned over and gripped the porter tightly by the shoulder. 'Don't play games with me,' he whispered. 'About eighteen months ago, a young man and woman were found naked with their throats cut, in the forest. You later found the corpse of a small lap dog nearby. You took the collar, sold the jewels for it and buried the remains at the foot of a scaffold.' Corbett watched the man become frightened. 'Now,' he continued, 'you may not be a murderer but you *are* a thief. You stole from the dead, and failed to deliver certain information to the King's Justices or to the Sheriff. I am prepared to forget all that *if* you agree to join us for a stroll on this fine summer's day.'

The porter threw one venomous look at Ranulf, slammed the jack of ale down on the bench, grumblingly unlocked the postern door and led them out on to the white, dusty forest track which snaked between the trees down to Godstowe village. The porter walked ahead, Corbett and Ranulf strolled behind. The clerk stretched and sucked in the clear morning air.

'Why do we need to visit the place?' Ranulf moaned.

'Curiosity,' Corbett replied. As they turned a corner on the path, the clerk suddenly stopped and grasped Ranulf by the arm. 'Listen,' he hissed as the porter walked on oblivious to what was happening behind him. Ranulf strained his ears, trying to ignore the sounds of the forest, the chatter of the birds and the rustle of the wood creatures under the thick green bracken. Then he, too, heard it: the sound of footsteps slithering across the loose shale of the track. The porter stopped and turned. Corbett indicated with his hand for him to stand still and be silent. The footsteps drew nearer.

'I think I know who it is,' Corbett whispered.

They heard heavy breathing and a figure appeared round the corner, clothed in the grey garb of Godstowe Priory. Corbett glimpsed red cheeks and sparkling eyes behind the wimple.

'Dame Catherine!' he exclaimed.

The nun stopped, jumped, and gave a small cry, her fingers fluttering to her mouth.

'Dame Catherine, good morning.'

'Good morrow, Master Clerk,' the flustered nun replied. 'I am going...'

Corbett stepped out from beneath the trees. 'Don't lie, Sister. The Lady Amelia would never allow you to go wandering off by yourself. I am sure you have no business at the village.'

The nun's face blushed a deeper crimson. Ranulf appreciatively watched the woman's plump breasts rise and fall beneath her grey, woollen gown.

'You are following us,' Corbett declared. 'I glimpsed you out of the corner of my eye when I was talking to the porter.'

'I...' The nun looked away. 'Yes, I was following you,' she confessed. 'I saw you talking to the porter, then suddenly leave. I was curious.'

'Why?' Corbett asked.

Dame Catherine's face hardened. 'You have come into our priory to insinuate that evil deeds have been committed,' she snapped.

'That's because they have, Sister.' Corbett turned and angrily waved at the porter to stay where he was. 'I do not believe that Lady Eleanor fell downstairs. I am suspicious about old Martha drowning in her bath, and you may tell the Lady Amelia that I am now curious about the two corpses found in the forest nearby.'

'Oh!'

Corbett stepped closer.

'You heard about that?' Ranulf interrupted.

'Yes, we all did. I believe the Lady Amelia has told you everything we know.'

Corbett ran his fingers through his hair. 'What exactly did the Lady Amelia tell us, Sister?' The clerk stared up at the clear blue sky. 'Come on,' he urged gently. 'You left the priory this morning on her orders, so tell me what you and Sister Amelia know about the corpses in the forest. It will save further questioning.'

The nun shrugged. 'About eighteen months ago,' she answered, 'the two corpses were found. They were put in canvas sacks and taken to the church in Godstowe for burial. The Sheriff and coroner came to the village and held the *Inquisicio Post Mortem* but they found nothing except that two travellers fitting the dead persons' descriptions had passed through the village earlier in the day.' Dame Catherine made a face. 'As I said, they were found naked, murdered, and no one came to claim their bodies.'

'Where were they travelling to?'

'We don't know.'

'Were two such visitors expected at Godstowe?'

'No. We have many visitors but most of them have the Prioress' permission to come and visit relatives. No such guests were expected. I...' Dame Catherine stopped and straightened her wimple. 'I am responsible for the preparations for such visitors. The Sheriff asked me the same question and I gave him the same answer as I have you.'

'What then?'

Dame Catherine licked her dry lips. 'The Sheriff concluded as we did, that the two unfortunates were travellers on the road and were ambushed by outlaws.' She stared into the green darkness of the forest. 'We have such wolfshead round here.' She smiled at Corbett. 'You are going to the place where their bodies were found?'

'Yes, the porter agreed to take us there,' Corbett lied.

'I'd better...' Dame Catherine stammered. 'I'd better return.'

'Dame Catherine?'

'Yes, Master Clerk?'

'Did you like the Lady Eleanor?'

'She was a royal whore!' The nun spat the words out. 'Make of it what you want, Clerk, she should not have been sent to Godstowe!'

'Yet the Lady Prioress agreed?'

'The Lady Prioress is a law unto herself,' Dame Catherine spitefully added. 'She has her own rules. She owes her position to her father's services to the Prince many years ago.'

'You dislike the Lady Prioress?' Ranulf asked curiously.

'The Lady Amelia can be strict,' Dame Catherine answered carefully. 'She banished pets and festivities from the priory. She is most strict on where we go and limits the number of our visitors. She has forbidden hunting or hawking, and then—'

'And then,' Corbett interrupted smoothly, 'she allowed the royal whore to come and stay in your midst?'

'Yes.'

'But did you like her?' Ranulf persisted. 'I mean, the Lady Eleanor?'

Dame Catherine pursed her lips. 'We left her alone. She was haughty, distant. The only people she spoke to were the Lady Prioress and Dame Agatha.'

Corbett nodded and clapped Ranulf on the shoulders. 'In which case, Sister, there is no further need for you to accompany us. You may tell Lady Amelia where we are going for our walk and that we will return shortly.'

They stood and watched the nun spin on her heel and waddle off with as much dignity as she could muster.

'Strange,' Corbett mused. 'I really do wonder where the Lady Prioress thought we were going.'

They continued their walk, rousing the surly porter from where he crouched at the edge of the track, chewing a piece of fresh grass.

'What did Dame Catherine want?' he demanded. 'You didn't tell her about the collar?'

'She came to wish us a safe journey,' Ranulf replied sarcastically. 'And no, we did not tell her about the dog collar. Or,' he added mischievously, 'the gems you stole from it!'

They must have walked for about another ten minutes and could glimpse the blue wood-smoke rising above the trees from Godstowe village when suddenly the porter stopped, turned left, and led them along a narrow beaten trackway into the forest. Ranulf shivered. He always felt uncomfortable amongst this dark silent wood, the strange shadows, the bursts of sudden sunlight and constant chatter and rustle of unseen birds and animals.

'I'd prefer a darkened alleyway in Southwark,' he muttered.

'Each to his own,' Corbett replied.

They followed the porter along the serpentine path, then suddenly they were through the trees and into a glade ringed by clumps of trees, silent except for the gurgle of a small brook as it splashed down some rocks which thrust up out of the ground like the finger of a buried giant.

'Be careful,' the porter murmured. He pointed to the near side of the small brook where the grass seemed darker, longer, and lush. 'Watch!' he insisted, and picking up a fallen bough, threw it into the midst of this dark greenness. Ranulf swallowed nervously as the bough hit the ground. There was a sucking noise, a small pool of water formed, and the branch sank without trace. 'A marsh,' the porter explained. 'There are a number in the forest.' He grinned with a display of broken teeth. 'Only fools would wander in here.'

'Where were the bodies found?'

'Well,' the fellow scratched his head, 'from what I gather, they had been rolled into the marsh but hadn't sunk. Two lovers from the village, looking for a quiet spot, found them and sent for help. We pulled them out.'

'How were they?'

Well, that's the mystery,' the porter replied. 'I heard about their discovery and hurried down from the priory. I was there when the bailiffs arrived. The bodies were naked as they were born, not a scrap of clothing, jewellery or any possessions. Yet their faces...' The man shook his head. 'A mottled black and white, their throats cut from ear to ear.'

'And no one claimed the bodies?'

'No.'

'And you expected no such visitors to the priory?'

'No.'

'Then how did you find the dog?'

The porter moved restlessly from one foot to another. 'Well, I was truly puzzled, so two days later I came back. I know the forest well. I thought there might be something worth finding.' He pointed over to the ring of trees. 'There, under the bracken, I glimpsed the dog. At first I thought it was a dead rabbit. I went over to look and knew it was a lap dog.'

'You didn't kill it?' Ranulf snapped.

'God be my witness, sir, I didn't!' The porter licked his lips nervously. 'The corpses must have been in the marsh for days, even weeks. The dog must have run away and, being such a pampered animal, crawled back and pined to death for its mistress. I took the collar off, removed the stones, put the rest in the sack and took it to the gibbet. The rest you know.' He glared again at Ranulf and looked down at his boots.

'Are there outlaws here?' Corbett asked.

The porter made a face. 'No, Master Clerk. That's what puzzled me and the other villagers. Oh, there's a few wild lads who do some poaching. But tell me,' he asked, defiantly repeating taproom gossip, 'what outlaw worth his brain would hide in a forest with a royal palace at one end and a priory full of powerful ladies at the other? Not to mention the village and the other farms. There are deeper woods than this for a wolfshead to hide in.'

Corbett stared round the eerie, silent glade. 'If only the leaves of these trees,' he murmured 'could turn to tongues, what story would they tell?'

Ranulf just shivered.

'A place to rest,' Corbett muttered. 'But perhaps not a place to die.'

'I don't know,' Ranulf replied, his face growing paler. 'I once knew a sailor, an old man from Gravesend. He said that on one of his voyages, he passed a floating island thronged with demonic blacksmiths who forged and hammered the evil souls of assassins!' Ranulf shook his head. 'I think this place is more suited for that than any island.' He stared at Corbett. 'I don't like it, Master. It stinks of death!'

'Then, Master Porter,' Corbett announced, 'it's best we leave.'

They walked back to the forest track where Corbett dismissed the porter. Then he and a calmer Ranulf sat on a log at the edge of the trees.

'What do we have here?' Corbett murmured as soon as the porter was out of earshot. 'Two travellers, ambushed and murdered in a forest glade—was it by outlaws?' He shook his head. 'The porter is right and Dame Catherine's explanation feckless. No outlaw would lurk so near a royal palace or so close to a powerful priory.'

Ranulf belched noisily. 'I'd agree with that,' he added apologetically. 'Nor would any outlaw strip the corpses so carefully: jewellery and silver maybe, perhaps the horses and their harnesses, but not to the extent the porter described. Nor,' he concluded, 'would any outlaw try to hide the bodies. He would take his ill-gotten gains and flee.'

Corbett rubbed his chin. 'And so the mystery deepens. Why kill them, Ranulf? Why not just demand their valuables and scamper off? It's almost as if,' he paused, 'the murderer wanted to disguise who his victims were. He takes their belongings, their horses, then tips their naked corpses into a marsh, except they don't sink properly.' He chewed his lip. 'There are other riddles.

These two travellers were apparently strangers in the area, yet how did they know about this forest path leading to a glade with the water to refresh themselves? And who would be strong enough to overcome a young man as well as a, presumably, fairly robust young damsel?'

'What are you saying, Master?'

'Well, the only conclusion is that they were lured to their deaths. They were taken to that glade to be murdered. And yet,' Corbett laughed abruptly, 'did they just offer their throats to the murderer?' He turned. 'Do you make any sense of it, Ranulf?'

'No, Master, I don't. I have the same questions. Who were they? Where were they going? Not to the priory, they weren't expected there.' Ranulf blew out noisily. 'And, as you say, Master, how were they lured to their deaths and why so meekly give up their lives?'

Corbett rose and brushed the moss from his clothes. 'A riddle within a riddle,' he murmured. 'But I can tell you this, Ranulf, even though I haven't a shred of evidence, I believe the deaths of those two young people have something to do with the murder of Lady Eleanor Belmont.'

Ranulf sat staring down at the ground.

'Master?'

'Yes, Ranulf?'

'Both Dame Catherine and the porter mentioned these two corpses being found in the wood which lies between the priory and the palace. Could the murderer have been from either of these?'

Corbett shook his head. 'It would be hard to prove, Ranulf. As the porter said, the corpses might have been lying there for days, even weeks. If it was the priory, why should a nun murder two travellers? And our noble lords at the palace would certainly have done a more professional job.' Corbett narrowed his eyes and squinted up at the sky. 'I suggest we are talking about a murderer rather than murderers. One person acting hastily who dragged the bodies to the marsh and hurried away.' He made a face and tapped his man on the shoulder. 'But, my dear Ranulf, that too causes a problem. Could one person overcome two able-bodied people?'

Ranulf rose and stretched. 'There're tensions at the priory, Master.'

Corbett grimaced. 'Of course there are. The Lady Amelia is unpopular. She put an end to the nuns' little treats and tricks, whilst at the same time allowing a whore to take up residence there. Moreover, we know our master the King, Ranulf. One day, I am sure, he will ask Lady Amelia to account for her stewardship.'

'And where to now, Master?'

'Well, I think we have finished at the priory for the moment, and the good villagers of Godstowe know very little. Perhaps it's time we visited our noble Prince of Wales and the Lord Gaveston at Woodstock.'

Ranulf groaned and closed his eyes.

'Look on the bright side,' Corbett sang out, walking briskly away. 'Where there's a palace there are pretty girls!'

Ranulf glared at his master's retreating back.

'Aye,' he muttered. 'And where there's Gaveston, there's the Devil!'

SEVEN

KING EDWARD OF ENGLAND sat in his purple silken pavilion which stood at the centre of his great camp on the green meadows beneath the formidable mass of Nottingham Castle. He was listening to the sounds of his army gathering; brown-jerkinned archers; men-at-arms in conical helmets carrying long spears and quilted jackets; the shouted orders of his serjeants and the neighing and whinnying of the proud-blooded warhorses.

The King, just past his sixtieth year, sat on one of the great pay chests, tapping the wood beneath him. He hoped his barons would bring the men he needed. He was intent on taking north the largest army he had ever gathered, to crush the Scottish rebels, hang their leader, the Red Comyn, trap the Scots in their glens and burn their villages. He would cover Scotland in a sea of flames, and teach those traitors a lesson they would never forget. He just wished his son were here...

Edward's heart, hardened against tears of self-pity, beat a little faster. Where had he gone wrong? He loved the boy, always had and always would. Perhaps it was his mother's death? Perhaps he had expected too much of him? Edward closed his eyes and remembered those golden summers now an eternity away. His son, silver-haired, delighted to see his father, tottering across some green meadow, sent to embrace him by his dark-eyed, olive-skinned mother, Eleanor. Oh, Christ! Edward closed his eyes tightly as memories came flooding back.

Oh, good God, he prayed, why did such memories always turn so bitter-sweet in his soul?

'I'd give everything I have,' he muttered aloud, 'for all that back.'

Edward's mood shifted quickly and he ground his teeth in rage. Gaveston would hinder that. The warlock, the perverted son of a perverted mother! Edward had considered banishing him but behind him loomed the spectre of civil war; his son would resist and there were those amongst his barons, especially the younger ones, who would be only too willing to follow his son. If there was civil war, the Scots would spill across the Northern March, the Welsh would rebel, and Philip of France would have his ships off Dover within a week. But Edward knew the real reason for his not banishing Gaveston—he could refuse his son nothing. Those blue eyes, their shimmer of innocence, the memories of sweeter, softer days...

'Your Grace! Your Grace!'

Edward opened his eyes. John de Warenne, Earl of Surrey, stood, legs apart, at the mouth of the tent, a flagon of beer in one hand, a half-eaten chicken breast in the other.

'You are too early, John.'

De Warenne saw the tears on the King's cheeks and looked away.

'What does it profit a king, John, if he conquer the whole world and suffer the loss of his beloved son?'

De Warenne stared blankly back and Edward grinned. Good old de Warenne, he thought, with his bluff red face and treacherous black heart. A good soldier but a bad general. His answer to everything was to mount and charge. He had even offered to kill Gaveston.

'What is it, John?'

'Nothing, except de Craon.'

Edward raised his eyes heavenwards.

'So Philip's envoy has searched me out,' he muttered.

'Snap out of your maudlin mood, Your Grace!' de Warenne rasped. 'Dry your eyes like a good girl and grasp your longest spoon, for the Devil has come to sup!'

'The Godstowe business?'

De Warenne nodded.

'It must be. The rumours are growing thick and fast as weeds and de Craon must be their sower. There is a whispering campaign. Even in the city they are saying the Prince killed his mistress to please his lover. De Craon is snuffling about for the juicier morsels, then it's back to Paris and heigh ho for Rome and our Holy Father.'

'Shut up, de Warenne!'

Edward kicked the earth with the toe of his boot. Oh, he could just imagine Philip's display of outraged innocence—and then the letter would come from the Pope. Edward knew how it would begin.

'Per venit ad aures nostras—It has reached our ears, most beloved Son in Christ...', followed by the usual sanctimonious phrases, then the allegations of sodomy, murder, the unsuitability of the Prince of Wales for an innocent French princess, the dissolution of the treaty, all culminating in bloody war. Hell's teeth! Edward thought. What was that inquisitive bastard Corbett doing, sending him warnings about an assassin, another de Montfort on the loose in England? Edward smirked. He did not fear that. Perhaps it was time he told Corbett so. No, it was the Godstowe business which

really troubled him. The crown had to be defended. His
son had to be protected. What on earth was his own spy
at Godstowe doing?

'If Your Grace wishes to go back to sleep... ?'

'I'll have your bloody balls, de Warenne!' The King
grinned. 'Show the bastard in!'

A few seconds later de Craon bustled in, his face
wreathed in an unctuous smile, bobbing and bowing
while his snake-like eyes scrutinised the King. Edward
thought the Frenchman looked slightly ridiculous in his
soft sarencet gown and tawny-coloured boots, but he
kept his face impassive. De Craon had strange tastes.
One of these days...

'Monsieur de Craon,' Edward deliberately dropped
the 'Seigneur'. 'We are pleased to see you. Your journey was comfortable? We have been eagerly awaiting
your arrival.'

De Craon half bowed.

'Not half as eager, Your Grace, as I have been to see
you! My master, King Philip, sends fraternal greetings.
He is deeply distressed by your problems in Scotland.
He offers to mediate and will do anything to assist.'

Like send a hundred ships full of men and munitions
to help the bastards, Edward thought. He hooked a foot
under a camp stool and dragged it over.

'Will you sit, Monsieur?'

De Craon noticed the stool's crooked leg.

'Your Majesty is too kind. I insist on standing. You
deserve that respect.'

De Craon decided to keep a wary eye on Edward. He
studied the cruel falcon face framed by the iron-grey
hair, watching those slightly slanted eyes, one half-
closed—a mannerism Edward had acquired as a young

man. It indicated a violent temper. De Craon decided to be more circumspect.

'Your Grace,' he began, 'my master sends greetings. He hopes all is well with his beloved sister Margaret?'

Edward thought of his whey-faced new bride, and grunted.

'The question of Gascony...'

'There is no question!' Edward snapped.

'Its rights and appurtenances?' de Craon meekly asked.

'They are mine.'

'By what right?'

Edward sighed.

'My dear de Craon, my troops are all over it.'

'Your troops have not been paid.'

'They will be!' the King bellowed.

'Yet, Your Grace,' de Craon spread his hands, 'all should be resolved by the marriage of your beloved son to the Princess Isabella.'

'You have seen my beloved son?'

'At Woodstock, Your Grace.'

'"At Woodstock, Your Grace."!' Edward mimicked back.

'Your Grace, has your son been detained there?'

'No, I just bloody well want him there!'

'To be near Godstowe?'

'To be near Oxford.'

'He mourns the death of Lady Eleanor.'

'Who is she?' Edward asked tartly.

De Craon smiled.

'Your Grace jests with me.' The Frenchman's face grew serious.

Here it comes, Edward thought.

'Your Grace, I am most anxious and deeply troubled by the rumours put about by evil men. Malicious, slanderous stories which claim the Lady Eleanor was murdered by your son so he could be with his beloved companion, the Gascon, Piers Gaveston.'

'They are lying traitors. I'll have any man who says that hanged, drawn and quartered!'

'Of course, Your Grace. But they whisper about how could a woman fall downstairs, break her neck, and yet keep the hood on her head undisturbed? They say that your son was sending potions, that the lady may have been poisoned.'

'My son knows nothing about Lady Eleanor's death. She died on a Sunday evening. The first the Prince of Wales knew of the unhappy event was the following Monday morning.'

De Craon blinked, his face now a mask of concern.

'Your Grace, I am sorry—your son knew about Lady Eleanor's death on Sunday evening.'

De Craon pushed his foxy face closer. Edward sat frozen, one of the few times in his life he had been genuinely frightened. My son a murderer! That's the rumour which will begin to circulate: a poisoner as well as a sodomite. A slayer of innocent women. I'll have Corbett's head! Edward thought.

Behind de Craon Edward saw de Warenne quietly pull a dagger from his sheath. All the King had to do was raise a finger and the Frenchman would be dead. Edward shook his head and de Warenne sheathed his knife.

'How do you know this?'

'Your Grace, your own son told me.'

'There must be some mistake.'

'No, there is not. His exact words were . . .' de Craon closed his eyes. 'I asked him about the Lady Eleanor and he replied: "She is near to death, a fall, an accident. She must have fallen downstairs."' De Craon smiled politely. 'It was after midnight, Your Grace. The Prince was in his cups, yet I thought it strange because the porter from Godstowe Priory did not arrive until the early hours of the morning.'

Edward turned to the jewel box beside him, opened it and took out a small gold ring with a precious ruby winking in the centre.

'Monsieur, please accept this as a gift. I will think about what you have said.'

De Craon stretched out his hand. The King grasped his wrist tightly, squeezing hard, not satisfied until he saw the Frenchman wince.

'A gift, Monsieur,' he whispered. 'And a warning to those who spread malicious rumours. If I can prove such scandalous stories are a tissue of lies, I will tell both my brother the King of France and His Holiness of their source. They will not be pleased.'

De Craon shook his head and the King released his grip. De Craon's face was red with embarrassment.

'Your Grace,' he replied hoarsely, 'I thank you for your gift and your message.' And, spinning on his heel, he strode out of the pavilion.

Edward gestured de Warenne forward.

'John, your fastest horseman?'

'Ralph Maltote, Your Grace.'

'I want him to go south immediately, to Godstowe. He is to take our swiftest horse as well as a fresh mount. He is to ride without stopping and take a message to my clerk, Corbett, at Godstowe Priory. That message must be delivered. You understand? Now get out!'

As soon as de Warenne had left, Edward put his face in his hands as he tried to control both his anger and his terror. What was happening? he wondered. Why hadn't Corbett cleared this mess up? And his own spy at Godstowe...? Edward's left eye now drooped almost to closing as he gnawed at his lip. Both Corbett and his spy would pay dearly if de Craon gained the upper hand.

Whilst Edward of England sat fuming over what he had learnt, Sir Amaury de Craon was nursing his bruised wrist and shouting orders to his retinue for a swift return to Oxfordshire. He had played his card. Now he must wait. Oh, he recognised Edward of England's warning and could only close the game if he had proof. But he had let his arrow fly, now he must see where it fell. He believed he could outmanoeuvre and trap the English King; he too had his spy at Godstowe to keep an eye on Corbett. Moreover, de Craon had received an urgent message from his master. Another shadowy player was also in the game: the de Montfort assassin. De Craon nursed both his pain and his pride. Soon Edward of England would be checkmated. The only danger was Corbett. The English clerk would work doubly hard, either to resolve the problem or carefully to hide it behind a tissue of half-truths. De Craon rubbed his wrist. Corbett he would have to stop. He looked into his tent at the two dark cowled figures squatting there.

'We go south again. There is something I have planned for you,' he called.

A FEW DAYS after Ranulf's encounter with the drunken porter, Corbett decided that, for the moment, there was little else he could learn in the priory. He also wished to leave because the nuns were still engaged in the obsequies preceding the funerals of their two dead colleagues. The storm was over, the weather still held fine, so he and Ranulf decided to walk rather than ride to Woodstock Palace. The porter, now half-sober, greeted them as old friends and, taking them out of the priory, sketched a description of the track across the fields and meadows.

Corbett enjoyed the walk, glad to be free of the baleful, mournful atmosphere at Godstowe. The route was simple to follow, cutting across the open meadows and farming land, past dark copses, and well within the hour the crenellated walls and turrets of Woodstock Palace came into view. They followed the track which ran on to the road. The main gate was open. A serjeant-at-arms wearing the royal livery stopped them and asked their business before allowing them through. The courtyard was a hive of activity. Grooms, ostlers and farriers were taking horses in and out of the stables; scullions and kitchen boys carried huge slabs of freshly cut meat into the kitchen.

'The Prince must be expecting us,' Ranulf sardonically observed. 'A banquet perhaps?'

'A feast certainly,' Corbett answered. 'But I doubt if he will be pleased to see me.'

Grooms took their horses whilst a pompous steward of the Prince's household led them up the main steps into the spacious hall. Corbett knew the King loved his luxury, and Woodstock, a large, timbered building, was the pleasantest of royal palaces. Its outside had been renovated recently: the black gables newly embossed with gilt, the wooden beams painted a rich dark brown, and the stucco plaster clean and white. Inside, the palace's splendour made Ranulf catch his breath. Bright tapestries gleamed with gold and silver motifs; rich silk

cloths were placed over tables, the backs of chairs and
the massive open sideboards. Jewelled cups, their precious stones glinting in the sunlight, and silver dishes
were laid out on handsome chests and cabinets. In the
great hall henchmen were laying tables for the banquet
and the air was thick with the tangy wholesome odour
of cooking from the kitchen which made both men's
mouths water. They were not allowed to tarry, however, but were taken upstairs, along a gallery and into a
small chamber, its simplicity in stark contrast to the
splendour they had just witnessed.

Both Gaveston and the Prince were there. The royal
favourite sat in a quilted window seat whilst young Edward lounged in a chair near him. They were both gaz-
ing out of the window like homesick boys, as if
desperately wishing to be elsewhere. The King, however, had ordered that his son should stay at Woodstock and, of course, where the Prince of Wales was,
Gaveston his shadow always followed.

Both young men loved ostentatious dress but today
they were dressed simply in hose pushed into soft leather
riding boots, lacy cambric shirts, and blood-red taffeta
jackets slung across their shoulders. Gaveston didn't
turn a hair as Corbett and Ranulf were announced. The
Prince, however, smiled falsely, straightening up in his
chair and running long white fingers through his blond
hair.

'Master Corbett, I remember you. You are my father's man.'

'And yours, Your Grace.'

The Prince smirked and indicated that a steward
should bring forward two chairs.

'Corbett, you and your wide-eyed servant may as well
sit. You wish for some wine?'

The Prince didn't even wait for an answer but turned to a small table beside him, slopped two goblets full of wine, rose and thrust them at his unwanted guests. Corbett murmured his thanks and sipped gently. Ranulf drained his cup in two noisy gulps. The Prince smirked and Gaveston turned, for the first time acknowledging their presence with a condescending sneer. Corbett refused to be ruffled. He guessed both men were drunk but Gaveston particularly, even half-asleep, was as dangerous as a slumbering boar. He studied the Gascon's dark effete face and the jewel-encrusted pearl which swung arrogantly from one ear lobe. In everything he was the perfect courtier. The King had told him that Gaveston aimed high, coveted an earldom, and wished to use his friendship with the Prince to found a dynasty as great as the de Clares, the Beaumonts, or any of the great lords who had followed the Conqueror across the Narrow Seas.

For his part, Gaveston scrutinised the clerk whilst running the tip of his tongue over full fleshy lips. He cursed the drink, his own maudlin thoughts, and the Prince for seeing Corbett. In his heart Gaveston knew that young Edward quite liked the clerk; admired the man's fidelity and unwillingness to criticise him to his terrible father. Gaveston feared no one, neither the King, de Warenne, or any great lord, but was wary of Corbett with his secretive face and hooded eyes. Soon the questions would begin and the Prince would have no choice but to answer. Oh, he could stand on his dignity, but Corbett would inform the King and the Prince would have to answer eventually. Gaveston clenched his hands in his lap. He and the Prince should be left alone! He glanced quickly at Edward and Corbett saw the flicker of annoyance on the Prince's face.

'Your Grace,' he asked, 'you object to my being here?'

'No, Corbett, I do not. What puzzles me is why?'

'Lady Eleanor's death.'

The Prince arched an eyebrow.

'There's some problem?' he asked. 'I understand she had an accident?'

'No, it is said she was murdered.'

Corbett stared coolly back, noting the agitation his stark comment had caused.

'You have proof of that?' Gaveston asked.

'My Lord, soon I will, but whatever evidence I have will not make any difference to the Prince's enemies. They will still allege he murdered her.' Corbett leaned forward. 'I am not saying I believe that. I report what I feel, as well as the rumour that is spreading. Accordingly, the more facts I have, the better I can combat the lies on the Prince's behalf.'

Edward stared at Corbett, and suddenly throwing back his head, roared with laughter. Gaveston looked perplexed. Corbett just sat motionless, impassive, until the Prince had recovered himself.

'Oh, that's rich, Corbett,' he said, wiping a tear from his eye. 'I am touched by your concern. Please accept my most sincere thanks for your interest.' His mood suddenly changed. 'I know why you are here. For God's sake get on with it!'

The clerk shrugged.

'Lady Eleanor, Your Grace, men say she was ill?' He hurried on, 'Of a malady of the breast?'

The Prince nodded.

'How long had that been so?'

'Oh, about a year.'

'Some people say longer.'

'Some people are liars! I am not responsible,' Edward snapped, 'for what people like to invent. They snout in the dirt with their long noses. They can make up what they want.'

'You did not visit Lady Eleanor at Godstowe?'

'No, I did not. I did not love her. For me the relationship was ended.'

'I am sure that was so,' Corbett replied drily, regretting the quip as soon as it was uttered, noticing the hostility flare in the Prince's light blue eyes. 'You must have been concerned?' he continued hastily.

'Lady Eleanor wanted for nothing. She had her comforts. She lived in luxury. The Lady Prioress looked after all her needs.'

'You sent her medicine, Your Grace?'

The Prince chewed thoughtfully on his lower lip.

'I know what you are thinking!' Gaveston intervened, rising from the window seat. 'It was I who sent the medicines. You may think they were tainted, but we know they were tested at the priory and I doubt Lady Eleanor would have taken them solely on the Prince's word.'

'I am sure My Lord Gaveston is correct,' Corbett answered. 'But what were these powders?'

'Look, Corbett,' the Gascon snarled, 'I am a courtier, and sometimes soldier. I am not a physician. They were simple potions, meant to relieve the pains in Lady Eleanor's chest and afford her sleep.'

Corbett, sensing he could proceed no further, decided to change tack.

'On the day Lady Eleanor died, Your Grace—'

'I was at Woodstock. I hunted in the afternoon and feasted in the evening. All who matter saw me here, including the French envoy, Sir Amaury de Craon.'

'Did you send any messages that day?'

'No, I did not. Piers here sent down potions. Oh, on the day before Lady Eleanor met with her accident.'

'Ah, yes, we are back to the potions. Did the Lady Eleanor ask for them?'

'Yes, she did,' Gaveston replied vehemently. 'She said they afforded her great relief.'

'Your Grace, on that matter, was the Lady Eleanor melancholic?'

'Yes,' the Prince replied, for the first time showing compassion. 'The poor creature was ill. She knew I did not love her, I did not hide my feelings. So, what more?'

Corbett quickly looked at Ranulf, who sat as if carved from stone, transfixed by their rapid questions like a spectator at some skilful swordfight.

'What do you think happened on the day Lady Eleanor died?'

'I know no more than you, Corbett. The facts are: Lady Eleanor kept to herself, put on her cloak to go for a walk and, in the half-light, slipped on the staircase at Godstowe, fell and broke her neck.'

The Prince yawned as if bored. 'Well, Clerk, that is all.' He rose, walked across and put a hand on his favourite's shoulder. 'So, Corbett, do you wish to know more?'

'Yes, Your Grace. Were you and the Lady Eleanor secretly married?'

Ranulf gulped noisily as he saw all the colour drain from the Prince's face. Gaveston stiffened like a dog ready to attack.

'No, of course we were not! Why do you ask?'

'Nothing, Your Grace, just scurrilous rumours. And you heard about Lady Eleanor's death on Monday morning?'

'Yes. The porter brought me the message. You know that, Corbett. Don't sit there and bait me!'

The Prince of Wales flicked a lace-cuffed wrist. 'Now, for God's sake, man, leave us!'

'No!' Gaveston spoke up, his face wreathed in false smiles. 'Your Grace, Master Corbett has been most busy. The priory at Godstowe has its attractions, but not for a man accustomed to the luxuries of this world.' He winked at Corbett. 'The Prince and I,' he continued, 'have arranged a sumptuous banquet this evening.' He grinned. 'We are the hosts as well as the only guests. I insist you join us!' He clapped his hands and the steward suddenly reappeared. Gaveston raised a hand to fend off Corbett's objections. 'We insist, don't we, Your Grace?'

Edward threw a sly glance at his favourite and nodded. 'Yes, we do,' he replied slowly. 'We insist you dine with us.'

Gaveston motioned to the steward. 'Take Master Corbett and his servant to the kitchen. Feed them well. They are our special guests.' Gaveston rose and came over, taking Corbett gently by the hand. 'Hugh,' he murmured, his soulless eyes fixed on those of the clerk, 'we do insist you stay. There are other matters we wish to discuss.'

EIGHT

THE STEWARD TOOK them down beyond the Great Hall into a vast, stone-flagged kitchen. The place was scrubbed clean though flies feasted on the huge globules of red blood spattered across the white-washed walls. Under its vaulted ceiling the place was a frenzy of activity; a baker and two apprentices, red-faced, the sweat streaming off them, laboured before a huge brick oven, sliding trays of soft white dough into it. Servants and other domestics scurried in and out, carrying roasting and grilling trays, dripping pans, fire shovels, brass pots, pewter vessels, and baskets full of herbs. A surly cook with an open sore on one wrist served Corbett and Ranulf pots of milk laced with nutmeg, two rather stale chicken pies and a dish of over-cooked vegetables. Corbett merely toyed with the food though Ranulf, hungry enough, munched away.

'We didn't learn much there, Master.'

Corbett smiled.

'We still might, Ranulf. Let's make hay while the sun shines.'

They finished eating and sauntered back upstairs. Corbett stopped the steward who was scurrying along a corridor, a pile of costly turkey cloths under his arm.

'My apologies,' Corbett smiled, 'but will the Prince go to Godstowe? I mean, to the Lady Eleanor's obsequies?'

The fellow stepped back, affronted by the question, but Corbett opened his hand and showed the two silver coins.

'Some money for your time, sir.'

The fellow looked furtively round, licked his lips, and beckoned Corbett and Ranulf into a shadowy window recess.

'What do you want to know?'

'Simple enough. How did the Prince learn of Lady Eleanor's death?'

The steward stretched out his hand and Corbett placed one piece of silver in it.

'A porter came from Godstowe.'

'Is that all?'

The man wetted his lips, looking hungrily at the second silver coin.

'There is a rumour,' he replied slowly, 'stories in the palace, that the Prince knew much earlier. One of his body squires heard him whispering about it to his Gascon favourite.'

Corbett stepped closer.

'You are sure?' he hissed.

'Sir, now you know what I do.'

Corbett handed over the coin, let the man go and leaned against the wall.

'Oh, God,' he muttered. 'Ranulf, if the Prince knew before the porter arrived here, there can be only one explanation. He must have had a hand in Lady Eleanor's death. And how,' he whispered, 'do we tell the King that his son is a murderer?'

'Corbett! Master Clerk!'

They both turned. Gaveston stood at the end of the gallery, leaning nonchalantly against the wall.

'Master Corbett!' he called. 'I have come to apologise. Your reception was not courteous, but the Prince and I had other matters to discuss. Come! Let me show you Woodstock.'

Corbett glanced warily at Ranulf and raised his eyes heavenwards.

Gaveston sauntered over. He smiled dazzlingly at Ranulf and linked his arm through that of the clerk.

'I understand the King has granted you a manor? You have stables? You like hunting?'

'I am more of a farmer, My Lord. More interested in the planting of crops and the clearing of scrubland, though, yes, I hunt.'

'Then I must show you something,' Gaveston replied. 'New hunting dogs from Ireland, great shaggy beasts. They are the Prince's pride and joy. Well,' he added mockingly, 'besides me!'

The Gascon led Corbett and Ranulf through a maze of corridors which led out to the back of the palace, across a deserted dusty yard into one of the large outbuildings there. Inside, the walls were cold, dank and rather slimy. Gaveston bustled about in the darkness, found a tinder, and a cresset torch flared into life.

Corbett became uneasy. He heard a howl which seemed to rise from the very bowels of the earth: long, cruel and haunting. He shuddered, his hand going to the bone handle of his dagger though he dare not pull back. Gaveston opened a door in the far wall and led them down some steps, dimly lit by torches fixed in iron brackets. These flickered and danced wildly as if blown upon by unseen lips.

Corbett glanced at Ranulf. In the pale light he noticed his servant's face was ashen, covered with a sheen of sweat. Corbett sensed menace and malevolence, and the hair on the back of his neck bristled. They went down the dark tunnel. They had not gone far when again the clerk heard that long, moaning howl. He quietly drew his dagger and braced himself. They turned a corner and Corbett had to hide his trembling at the appearance of the small, squat, one-eyed man who seemed to rise out of the darkness before them. His head was covered by a tarred leather hood. He wore a dirty brown apron and sweat gleamed on his naked forehead. The black patch hiding one eye gave his cruel, sharp face an even more sinister aspect.

'Ah, Gyrth!' Gaveston talked as if they were in some pleasant garden. 'I have brought our guests to see the dogs.'

The fellow grinned. He had no teeth; nothing except dripping black-red gums. He opened his mouth wider, making a strange grunting noise.

'Gyrth has no tongue,' Gaveston observed. 'The unfortunate result of a disagreement, is it not, Gyrth?'

The mute looked warily at the Gascon and nodded his head.

'Come, man!' Gaveston said. 'We wait. The door!'

The creature scuttled ahead of them like some small black spider, opened the padlocked door and waved his guests forward. As he did so the most furious howling broke out. Corbett walked forward. Beyond the door was a slight recess blocked by a thick metal iron grille, and behind it four pairs of cruel red eyes gleamed in the darkness. Gaveston pushed Ranulf behind him.

'You stay,' he whispered, and walked gingerly forward.

The four huge black mastiffs came to life, smashing their great muscular bodies against the grille, lips curled, white teeth flashing, jaws slavering. They would

have torn Corbett to shreds if the grille had been raised.
He stood his ground, carefully inspecting the dogs. He
had seen this breed before. King Edward had used them
in Wales as war dogs but later had them killed because,
in their blood lust, they had failed to distinguish between friend and foe.

The four dogs were massive, the muscles bunched
high in their shoulders above long, strong legs. Their
heads were rounded, ears flat. They gave the impression of being nothing more than killing machines with
their huge jaws, white jagged teeth and mad, red eyes.
They stopped their howling, eyes fixed on Corbett, and
again, as if controlled by one mind, threw themselves
against their iron cage, the leader of the pack standing
on his hind legs and pounding his muzzle against the
grille.

Corbett estimated the dogs were taller than any man.
He smelt their fetid breath and tried to control the
shuddering of his body, fighting against the nauseous
panic which curdled his stomach and made his legs so
weak he longed to sit down. Gaveston was playing with
him, testing his nerve in this cruel game. He could hear
the Gascon behind him, taunting Ranulf, inviting him
to draw closer, and his servant's angry refusal.

'Ranulf does not like dogs.' Corbett turned and spoke
over his shoulder. 'Ever since he was a boy he has had
a fear of them. He was attacked by a vicious mongrel.'

Corbett looked around: near the foot of the grille was
a tub packed with juicy red chunks of meat. He stepped
over, pierced one of the raw chunks with his dagger and
held it up before the mastiff. The dog whimpered. There
was a square in the grille larger than the rest, probably
used to feed the dogs. Corbett pushed the meat through
and watched the leading dog seize it in his huge jaws,

throwing it up and devouring it, the blood streaming down his black, slavering mouth. Corbett cleaned his knife on the toe of his boot, resheathed it and walked back.

'Fine beasts, My Lord! You are to be complimented, though I urge caution. They may well be animals who bite the hand which feeds them!'

Gaveston laughed and clapped his hands gently.

'*Un bon mot*, Clerk,' he said. 'Come! You have seen enough.'

They walked slowly back up the tunnel. Behind them the howling of the dogs rose like some demonic music. Gaveston led them back to the heart of the palace whence a servitor took them up to a chamber high in the building. A simple room with stark white plaster, but at least they were provided with rosewater, a set of clean napkins, and a jug of wine which Corbett told Ranulf not to touch. They whiled away the time, Ranulf playing dice against himself, the only time he ever lost. Corbett lay dozing on the bed, idly wondering what Maeve was doing, and thought again of Sister Agatha. She and the other nuns would still be involved in the official mourning for Lady Eleanor and Dame Martha. He stirred uneasily at the suspicions the steward had provoked. How could the Prince have known of Lady Eleanor's death so early? Corbett viewed the mystery as a logical problem. There were two routes to follow: on the one hand he could try and solve the murder, but that might make a bad situation worse. On the other he would concede the Prince was involved, perhaps even guilty of Lady Eleanor's death, in which case, for the sake of the crown, the scandal would have to be hidden.

Swallows fought under the eaves outside the window, a lonely bell sounded, and Corbett heard faint shouts from the courtyard. He dozed but woke with a start, dreaming that the Hell-hounds he had just visited were snuffling at the door, but it was only Ranulf dragging a stool across the dusty rushes. A servant knocked and announced that the banquet would begin in an hour. Corbett rose, washed, and made himself as presentable as possible. Ranulf scooped his dice into his leather wallet and they went down the spiral wooden staircase and into the hall.

The banquet was a sumptuous, luxurious meal. Huge banners hung from the heavy, black beams bearing the Royal Arms of England, the Golden Leopards snarling next to the White Lilies of France and the Red Dragon of Wales. Trestle tables had been arranged in a square and covered with white lawn sheets. Multi-bracketed candelabra placed along the centre helped the sconce torches to bathe the room in light. Corbett could smell the heavy, thick fragrance of those mouth-watering dishes he had seen being prepared in the kitchen. Servants in the blue and gold livery of the Prince and the Lord Gaveston scurried round with silver plates which the guests would use as dishes instead of the usual traunches of thick square slabs of stale bread. Musicians played quietly on tambour, rebec and lute in the minstrel gallery at the far end of the hall, accompanied by a group of beautiful young boys all dressed in silver and gold who softly sang some troubadour's lay. A greyhound cocked his leg against the table and was promptly shooed away.

A chamberlain showed them to their seats just beneath the high table, which was dominated by a pearl-encrusted silver salt cellar. Corbett looked around. The other diners were all henchmen of either the Prince or Lord Gaveston: clerks, household officials, captains from their mercenary retinues, and the occasional priest or almoner. He and Ranulf were ignored, which made him uneasy. A flourish of silver trumpets, their shrill fanfare stilling the chatter, and the Prince entered, holding Gaveston's hand. Both wore silver chaplets and were clothed from head to toe in robes of gold. Their appearance drew 'Oohs' and 'Ahs' from the group of sycophants. The Prince acknowledged their greetings as he and his favourite sat in the two great throne-like chairs at the high table. Corbett shuddered and looked away. If the old King saw this he would have apoplexy, for the Prince was openly treating Gaveston as if he was his wife. Another braying of trumpets and the banquet began. The French chefs in the Prince's kitchen had used all their arts and skills; soups and broths thick with herbs, pheasant and quail meat, were served, followed by salmon, turbot, pike and tench. Boar's heart stuffed with cloves, lamb garnished with mint and marjoram, a swan cooked and restored so it sat upon the silver platter as if swimming on some magical pool. Haunch of venison, jellies and sugared pastries, and jug after jug of the best Bordeaux or chilled white wine from the Rhinelands completed the feast.

Of course, Ranulf ate as if there was no tomorrow, Corbett more sparingly. He felt uncomfortable, uneasy at the way the Prince and Gaveston hardly spared them a glance whilst their companions at table treated them as if they simply did not exist. The wine bowl circulated more freely, the conversation and laughter grew louder, the silver-white cloths became stained. A jester, a tiny woman no taller than three foot, appeared, doing somersaults along the table whilst dodging the bowls

and bits of food thrown at her. Corbett suddenly realised he was in the corner of the hall. If a quarrel was
provoked, he and Ranulf would be trapped. Gauging a
suitable moment, he dragged his servant to his feet,
bowed towards the Prince and quietly withdrew. Once
outside he sent Ranulf back to their chamber. The servant came hurrying down with his cloak but only one
glove.

'I could only find one, Master.'

The clerk shrugged.

'No matter. I may have lost it, and I am certainly not
wandering around the palace looking for a glove!'

'We could go and try to borrow horses from the stables?'

Corbett shook his head.

'No, Ranulf, I feel uneasy. The sooner we are out of
here, the better. The night is fine, the walk short, and
the evening air will clear both our heads.'

They slipped through a side door and made their way
out via one of the postern gates of the palace. They
easily found the track they had followed earlier in the
day. A full harvest moon bathed the sleeping countryside in a silver light, the night air was warm and the
fields slept under clear autumn skies. Corbett and
Ranulf followed the dusty track past green hedgerows
and up a hill. The clerk listened with half an ear to
Ranulf's chatter about the banquet and the Prince's
open display of affection for Gaveston. They had
reached the top of the hill when they heard the first
soul-chilling, baying call. Both stood still, the warm
blood freezing in their veins. Corbett felt his head and
neck tense as if someone had slipped an iron helm over
his hair. He wanted to turn round but dared not do so.
Again the howl, as if one of Satan's demons was rising

from the pit of Hell. Corbett turned and looked back down the moonlit path. He felt he was in a nightmare. His heart hammered in terror as he glimpsed those shaggy, hulking shapes of shadowy grey speeding across the meadows. He remembered those mad, red eyes which had glared at him earlier that day through the grille, and those great death-bearing, slavering jaws. He grabbed his servant.

'Run, Ranulf!'

Corbett undid his cloak and dropped it on the ground. Ranulf hesitated as if intending to pick it up.

'Leave it!' Corbett screamed. 'It will divert the dogs for a while. Run!'

Ranulf needed no second bidding but sped off like an arrow. Corbett followed, past the dark, open fields and into the trees that stood like silent soldiers in some bewitched army. They fled for their lives as the great Hellhounds caught their scent and bayed in savage glee. A howl showed that the dogs were beginning to close. The cool night air burned in Corbett's straining lungs. The trees thinned and they fled across an open meadow. He looked up and, in the clear moonlight, glimpsed the roofs and towers of Godstowe Priory. They stopped just over the brow of a hill.

'Ranulf!' he gasped. 'It's my scent. The glove—it was taken. You go for some tree. Climb and hide!'

Ranulf, his face white as a sheet, hair matted with sweat, shook his head.

'If I'm to die, Master, I prefer to be with you. There might be huntsmen who could bring me down.'

Corbett nodded and they staggered on, bodies soaked in sweat, eyes blinded with panic, legs and feet threatening to turn into the heaviest lead. They ran on, sobbing for breath, across a ploughed field. Corbett could

have sworn that momentarily he glimpsed another figure, shadow-like, but fled on. Behind him the dogs
bayed in triumph, then suddenly there came a terrible
scream which clutched Corbett's heart—a cry of
dreadful despair. He turned. The hounds had not
breasted the hill. Ranulf...where was he? He looked
around and felt so dizzy he had to steady himself. He
saw Ranulf on his knees, his arms wrapped around his
straining chest.

'I cannot go on, Master!'

'Yes, you can!' Corbett snapped.

He picked Ranulf up, hustling him towards the wall
of the priory. They leaned, sobbing, against it. Behind
them the dogs had fallen strangely silent.

'It's too high to climb,' Corbett hissed. 'Come on!'

He pushed Ranulf round the wall, past the Galilee
Gate, which was locked, to the main door. The clerk
hammered on it with the pommel of his dagger.

'Open up!' he screamed. 'For the love of God, open!'

The drunken porter opened the postern door. Corbett dragged Ranulf inside, turned and kicked the gate
shut.

'Secure it, man!' he roared.

The porter looked at him drunkenly, then heard the
low, mournful howl of the dogs and quickly pushed the
bolts home. Corbett ran inside the porter's house. The
two soldiers were sprawled there half-asleep. He took a
torch from its iron bracket, picked up an arbalest leaning against the wall, as well as a stout leather quiver
filled with vicious barbed quarrels. He hurried up the
narrow steps on to the parapet of the curtain wall. He
leaned against it, winching the arbalest back, cursing,
his eyes stinging with sweat as he placed the quarrel.
Corbett heard a savage barking and two of the great

dogs pounded round the corner of the wall beneath. Corbett picked up the torch and threw it down. Both animals stopped, looked up and snarled. In the flickering light Corbett could see their muzzles caked in blood.

'Bastards!' the clerk bellowed. 'Devil-sent bastards!'

The hounds threw themselves at the gate. Corbett suddenly found himself laughing.

'That's right, you bastards!' he screamed. 'Stay there!'

He positioned the arbalest, leaned over the wall and released the catch. He heard the whirr of the bolt and shouted with pleasure as it struck the leading dog just behind the head, digging deep and slicing its spinal column. The animal suddenly leapt in the air in a terrifying spasm of pain before collapsing, choking on its own blood. Corbett, muttering to himself, fitted a second bolt. This time he was too clumsy. The crossbow bolt whirred out, nicking the hindquarters of the second dog, which turned and fled howling into the darkness. Corbett leaned against the wall and promptly vomited. He paused for a while to compose himself then staggered down to the porter's lodge.

Ranulf sat just within the door, his back to the wall, his face ashen and wet with sweat, the front of his jerkin stained with vomit. The porter crouched beside him, too drunk to offer any succour. Corbett filled the wine cup, drank some himself and then forced the goblet between his servant's lips, snarling at the porter to bring a blanket.

There was a knock at the door. Lady Amelia, accompanied by Dames Catherine and Frances, bustled in. They were shrouded in blankets, their faces pale and heavy-eyed with sleep.

'What is it, Clerk?'

'Nothing, woman!' he rasped angrily.

He saw the colour come back into Ranulf's cheeks and stood up.

'I am sorry,' he muttered. 'We were returning from Woodstock and were chased by war dogs.'

Lady Amelia gazed back, her eyes puzzled.

'Hounds,' Corbett said slowly, 'trained to hunt and kill men. You must not open the gates tonight. They would have killed us. I tell you this—somewhere out in the darkness, some poor unfortunate, a tinker or vagabond, paid for our escape with his life!'

As if to mock his words a low, moaning howl came out of the darkness beyond the wall. Lady Amelia stared coolly in the direction of the noise.

'Dame Catherine!' she snapped. 'You are to rouse the labourers. Sound the tocsin! Everything is to be secure; all gates are to be kept closed and locked. No one is to leave. Corbett, follow me!'

To the sound of hurrying footsteps and the clanging of the tocsin, Corbett and Ranulf were led across to the infirmary, a pleasant, two-storey house just past the refectory. An old battle-axe of a nun wrapped them both in heavy blankets, forcing cups of mulled wine down their throats. It was only as his eyes closed and he drifted into sleep that Corbett realised the wine must have been lightly laced with a sleeping potion.

He woke clear-eyed late the next morning. Ranulf was already up, squatting on the side of his bed, his face clean and washed. He had donned a new set of clothes and brought fresh doublet and hose for Corbett.

'A nightmare, Master?'

'Yes, Ranulf, a nightmare.'

He cast the blankets aside, pleased that he felt no ill effects from the terrible chase of the previous night.

'Now,' he said, 'I am going to wash, shave, change my clothes and eat honest food, then it's back to Woodstock, Ranulf, mounted and armed. I am going to have that bloody pervert's head!'

Ranulf grinned. Corbett rarely lost his temper and when he did it was always a pleasure to watch.

'Is that safe, Master?'

'As you would say, Ranulf, I don't give a rat's arse! The King still rules here and I am his envoy. We can take those two soldiers from the porter's lodge with us. It's time they earned their wages!'

Ranulf felt pleased. This time it would be different. He would have sword, dagger and crossbow. He blinked rapidly.

'Master, I am sorry, you have a messenger. A Ralph Maltote. He comes from the King's camp at Nottingham and bears urgent messages. He arrived just after dawn. The Lady Prioress has also sent out riders. They found no trace of the dogs except the body of the one you killed and the Lady Prioress has ordered that to be burnt in the forest. They also found,' the servant coughed and looked away, 'the mangled remains of a corpse.' Ranulf stopped. 'One of the labourers recognised him. The landlord of The Bull will not go poaching again.'

Corbett whistled softly through his teeth.

'God rest him,' he muttered. 'I suspect our landlord was our porter's poacher friend. You had better bring Maltote in.'

Ralph Maltote proved to be a stout young man who looked rather ridiculous in his boiled leather jerkin, military leggings and boots. His face was as round and as red as an autumn apple. His sparse blond hair was dark with sweat, and his surprised blue eyes and hang-dog look made him the most unlikely royal messenger Corbett had ever seen. He stood with the conical hel-met cradled clumsily under his arm.

'You rode far and fast, young man?' Corbett asked, glaring at Ranulf, who was sniggering softly beside him.

'Yes, My Lord.'

Maltote slumped down on the stool, his long sword catching him between the legs and nearly tipping him over on his face.

'And?'

The young man looked puzzled.

'The message?' Corbett asked. 'You haven't trav-elled all the way from Nottingham for nothing?'

Maltote shook his head nervously, gulped, and dug into the inside pocket of his half-open jerkin. He handed a small scroll across to Corbett, who checked the purple wax seal of the King before breaking it and unrolling the vellum. The message was short and cryp-tic and Corbett's worst fears were realised. The King was bluntly informing him that he was ill pleased at the lack of progress Corbett was making. Indeed, the French envoy de Craon knew more, claiming the Prince had told him about Lady Eleanor's death long before the porter had even reached Woodstock. Corbett handed the letter over to Ranulf.

'Read it and burn it!' He nodded towards the mes-senger. 'Then take Maltote to the kitchen and get him something to eat. Afterwards we leave for Woodstock.'

Ranulf sauntered out, the young messenger trailing behind him like a lost puppy. Corbett was finishing his ablutions when he heard a knock at the door.

'Come in!' he barked, regretting his harsh command as Dame Agatha entered, bearing a tray covered by a napkin.

'You wish to break fast, Master Corbett, before you go?'

Corbett smiled.

'Good morning, Dame Agatha. Who told you I was leaving?'

'Your servant. You will eat?'

Corbett nodded, rather embarrassed as Dame Agatha bustled round the room, laying the tray on a small table and dragging across a stool. She had brought a bowl of hot chicken broth, freshly baked white manchet loaves and a tankard of watered ale. She did not leave as Corbett took up the pewter spoon and began to eat.

'You are unhurt?' she queried anxiously.

'Yes, except in my pride, Sister.'

She walked across and placed her soft, white hand on his arm. Corbett looked up. It felt strange to be alone in a chamber with such a solicitous, beautiful young woman.

'Take care,' she whispered. 'Do not be rash. Gaveston will be cunning. Lady Amelia says the dogs were loosed by him but we have no proof. Do not give him a pretext to strike you down.'

She withdrew her hand and grazed his cheek softly with the back of her fingers. Corbett blushed and, tongue-tied, went back to eating, not daring to raise his head until he heard Dame Agatha's soft footfalls and the chamber door close behind her. He was touched by her care and concern but found it difficult to accept. He felt guilty as he thought of Maeve's sweet face, and embarrassed that he should be so powerfully attracted to a woman dedicated to God. Nevertheless, Dame Agatha's advice was wise and Corbett felt his temper cool. He decided he would show Gaveston he was not frightened but be wary of making any rash moves. Gaveston was the favourite of a Prince of the Blood and even to draw steel in the Prince of Wales' presence could be construed as treason.

Corbett chewed absent-mindedly on the bread whilst analysing the problem which faced him. In logic he had been taught to reach an acceptable conclusion by revising the steps which led to it. How could he do that now? He smiled and went over to the bag Ranulf had hidden beneath the bed. Corbett, laughing softly to himself, examined his servant's venture into selling physic. He took a small jar of ointment, went down the stairs and out across to the convent building. No one was around. He slipped quietly up the stairs and gently tapped on Dame Elizabeth's door.

'Come in! Come in!' The old nun was as imperious as ever but she visibly thawed when she saw Corbett and beamed with pleasure at his gift.

'A rare potion,' Corbett announced slyly.

Oh, Lord, he thought, what does it contain? Ranulf was harmless but the potion could be dangerous.

'It's ointment,' he lied, 'culled from the hoof of an elk and mixed with herbs. Smear it on your four bedposts every night. It will purify evil vapours from the air, make you breathe more easily and allow more restful sleep.'

The old nun nodded wisely and Corbett felt a twinge of guilt at his incredible lies. He placed the ointment on the table beside her, rose and walked over to the window. He peered down.

'What are you looking at, Master Clerk?'

'I am just remembering how you and Dame Martha saw Lady Eleanor on the night before she died. You are sure it was her?'

'Oh, yes!' The old nun chewed on her gums. 'You see, Dame Martha was standing where you are. She called me over and pointed down. "Look," she said, "there's Lady Eleanor!"'

'When was that?'

'Oh, just before Compline.'

'And what happened then?'

'We tapped on the window and called out. Lady Eleanor turned and waved up at us.'

'You could hear her voice?'

'Oh, yes. Dame Martha had opened the window and asked where she was going. Lady Eleanor replied she was going for a walk behind the church.' The old nun's eyes narrowed. 'She was always going there.'

'You are sure it was she?'

'Of course!'

'What was she wearing?'

'One of her blue gowns. Blue was her favourite colour.'

'But you saw her face?'

'Oh, yes, she had her hood up but she turned and shouted back at us.'

'Did you see her return?'

'No, but of course she must have.'

Corbett felt a twinge of disappointment.

'Master Corbett!'

The clerk spun round. Lady Amelia, accompanied by her ever present acolytes, Dames Frances and Catherine, stood in the doorway, quivering with righteous anger.

'You may be the King's Clerk, Master Corbett, but this is a convent building. You have no right to be here. Even though you are talking to an old nun!' She threw a look of contempt at Dame Elizabeth.

'Dame Elizabeth is my friend,' Corbett snapped. 'I am a man of honour as well as a royal emissary.' Corbett felt his own anger boil at the Prioress' air of righteous indignation. 'I will leave this chamber when I have finished and, Lady Prioress, I should be grateful if you would wait for me in your own chamber. I have further questions to ask you.'

The Lady Prioress looked as if she was going to refuse but Corbett stood his ground and glared back. Lady Amelia, with one more disdainful glance at Dame Elizabeth, stepped back and closed the door behind her. The old nun rose and scuttled across to him. Clasping her hands to her chest, she gazed up in round-eyed admiration.

'You are brave, Master Clerk,' she murmured. 'No one else dares to speak to the Lady Prioress like that.'

Corbett gently patted her hand.

'Rest easy, Sister,' he said. 'She had no right to say what she did, and I never could stand a bully.'

He scooped the old lady's vein-scored hand to his lips. 'But enough. I bid you adieu.' He walked towards the door.

'Master Corbett!' Dame Elizabeth scurried toward him. 'I shall tell you a secret,' she whispered. 'One I have told no one else.'

'What is that, Sister?'

'On the afternoon Lady Eleanor died, I saw horsemen in the trees.' She pointed to the window. 'There in the forest, beyond the walls.'

Corbett walked back to the window. The convent building was high and Dame Elizabeth's chamber on the second storey. He could see, just over the wall, the line of trees which marked the beginning of the forest.

'Where exactly were they?'

Dame Elizabeth came alongside him.

'There,' she murmured. 'I was staring out, just after mid-day. I was watching a hawk above the trees when suddenly I saw something move. My eyes are not very good,' she apologised, 'so I stood and watched closely. I saw the horses, and three or four men just sitting there. If one of them had not been riding a white horse I would never have noticed them. Shadowy figures,' she whispered, 'who hardly moved. I went back to bathe my eyes and when I returned I could not see them.' She chuckled. 'I have told no one. I am not like Dame Martha. I don't chatter and allow myself to be dismissed as an old fool!'

'Did anyone else see them?'

'No, not that I have heard.'

Corbett gazed at the distant line of trees. Anyone with good eyesight would certainly have seen the riders, but to someone like Dame Elizabeth their presence might only be betrayed by a flash of colour.

'Did you see them again?'

'Oh, no.'

'Did they wear any livery?'

She shook her head. Corbett rubbed his chin thoughtfully.

'Tell me, could these riders have entered the convent?'

'Oh, no. The gates would have been locked, and the porter may be a drunkard but he has his orders.'

'They could have climbed the walls?'

Dame Elizabeth laughed.

'I doubt it. One of the labourers or lay sisters would have seen them. Anyway,' she said, 'you know what men are. They would have clattered upstairs along the gallery and woken both me and Dame Martha.'

Corbett thanked the old nun and slipped quietly out of the chamber in search of the Prioress. Lady Amelia had regained some of her composure. He found her sitting behind her great oak desk, chatting to the two Sub-prioresses, a roll of accounts before them. She gestured to Corbett to sit.

'Master Clerk,' she began, 'I apologise for my outburst but, despite what has happened, this is a convent.' She took a deep breath. 'You have more questions?'

'Yes. Did any of the sisters see anything untoward the day Lady Eleanor died?'

'No.'

'You are sure?'

'In an enclosed community, Master Corbett, people chatter—to themselves, to their sisters, to me, or even to you or your ubiquitous servant, Master Ranulf.'

'Then tell me, Lady Prioress, at Sunday Compline who was in church?'

'I have told you that—everyone.'

'No, I mean beforehand.'

'The Lady Prioress was in church with me,' Dame Catherine blurted out.

'Whilst I was in the sacristy with Dame Agatha,' Dame Frances added quickly.

'You are sure of that? You were all there before Compline?'

'Ask anyone you like,' Lady Amelia broke in. 'Other sisters saw us there.'

Corbett bit back his disappointment.

'And what happened to Lady Eleanor's possessions?'

'The day after her death,' Lady Amelia repeated, 'the Prince sent down one of his henchmen with strict orders. Lady Eleanor's jewellery and other precious trinkets were to be handed over. The rest...' She shrugged. 'I thought it was rather spiteful but the Prince ordered me to burn them. I did so immediately. Are there any more questions, Master Clerk?'

'Yes.' He smiled bleakly at the Sub-prioress. 'Lady Amelia, you admitted that you found Lady Eleanor's corpse in her room and, together with these sweet sisters, moved it to the foot of the stairs to make her death appear an accident. Yes?'

'I have said as much.' Lady Amelia glared back.

'Did you find any trace of a struggle in Lady Eleanor's chamber?'

'No.'

'The door was open?'

'Yes.'

'But nothing was untoward?'

'No, I've told you. I thought at first that Lady Eleanor had fainted. Are there further questions?'

Corbett shook his head.

'Then, Sir, I bid you adieu.'

After he left the sisters, Corbett went out to the stable yard where Ranulf and Maltote were waiting with the two retainers from the porter's lodge. The latter looked angry at being dragged from their life of leisure but both were well-armed, having donned helmet and hauberk, with swords and daggers pushed into their belts. Maltote, too, looked surprised at his new duties.

'Master, is this necessary?'

'You are the King's man, aren't you?'

Maltote nodded mournfully. Corbett pointed to the arbalest which swung from his saddle horn.

'You can use that?'

Maltote just stared back. Corbett, intrigued, walked closer.

'You can, can't you? You are a royal serjeant-at-arms.'

He pointed across the stable yard at an old, disused door propped against a wall. A few straggly chickens pecked the dirt around it.

'Aim low, loose and hit the door,' Corbett ordered. 'Hit it dead centre.'

'Master!' Maltote pleaded.

Corbett placed a hand on the messenger's stirrup.

'You know the rules, man. You are under my orders now. The King sent you to me. Do as I say!'

Maltote, watched by all, loaded the arbalest and aimed at the door. Corbett wasn't too sure what happened next. He heard the bolt whirr as it was loosed but, instead of hitting the door, Maltote sent it crashing into an unfortunate chicken, which collapsed, squawking, in a pool of blood and feathers. The two retainers sniggered. Ranulf gasped, open-mouthed.

'Good God, man!' Corbett whispered. 'You are the worst archer I have ever seen. Was that deliberate?'

Maltote, looking even more ridiculous under his conical helmet, shook his head mournfully.

'Now you know, Master Corbett, why I am just a messenger. Where weapons are concerned, I am as much danger to friend as to foe.' He smiled broadly. 'But the King says I am the best horseman in his army. I can ride any nag and get the best out of it.'

Corbett nodded and, taking his heavy sword belt from Ranulf, clasped it round his waist.

'I'll remember that, Maltote.'

'And so,' Ranulf added drily, 'will the chickens!'

NINE

AFTER GIVING HIS small escort strict instructions, Corbett, accompanied by Ranulf and Maltote, left by the Galilee Gate and thundered along the track, through the silent village and up the road to Woodstock. He hadn't decided what exactly to do. He wanted to confront Gaveston, and was determined to question the Prince on why he knew about Lady Eleanor's death long before any messenger arrived from Godstowe.

The guards at the palace's main gate swiftly let them through but, as they debouched out of the tree-lined path front of the palace, a gruesome sight awaited them. A huge, makeshift scaffold had been erected in front of the palace, a long, thick ashen pole fixed into two uprights at either end. Corbett stopped, calming his horse which grew skittish at the sight. From the pole hung four corpses; three of the great, black mastiffs and, in between them, his neck broken and twisted, eyes protruding, the body of Gyrth, their keeper.

Corbett dismounted slowly, ordering Ranulf to look after the horses as he went to meet the chamberlain, who had come out to greet him. The fellow treated Corbett as if he were a Prince of the Blood and took him swiftly into the hall, which an army of servants were now cleaning after the previous night's banquet. Corbett was led down a maze of corridors and into a chamber where the Prince of Wales and Gaveston, both white-faced and sober, stood waiting to receive him.

Before Corbett could open his mouth, Prince Edward came forward and took him firmly by the hand.

'Master Corbett—Hugh,' he said, his eyes pleading with the clerk, 'the dogs...it was a mistake. My profuse apologies. The beasts and their handler have been hanged.' The Prince swallowed nervously and looked away. 'It was a mistake, an accident, wasn't it, Piers?'

'Yes, it was,' Gaveston replied. 'A terrible accident.'

Corbett glanced at the favourite, noting how pale his face had become. An accident? the clerk thought. Perhaps some drunken jape which got out of hand, or perhaps a calculated act of attempted murder.

'We found out this morning,' the Prince continued hurriedly. 'The Lady Prioress sent messages. Both the keeper and his hounds were instantly hanged. The fellow was drunk and released the dogs as you left the palace. They picked up your scent...' His voice trailed off.

The Prince of Wales' concern was genuine. Was it remorse? Corbett wondered. Or even complete ignorance on the Prince's behalf? Had Gaveston acted on his own? Corbett understood their fear. He had no illusions about the King. If Corbett was killed in the royal service, the King would accept it. But a deliberate attack on one of his messengers? Edward would have hurried troops south and burnt Woodstock to the ground. Corbett was going to ask about his lost glove but decided not to. Gaveston would have a ready explanation.

'Your Grace, I must see you alone.' Corbett ignored the look of annoyance on the favourite's face. 'Your Grace,' he persisted, 'you owe me that. I must talk to you. It is on your father's orders,' he lied.

The Prince looked across at Gaveston. 'I agree,' he replied. He grinned sheepishly at Corbett. 'I have to change. The French envoy, Monsieur de Craon, has returned.'

'You do not like the French envoy, Master Corbett?' Gaveston sardonically observed.

'Monsieur de Craon does his job and I do mine,' Corbett replied drily. 'But, Your Grace, I insist you must not trust him. Monsieur de Craon could catch spiders in the webs he weaves.'

The Prince nodded briskly and looked round.

'Be my guest, Master Corbett. In an hour I will meet you in the scriptorium.'

Corbett bowed, withdrew, and spent the rest of the time kicking his heels in the antechamber before a servant imperiously summoned him up the great staircase and ushered him into a brilliantly decorated room. The floor was of polished wood and the new wainscoting bore elaborate designs: vines, strange flowers, and exotic creatures such as dragons and wyverns. Around the painted blue walls were shelves and small cupboards full of different books, all bound in calf-skin of different colours, red, blue and tawny brown, their clasps of wrought gold and silver. Corbett noticed how each of these precious manuscripts was fastened to the wall by silver chains. He knew the Prince was a connoisseur of luxury, deeply influenced by the new designs from the prosperous Italian states. It was the only chamber Corbett had ever seen where there were no torches fixed to the wall. Instead heavy bronze candelabra stood on polished oak sideboards and dressers around the room. Nor were there any rushes on the floor with their usual fleas and dirt but thick woollen carpets of the purest white.

At the far end of the room on a small dais stood a polished round table with high-backed, ornately carved chairs. The Prince was sitting quietly there, his hands clasped, staring down at the table, so silent he could have been taken for some studious monk; his robes, however, were splendid, his fingers covered in precious rings, and his hair and golden beard carefully combed and oiled. He looked up and gestured Corbett forward. As he approached, the clerk noticed that the Prince's doublet was of pure white satin with gold buttons. On his legs were hose striped with red and gold, while his feet were hidden in crimson velvet slippers with silver roses on the toes. Judging by the Prince's appearance and demeanor, Corbett sensed that Gaveston had advised him to stand on his dignity in his dealings with both him and de Craon.

The Prince rose and waved him round the table to the chair next to his before serving them both the best wine the clerk had tasted in months. He sat down and sipped carefully from the cup. The Prince was not as temperamental as his father. Indeed, when he so wished, the young Edward could be dazzlingly courteous and charming. But, like all the Plantagenets, his moods were fickle, his temper unsure. Corbett had always liked Prince Edward; he had a roguish air, coupled with an almost childlike innocence. He could be a good friend or the most dangerous of enemies. Edward settled himself in his own chair, turning to look directly at Corbett.

'Well, Hugh?' he began. 'You wish to see me "*in secreto*". I respect you, otherwise my Lord Gaveston would be present.' He glanced away. 'Piers can be wicked,' he remarked softly. 'What happened last night was unforgivable. My father—must he know?'

'*Alea iacta*,' Corbett replied evening. 'The die is cast.' His eyes caught the cornflower blue of the Prince's. 'As Your Grace remarked, it was probably a terrible accident.'

The Prince smiled his thanks and held his hand out so that the sunlight streaming through the stained glass windows caught the gems in his rings and made them sparkle.

'So, Hugh, what is it?'

'Two questions, Your Grace.' Corbett sipped again from the wine cup. 'On the day Lady Eleanor died, did you send any of your men to Godstowe Priory?'

The Prince shook his head.

'No, I did not.'

'Well, Your Grace, did anyone else, perhaps unknown to you, send retainers there?'

The Prince, still shaking his head, rose and walked over to a carved bookstand which was similar to a lectern in a church. He placed his hand on the huge bible lying there.

'You may tell my father,' he replied, 'my hand on the bible, and I will repeat this oath before the Commons and the Lords Spiritual and Temporal—I swear this: neither my people nor the Lord Gaveston went anywhere near Godstowe Priory on that day.'

'Your Grace seems so certain?'

Edward turned, a stubborn look on his face.

'I forbade my Lord Gaveston to have anything to do with that woman!'

'Your Grace, is it true that the first you heard of the news was when the porter from Godstowe arrived here?'

Corbett noticed how quickly the Prince took his hand from the bible and walked back towards him.

'Yes, it was, as far as I know,' he replied, and sat on the edge of the table, looking down at Corbett, one leg swinging lazily before him. 'Why do you ask?'

Corbett took a deep breath.

'I must inform you, your father knows different. There is a rumour that you knew about Lady Eleanor's death long before any drunken porter arrived here.'

Edward chewed his lip.

'I was also drunk,' he murmured. 'But not that drunk,' he continued. 'I did hear something, or was I told...? Yes!' the Prince said excitedly. 'If Monsieur de Craon alleges *I* told *him*, then he is a liar! Indeed, Master Corbett, I am sure it was the Frenchman who informed me.'

'Then how did *he* know?'

The Prince shrugged.

'I can't tell. And if I questioned him, he would simply deny it. De Craon comes here,' he added bitterly, 'with his false face and lying tongue...the fellow wouldn't know the truth if it jumped up and pulled him by his pointed nose!'

The Prince went back to the bible and put his hand on it.

'I swear I have told you the truth. I swear I did not send men to Godstowe, though I would love to know who did. Were they wearing my livery?'

Corbett shook his head.

'I cannot say.'

'I also swear,' Prince Edward declared, 'that if I knew about the Lady's...death—'

Corbett was sure he was going to say 'murder'.

'—if I knew of the lady's death before Monday morning, I learnt of it from Monsieur de Craon.'

'Your Grace, were you married to the Lady Eleanor?'

The Prince kept his hand on the bible.

'That is none of your business,' he replied testily. 'What is your business, Corbett, is to clear my good name. De Craon awaits in a chamber down the hall. I want you to question him. He can stay there until you are ready to do so!'

And with that the Prince flounced out, all courtesy and good humour forgotten. Corbett smiled drily and leaned back in his chair, half-listening to the Prince's footsteps in the gallery outside. He believed the Prince that it was de Craon who had informed him on the Sunday night but how had the Frenchman known? Did he have a spy at Godstowe? If so, who? But the Lady Prioress had maintained that de Craon had been turned away from Godstowe. Corbett moved restlessly, then laughed to himself. Of course! He rose, went to the door, and beckoned a waiting servitor towards him.

'The French envoy, Monsieur de Craon—the Prince wishes me to speak to him.'

The fellow led him down the corridor, stopped before another door and tapped gently on it. The door was half open and Corbett, not waiting for the servant to knock again, simply pushed it open and swaggered in. De Craon was sitting in a high-backed chair near the window, a small scroll of parchment on his lap, apparently waiting for the Prince to summon him to an audience. He looked up as Corbett entered, smiled and half-rose before slumping back into the seat again as if he really could not be bothered. The scroll he had been studying disappeared quickly into the folds of his voluminous robes.

'Monsieur Corbett! I am delighted to see you. Do sit down.' He airily waved towards a footstool.

'De Craon, you're a lying bastard! You're about as
pleased to see me as a peasant is to meet the tax-
gatherer!'

Corbett walked over, arms folded, and smiled icily
down at his inveterate enemy.

'Hugh,' de Craon spread his hands expansively, 'why
do you insult me? Like you, I carry out orders.' He
sighed wearily. 'Diplomacy can be such a tangled web.'

'With you, de Craon, anything would be tangled!'

Corbett leaned over, putting his hands on the arms of
the chair, his face a few inches away from de Craon's.

'As I said, you're a lying bastard! You are the father
and mother of liars! You're up to your blood mischief
again, aren't you? The business at Godstowe...'

De Craon rounded his eye in mock innocence. Corbett noticed how dead they looked, as if de Craon was
two people. There was the physical husk, and something else: a sly, malevolent presence. Corbett decided
to test him.

'The Godstowe business is not going well for you, is
it?'

'What on earth do you mean?'

Corbett turned on his heel and walked back to the
door.

'What I mean, my beloved Frenchman, is that I know
the truth. I also know that your informant there has not
told you the truth. You have paid, Monsieur, for nothing more than a pack of lies.' Corbett opened the door.
'But there again,' he tossed airily over his shoulder, 'it's
a pack which suits you well!'

Corbett slipped through the door. Behind him de
Craon had dropped his mask of good humour. His lips
were moving quietly as he mouthed to himself what he
would do if ever he had Corbett in his power. The clerk,

however, had slipped quickly down the stairs and out into the courtyard where Ranulf and Maltote were waiting. His servant was trying to show the messenger how to hold a dagger, and Corbett shook his head in silent wonderment. Never, in all his life, had he witnessed anyone as clumsy or more dangerous to himself than Maltote with a weapon. Nevertheless, he liked this good-natured plough boy who knew nothing except horses.

They mounted and left the palace, following the track down to the village. Corbett sniffed the sweet tangy air and realised autumn was coming in. Maeve would be seeing to the barns, ensuring stock was slaughtered, the meat dried, salted and hung high in the kitchen to smoke, preserving it for the long winter months. Autumn had come, slipping in like a thief, turning the countryside into one brilliant flash of orange, gold, russet and sombre red. The sun now had a golden haze around it and the fields, the grass standing high and lush, were enjoying one last flurry of life before the frosts.

They passed an old horse pulling a cart full of apples, the driver not even bothering to turn to acknowledge their presence. On the top of the cart, as if resting on a bed of cushions, a young boy with breeches cut high above the knee lay fast asleep. The riders turned a corner and went down into the village. They paused as they heard the silver tones of a bell and, peering through the trees, saw a procession of villagers crossing the fields. It was led by Father Reynard, his russet gown now hidden beneath a gold and scarlet cape. The priest was preceded by a cross bearer and two young boys, one holding a bell, the other swinging a thurible. Corbett caught a whiff of the fragrant incense. He watched the priest, a stoup of holy water in one hand and an asperges rod in the other, bless the fallow fields. Corbett realised that soon it would be Michaelmas and these were the Rogation Days when the priest blessed the soil and asked God's help for the sowing and future harvest.

Corbett continued on into the village, Maltote and Ranulf behind him, chatting about the lies of the horse-copers at Smithfield Market and how best to detect their tricks. Corbett left them at The Bull, its narrow windows draped with black crepe in mourning for the landlord whose coffin now stood outside the main door, perched rather crazily on its wooden trestles. Around it some villagers were drinking their departed companion's health, and by the looks of them were almost as senseless as the corpse they were mourning. Whilst Ranulf and Maltote stayed with the horses and pulled long expressions so they could join the mourners, Corbett strode across the leaf-strewn village green and through the wicket gate of the church. He sat on a small stone bench opposite the priest's house, half dozing, still relishing the memory of his meeting with de Craon. He heard the procession return and, after a while, Father Reynard appeared out of the side door of the church. He stopped and groaned when he saw Corbett.

'What do you want, Clerk?'

'A few questions, Father.'

The priest blew out his cheeks, unlocked his door and gestured Corbett in after him. He waved the clerk to a seat and served him a cup of watered wine. The priest sat on a bench, facing him across the rough table.

'I have work to attend to, Master Corbett. The inn-keeper's body has been coffined and has now to be churched before the villagers become too drunk and dump him in the pond.' The friar smiled wanly. 'The landlord was a good poacher but a bad taverner. He was always watering his ale, and so many of the villagers believe his body should be buried in water. A fitting epitaph!'

'Is it always so dangerous,' Corbett asked abruptly, 'to be out at night around Godstowe?'

The priest shrugged.

'It depends. The landlord was poaching on palace ground.'

'And the other two? The young woman and man found naked and murdered some eighteen months ago?'

The priest grimaced.

'The roads can be dangerous.'

'You saw the corpses? Describe them.'

The priest sucked in his breath.

'The young man could have been no more than sixteen summers, olive-skinned and with black hair. Like his companion's, his throat had been cut. He wore no jewellery or stitch of clothing. The girl must have been a little older, also dark-skinned.' The priest paused. 'They may well have been foreign.'

'What makes you say that?' Corbett asked.

'The darkness of their skin. They were also well bred, and that surprises me.'

'What do you mean?'

'Well, the girl's hands particularly were soft, well kept. She had certainly done no manual work. I realised that when I anointed them. The same for the feet. Soft, uncalloused, as if she always wore hose and shoes. The poor girl's hair was mud-caked but it had once been well combed and dressed with oil. I also wondered how a high-born lady could disappear and no one raise the hue and cry.'

Corbett remembered the motto he had seen on the leather dog collar.

'Does the phrase "*Noli me tangere*" mean anything to you?' he asked.

Father Reynard shook his head and stirred restlessly on the bench.

'Surely you came to discuss other matters, Master Corbett?'

'Yes, I did.' The clerk stared at a point above the priest's head.

'Well?' Father Reynard asked.

'On the night Lady Eleanor died,' Corbett began, 'you went to Godstowe to anoint her body?'

Father Reynard nodded.

'And after that?'

Corbett caught the wary look in the priest's eye.

'I came back here,' he mumbled.

'No, you didn't!' Corbett snapped. 'You borrowed a horse from the tavern stables and went to Woodstock with the news.'

'I would have nothing to do with the Prince or his catamite!'

'Oh, not the Prince,' Corbett replied. 'But with your good friend and benefactor, Monsieur Amaury de Craon, who had sent you a secret message saying he was staying at the palace! You see, Father,' Corbett continued, 'some time ago Monsieur de Craon tried to gain access to Godstowe and was refused, so he looked around for someone to keep him appraised of developments at the priory, particularly Lady Eleanor's movements. He wanted a person he could trust. Someone who had access to that information. He chose you.'

Corbett noticed that the priest's face had paled.

'When de Craon was refused entry to Godstowe, he came here and offered you money: gold and silver for your church and parishioners. And you took it. Not as a bribe,' he added softly, 'but for alms. After all, what was the gossip of princes and their doxies to a priest? I am right, am I not, Father?'

Father Reynard placed both hands on the table and bowed his head.

'Well, Father?'

'You are right,' the priest replied. 'What you say is close to the truth. De Craon was charming. He paid gold for simple chatter.' He glanced up. 'You have seen the poverty, Clerk. The riches of the priory, the opulence of the palace. The people there don't give a fig. They have no sense of God. De Craon is no better but at least he gave me gold. Not for myself,' he added hastily, 'but for the widow with hungry mouths to feed, the boy who wants to become a scholar. I am no spy.'

Corbett felt pity but resolved not to weaken.

'If the King's serjeant-at-arms or the lawyers in King's Bench heard of this,' he replied, 'they would say you were a traitor. It is treason, Father, to correspond with the King's enemies beyond the seas.'

'I am no spy and no traitor,' the priest said quietly. 'Have you ever seen a woman yoked to her husband pulling a plough because they can't afford an ox or a horse, while their baby lies under some hedgerow, wrapped in rags, sucking a crust and whining because it is too weak with hunger to cry?' His eyes flared. 'I tell you this, Clerk, one day the poor will rise and there will be a terrible reckoning. Tell me, what would you have done in my place?'

Corbett leaned across and put his hand on the priest's elbow, glad that Father Reynard didn't flinch.

'I suppose,' he replied, 'I would have done what you did, Father.' He withdrew his hand and sipped the watered wine. 'I know you are no spy or traitor, but de Craon is dangerous. He has no morality, no God, no code of chivalry except service to the French King who sees himself as the new Charlemagne. If de Craon has spun his web round you, then you are in danger, Father.'

The priest made a rude sound with his mouth and looked away.

'Father, de Craon suspects I know the identity of his informant. He will strike against me and may well try to hurt you. Fear nothing from our King, I can get you letters of safe conduct, but you must go into hiding for a while. You should not stay here!'

Father Reynard shook his head and looked up, the fanaticism gleaming in his eyes.

'I am the good shepherd,' he replied, 'not the hireling. I will not flee because the wolf is on the prowl.' He smiled and relaxed. 'Anyway, Corbett, you forget I was once a soldier.'

Corbett shook his head.

'I cannot force you, Father, but heed my warnings.' He paused. 'What does de Craon know?'

'What I told him—that the Lady Eleanor died.' The priest smiled. 'Died in the most suspicious circumstances. You know, Clerk, I have seen many a corpse. A woman doesn't fall down steep stairs then lie at the bottom as if she is fast asleep.'

'Anything else, Father?'

'No. What I know, you know.'

Corbett rose.

'Then I bid you goodnight, and warn you to take care.'

Father Reynard looked away, dismissing his warning with a smile. Corbett went out through the deserted churchyard. The sun was now sinking, a fiery ball of light in the west, its dying rays lighting up the greens and russet browns of the graveyard. Somewhere, high in one of the elm trees, a lonely bird sang its own hymn for the dead. Corbett looked around. Father Reynard had said that the corpses of the young woman and her companion were buried beneath an old elm tree. Who were they? he wondered. What secrets did they hold? He stared around and he wondered. A silent, peaceful place but he had a premonition of something terrible. Was he being watched? He was used to the feeling in the dark, winding streets of London, but here near God's house? A twig snapped. Corbett spun round, looking beyond the priest's house.

'Is there anyone there?' he called softly.

No sound, nothing but the gentle flurry of leaves as the wind lifted and scattered them like pieces of gold across the grass. Corbett strained his ears and grinned. The evening breeze also brought the sounds of singing and he recognised the lusty bellowing of Ranulf.

He went back through the wicket gate, crossed the darkening village green. As he had guessed, Ranulf had led Maltote into temptation. Both were standing, foaming tankards of ale in their hands, in the middle of the group of mourners around the makeshift coffin, leading them in raucous song about the fate of an innkeeper's young daughter. Corbett joined them and waited for the tankards to empty before good-naturedly bullying Ranulf into collecting their horses and making their way back on to the deserted track to God-stowe.

Of course, Ranulf and Maltote were now firm friends, the servant innocently enquiring whether the messenger ever played dice? A game, he confessed, in which he was interested but had very little skill. Corbett was about to alert Maltote to the truth when he tensed. Something or someone was following them, treading through the trees on the side of the track. He reined in his horse and gestured to Ranulf to keep silent. He stared into the green darkness behind them. Someone was watching from the shadows of the forest.

'What is it, Master?' Ranulf whispered.

'Nothing,' Corbett murmured. 'But when I lower my hand, ride as fast as you can!'

He half turned, dropped his hand and kicked his horse into a gallop. Ranulf and Maltote following suit just as the two crossbow quarrels came whirring out of the darkness, skimming the tops of their heads. They needed no second bidding but rode as fast as they could, not pausing until they thundered through the half-open gate of Godstowe Priory, putting the porter into such serious agitation he appeared almost sober for once.

'Close the gates!' Corbett rasped. 'Bolt them, and let no one through without my orders!'

He suddenly looked round and remembered the two retainers.

'When did they leave us?' he asked Ranulf.

'At Woodstock, Master. They said their duty was to guard Godstowe Priory.'

'Is that so?' Corbett retorted. 'Then, Master Porter,' he raised his voice so the two soldiers hiding in the porter's house could hear him, 'tell them I will check that they are carrying out their duties. If I smell so much as a drop of ale on their breaths, they will answer to the King's Provost Marshal!'

He left Ranulf with the horses and walked round to Lady Amelia's chamber. He found the Lady Prioress closeted with Dames Frances and Catherine.

'Master Corbett!' She rose from behind the desk, her face full of surprise. 'Do come in.' She ushered him to a window seat. 'More danger, more problems?'

'On the way back from Woodstock we were attacked.'

The Lady Prioress drew her imperious brows together.

'Outlaws? Wolfshead?'

'I would like to think that, My Lady,' Corbett tactfully replied. 'But I think they were sent to kill me.'

He gazed at the two Sub-prioresses who were staring fixedly at him. Ranulf was right, he thought. Dame Catherine did have a lecherous look in her eyes.

'Lady Amelia, I have a request. Does the phrase "*Noli me tangere*" mean anything to you?'

'Do not touch me!' The Lady Prioress grinned mischievously. 'A family motto, Master Corbett. And hardly suitable to a nunnery. Why should it mean anything to me?'

She shook her head.

'In which case,' replied Corbett, 'I must crave your indulgence.' He looked across at the hour candle on the table. 'Soon the sisters will gather for Compline, I believe?'

'Of course.'

'May I speak to them?'

'About what?'

'About the motto. Whether they have heard it or not.'

Lady Amelia glanced at the Sub-prioresses and shrugged.

'It's most uncommon,' she murmured.

'The King would be pleased,' Corbett added.

'In a little while then, Master Corbett. Perhaps you will take refreshment first?'

Corbett agreed, allowing the Lady Prioress to serve him a full cup of malmsey whilst chattering about everyday matters and his recent trip to Woodstock. A bell tolled, the sign for Compline, and Lady Amelia led him down through the darkened cloister out across the grass to the church. Corbett sat on the same bench he had occupied the previous Sunday watching the nuns file in. At last, when all the stalls were full, Lady Amelia gestured to the cantor not to begin the usual psalms and caused a stir when she herself rose and swept up to the lectern.

'Sisters in Christ,' she began, 'tonight we have a change in the regular order of our routine. Master Hugh Corbett, Clerk and Special Emissary from our King, wishes to address you. He has a question which on your loyalty to God, the King and this Order, you must answer if you can.'

Corbett stared around whilst the Lady Prioress was speaking and noticed how troubled Dame Frances looked, but then the Lady Prioress snapped her fingers and imperiously summoned him forward. Drawing a deep breath to hide a flicker of nervousness, he stood at the great carved oak lectern and looked along the stalls at the nuns who sat before him there, so composed in their wimples of white and the dark garb of their Order. He glimpsed Dame Agatha smiling mischievously at him and felt comforted by her friendship.

'Lady Amelia...' Corbett felt his nervousness return at the wall of silence which greeted him. 'Lady Amelia,' he repeated, 'Reverend Sisters, eighteen months ago in the neighbourhood of Godstowe, a terrible murder took place. A young woman and her male companion were barbarously killed.'

A gentle, collective sigh greeted his words.

'I wish to ask you a question, and ask it on your allegiance to God, the King and this Order.' Corbett quietly cursed his own pomposity. 'Do any of you know the true identity of the victims, or does the phrase or family motto "*Noli me tangere*" mean anything to you?' Corbett quietly prayed no wit would cap his remark with some repartee, and blushed as he heard a few of the sisters giggle. 'I ask you again,' he felt his cheeks growing hot, 'does that phrase mean anything to you?'

He looked along the rows of silent sisters. Some gazed back, wide-eyed and open-mouthed. Dame Agatha had her face in her hands and Corbett wondered if she was laughing at him. There was no response. Corbett bowed towards Lady Amelia, stepped from the lectern and walked quietly out of the church. He stood for a while in the darkness, hoping that perhaps one of the nuns, Lady Amelia or Dame Agatha, would follow him out, but no one came. So he walked back to the guest house where Ranulf and Maltote were locked in a fierce game of dice.

'Beware of Ranulf!' Corbett called out. 'With him nothing is what it seems to be.'

The dice players ignored him so Corbett lay on his cot bed and tried to marshall his thoughts.

Item—Lady Eleanor had died during Compline when the other sisters had been in the chapel. All had gone from there to the refectory.

Item—Lady Eleanor had been seen alive just before the service began by Dame Martha and Dame Elizabeth. However, the former had seen something amiss but hidden her thoughts behind the riddle '*Sinistra non dextra*', literally translated: 'On the right not the left.'

Item—there had been horsemen seen near the priory, but who were they and who had sent them?

Item—Lady Eleanor was preparing to leave the priory and go to her secret admirer, but who was he?

Item—somehow de Craon was involved in all this and had bribed the unwitting Father Reynard.

Item—the Prince had claimed he had no involvement in Lady Eleanor's death but both he and his favourite appeared nervous.

Item—Gaveston had hated Lady Eleanor, and he, so Corbett secretly believed, was capable of cold-blooded murder.

Item—he believed the deaths of the mysterious young man and woman some eighteen months previously held the clue to the riddle surrounding Lady Eleanor's demise, but who were they and what did the motto '*Noli me tangere*' signify?

Corbett turned these questions round in his head. He thought of Maeve and realised how desperately he missed her. He also thought of Dame Agatha's smiling face before drifting into a dreamless sleep, leaving Ranulf and Maltote to argue over the fortunes of dice.

TEN

IN HIS PRIVATE CHAMBER in the priest's house Father Reynard was also lost in his own thoughts. Had he done wrong in taking the gold and silver from de Craon? He thought of the widow in her ramshackle hut at the end of the village and the gratitude in her eyes when he gave her a purse of coins. No, he considered it all worthwhile. Father Reynard lifted his head and listened to the sounds outside. Autumn, the season in which he had been born, was here again. The wind was growing stronger, whipping the branches of the trees and shredding them of their fading leaves. Soon it would be Michaelmas, then the feast of All Souls, a time to remember the dead.

He felt a flicker of disquiet. Those corpses, the ones he had buried in their makeshift grave under the old elm tree—who were they? Why had they been killed so barbarously and so mysteriously? He rubbed his mouth with the back of his hand. What would a high-born lady be doing in the wilds of Oxfordshire? Visiting a friend at the university or maybe one of the towns like Abingdon? Yet, if so, why had no one come forward to claim the corpses? Or were they connected with Godstowe?

'Father Reynard!'

The Franciscan felt the hair on the back of his neck stir as he looked towards the door. Someone was standing outside in the cemetery calling his name. It sounded like a child's voice, lilting and clear.

'Father Reynard! Please, Father Reynard, help me!'

The Franciscan made the sign of the cross in the air. Was it a ghost? An apparition? An earth-bound soul? The ghost of the dead Lady Eleanor?

'Father Reynard, come out!'

The voice was becoming petulant. The Franciscan rose and walked cautiously towards the door, picking up the thick cudgel which leaned against the wall.

'Father Reynard, do come! Please!'

Again the lilting voice cut through the darkness and the priest paused with his hand on the latch. Was it some demon raised by a witch or warlock? On his arrival in the village, the Franciscan had had some trouble with those who practised the black arts and used the cemetery for diabolical activities. There had been strange lights and incantations, the sacrifice of a black cock at midnight, but he had cleared them out and barred the graveyard, threatening the congregation with the pains of excommunication in this life and Hell fire in the next.

'Father Reynard, I mean no harm.'

The priest grasped the cudgel tighter, opened the door and stepped into the darkness. The wind caught his face as he closed the door behind him. He stared into the blackest night.

'Who's there?' he shouted. 'In God's name, child, who are you? What do you want?'

Only the wind moaning through the trees answered his cry. Father Reynard walked across to the cemetery, making out the dark shapes of the wooden crosses, mounds of earth and ghostly elm trees.

'Who are you?' he repeated. 'Where are you?'

He strained his eyes and glimpsed a shadow darker than the rest. He gasped in horror. A child, a small, dark, hooded figure was sweeping across the grass to-

ward him with hands joined as if in prayer. Father
Reynard too began a prayer and was half-way through
it when the crossbow quarrel hit him full in the chest,
ripping open skin, bone and muscle. The priest collapsed, the blood pouring through his mouth and nose
tasting like iron. He felt the soft grass against his cheek.
He saw himself as a child, running towards someone.
His mother was holding out her arms to him. He knew
he was dying.

'*Absolve me, Domine!*' he muttered as his eyes closed
and his soul was extinguished.

THE NEXT MORNING Corbett was up early, shaking
awake a tousled-headed Ranulf and a heavy-eyed Maltote.

'Come on,' he shouted good-naturedly. 'Maltote, you
will stay with us. We go to London and then on to
Leighton.'

Ranulf sprang up, pleased to abandon the fresh air of
the country and head back to the seamy streets of London and the rounded pleasure-giving body of Mistress
Semplar. Maltote staggered to his feet and went down
to relieve himself in the necessary house. Corbett met
him coming up the stairs.

'Master, shouldn't I return to the royal camp?'

Corbett noticed his surprised expression.

'No, Maltote.' He put his hand on the messenger's
shoulder. 'I need a man-at-arms, someone to protect
me.' And, before the young soldier could ask whether
he was being sarcastic, Corbett slipped by him.

The nuns were just leaving their convent church.
They glanced shyly at him out of the corner of their eyes
and giggled, remembering his appeal of the night before. Lady Amelia, majestic as a queen, swept by. Cor-

bett bowed respectfully and, pushing by the labourers and other villeins coming in from the fields to break their fasts, went out of the Galilee Gate, across the track and into the woods. There he positioned himself, trying to glimpse Dame Elizabeth's chamber from where she had alleged she had seen the horsemen waiting in the trees. At last Corbett achieved the correct position. If Dame Elizabeth, as she surely must be, was staring curiously out of her window now, she would be able to see him.

Corbett squatted down and examined the ground, sifting carefully through the fallen leaves and twigs. At last he found what he was looking for: horses had stood there. He picked up the dry droppings and crumbled them in his hand. He could not say when, but the horse dung and the faint indentations in the dry earth showed riders had stood there for some time. Dame Elizabeth had not been dreaming or seeing things.

Corbett rose, wiped his hands and went back into the priory. He heard the lamentations and cries as he walked through the Galilee Gate, and hurried around to the main entrance where a distraught Lady Amelia was being supported by the two Sub-prioresses, their own cheeks wet with tears. A young peasant boy had remounted his lathered horse and was galloping away from the priory.

'Lady Amelia, what is wrong?'

The Lady Prioress raised tearful eyes, shook herself free from the clinging sisters and wiped her cheeks.

'God rest him, we argued enough,' she muttered. 'But the poor man is dead.'

'Who, My Lady?'

'Father Reynard,' she whispered. 'He was found murdered in the cemetery this morning. A crossbow bolt in his heart.' She clasped her hands and stepped closer. 'What is happening, Corbett?' she asked. 'Such a peaceful community once, now murder and death at every turn.' She stepped back, her eyes hard. 'Is it you, Clerk? Are you a deathbringer? Does murder slide behind you?'

'No, My Lady,' he replied sharply. 'But we are in the eye of a gathering storm. Unless I find a solution to the puzzle, hundreds—perhaps even thousands—more will die in Gascony, on the Narrow Seas, and in our towns along the southern coasts. Now, My Lady,' he took her cold hand and raised it to his lips, 'I bid you adieu. I will return. If you have further information, send the fleetest messenger you can hire to my manor at Leighton. It can be found by following the Epping road down to London.'

Corbett nodded at the two hard-faced Sub-prioresses and went to order Ranulf and Maltote to saddle their horses as swiftly as possible. He told them briefly what had happened and, satisfied that they had packed everything, led them out towards the Galilee Gate.

'Hugh—Master Corbett!'

The clerk turned. Dame Agatha was hurrying towards him. She, too, had been weeping.

'I heard,' she said breathlessly, 'about Father Reynard's death.' She thrust a small linen-bound bundle into his hand. 'Some food for your journey. Take care!' she whispered. 'You will come back?'

'I will come back.'

He glimpsed the tenderness in her eyes and looked away, embarrassed.

'God be with you, Sister.'

Corbett returned to a grinning Ranulf, who was holding the heads of the horses.

'Mount!' he ordered gruffly. 'You find something amusing, Ranulf?'

The mischievous grin disappeared.

'No, Master,' he replied innocently. 'I just wondered if we could invite some of these sisters down to Leighton. The Lady Maeve would relish such company.'

Corbett gathered the reins in his hands and leaned towards Ranulf.

'Mark my words,' he snapped. 'If you so much as whisper a word about Dame Agatha to the Lady Maeve, you will regret the day I ever plucked you out of Newgate!'

Ranulf drew back, eyes rounded innocently.

'Of course, Master,' he replied slyly. 'I was only trying to help.'

They cantered down into the village and led their horses into the graveyard. A small crowd had gathered outside the church. Corbett gave a child a penny to hold the horses and they went into the priest's house. The villagers had laid Father Reynard out on the table and an old woman, tears streaming down her face, was gently bathing the corpse before it was sheeted for burial. Corbett went across, saw the horrible wounds and glimpsed the short, feathered quarrel still embedded in the man's chest.

'God have mercy on him,' he muttered. 'Did I cause this?' He gazed down at the now peaceful face of the priest. 'Why didn't you go?' he whispered. 'Why didn't you go when I told you to?'

'Master?' Ranulf muttered, 'the assassin must have been very close. The quarrel is embedded deep.'

'Strange,' Maltote interrupted, his face drawn and white as he stared down at the gory, blood-spattered wound. 'Strange,' he repeated. 'The assassin must have been lying on the ground or Father standing on some steps? Look, the crossbow quarrel is turned upwards.'

Corbett peered closer and agreed. The quarrel was embedded at an angle.

'Was Father Reynard found in the cemetery grounds?' Corbett asked the grizzled woman. She blinked away a tear and nodded. Corbett dug into his purse and handed her some coins.

'Prepare him well,' he said. 'He was a good man, a dedicated priest. He deserved a better death.'

They went back out into the cemetery. At Corbett's bidding an old man showed them the blood-spattered piece of ground where their priest had been found. Corbett walked over the soft rather damp clay of the cemetery, Ranulf and Maltote on either side.

'Look, Master, here!' Ranulf squatted down and pointed to the small indentation of a boot. He looked up at Corbett. 'Like a child's,' he whispered. 'But what child wears boots in an Oxfordshire village?'

'It could have been a woman,' Maltote interrupted.

Corbett just stared back and shook his head. A vague idea formed at the back of his mind.

'Father Reynard's death,' he concluded, 'however distressing, must wait for a while. Come,' he announced, 'we have far to ride.'

Within the hour they were out into the countryside, following the track which would lead them down to the old Roman road. The clear autumn day drew to a close and Corbett made them rest their horses for a while. Ranulf and Maltote, lost in their own thoughts and conversation, allowed him to walk ahead. The clerk wanted peace and calm after the shock of Father Reynard's death. He was glad to be free of Godstowe and the cloying, hidden menace which seemed to permeate the place like some unwholesome stench. Moreover, Corbett loved this time of the year and realised how much he missed Maeve and the serenity of his own manor house. Like here, the leaves at Leighton would be turning a reddish-gold, there would be the faint smell of wood smoke, and Corbett wondered if his wife was also out in the fields enjoying the last lingering warm embrace of summer.

They cleared the thick, wooded hills of Oxford and went down into the open countryside. Corbett stopped his horse to watch some labourers in the fields below working to bring in the last of the crops. In an adjoining field a sower, a basket cradled in his hands, scattered the life-bearing seeds, whilst behind him two young boys danced and cavorted, swinging their slings to drive off the marauding crows and ravens. Somewhere a dog howled and Corbett shuddered. He remembered that ghastly hunt across the fields at Woodstock and bit his lip at the despair he felt. So far he had found no way to resolve the conundrum facing him. There were pieces missing. Why were Lady Eleanor's saddle bags packed? Who was her secret admirer or friend? And was Lady Eleanor planning to flee to him? Corbett blinked and felt tired. He must study this mystery, take each strand and follow it through.

Behind him Ranulf laughed and Corbett looked back. The evening dusk was falling, the breeze rather cold. They had to hurry on. Corbett wished he was back in his chamber at Leighton Manor, Maeve with him. He could listen to her gentle teasing before going into his secret room and memorandising the questions which bedeviled him. He turned and smiled at Ranulf.

'Come!' he shouted. 'Let's ride a little faster to the nearest tavern. Some food and drink before we decide whether we shall continue our journey.'

They mounted and spurred their horses into a gallop, thundering along the rutted track past the crossroads where a decaying skeleton swung, the neck and head twisted, a macabre dancer against the darkening sky. Corbett fleetingly wondered if it was a portent.

They stayed at a tavern that night as the weather turned foul. Heavy rain clouds gathered and the roads next morning were clogged with thick, heavy mud. Nevertheless, they were in London just before mid-day, following White Cross Street through Cricklegate. They broke their fast in a small tavern near Catte Street, Ranulf revelling at being back in London, straining like a dog on a leash, wanting to be off on his own personal business.

Corbett warned him: 'Stay with me, Ranulf, and you too, Maltote. Whoever killed Father Reynard shot at us the previous evening. He may well have trailed us back into London.'

Maltote was only too pleased to agree though Ranulf sulked for a while. They stabled their horses and pushed their way through the noisy, colourful streets. There Ranulf quickly regained his good humour: he pointed to a group of Spaniards in their multi-coloured hoods, mantles and stupendous codpieces. He and Maltote quarrelled about what was genuine fur, and what the jewelled embroidered motifs and the bright hues on the cloaks of some retainers really signified. All around them were the cries of tradesmen and costers, the distant shrill braying of trumpets as the household of a noble moved majestically through the city under flapping banners down to Westminster. Ranulf, nudging

Maltote, leered at the pretty ladies in the fillets and low-waisted dresses; sometimes his words were drowned by the clamour of the crowd and the mid-day peal of the bells of London tolling for prayers from their great stone-washed, stately towers.

They passed into West Chepe where the throng was greatest. This broad, cobbled area, the main market place of the city, was packed with carts bringing in wine from the vintners, lawn for the cloth guilds, and vegetables packed high for the stalls and booths in the Poultry. They went through the Shambles where the butchers, ankle-deep in blood and gore, slit open the swollen bellies of cows, pigs and sheep. They allowed the blue entrails to fall on huge platters which were scooped up by young, ragged-arsed apprentices to be cleansed in vats of scalding water. A group of chandlers stood next to a long line of gutted pigs, arguing with their owner about the price of the fat which they would buy to make tallow candles. The noise was terrible and the stench made them retch. The cobblestones were soaked by streams of black blood over which swarms of fat flies hovered.

They continued on past Newgate prison, the stench from the inmates even more revolting than that from the Shambles. A beggar, the lower part of his face eaten away by sores, did a strange dance, hopping on one leg while a small, skeletal boy clothed in rags played a haunting tune on a reed pipe. Ranulf threw him a penny, then cursed as he slipped on the decaying corpse of a rat. They hurried past Fleet ditch, the corpses of dead dogs floating in the slime, and along twisting lanes which ran through the high four-storey houses, the upper floors projecting out on wooden pillars so the rooms above could catch the sun. Here, hawkers and coster-mongers pushed their little handcarts, crying 'Bread!', 'Eels!', 'Fish!' and 'Meat pies!' and on every corner stood tipplers who sold drinks to passersby out of small, iron-hooped barrels.

'Master, where are we going?' Ranulf called.

'Smithfield!' Corbett shouted back, pushing away an apprentice who offered him spiced hot sheep's feet. At the mouth of Cock Lane a group of young prosti-tutes—slim-waisted and lecherous—shouted out their lies and danced with sheer delight at the prospect of mischief. One of them apparently recognised Ranulf and called out honey-phrased invitations as to what she would offer for a silver coin.

'I have no silver!' he shouted back, ignoring Cor-bett's warning frown.

'Nor any balls, by the look of it!' one of the whores retorted.

The ladies of the town shrieked with laughter whilst Ranulf, his face flushed, hurried on as fast as he could. They crossed the open dusty area of Smithfield to where the hospital of St. Bartholomew stood. Corbett asked the others to stay at the great gate whilst he went across the open square. He relished the coolness, the raised beds of flowers and herbs, and the elaborately carved fountains splashing in the centre. He caught the tangy smell of soap, though he also sniffed the stench of cor-ruption and the dank smell of a charnel house which stood in one corner of the grounds.

Corbett went up the great steps of the hospital, past the group of old soldiers, their limbs grotesquely am-putated, who enlivened each other with stories of their past. A young boy with a ladle and a stoup of water wetted their grizzled mouths. Corbett stopped a lay brother.

'Is Brother Thomas here?' he asked.

The little man nodded his bald head, his eyes simple as a child's. He beckoned Corbett to follow him along white-washed corridors to the herb-scented chamber of Brother Thomas. The apothecary was sitting at his small desk under the open window but rose, laughing and clapping his hands as he recognised Corbett. He threw down his goose quill and grasped the clerk's hands, pumping them up and down vigorously.

'Hugh, you have returned! Come in!'

He almost pulled him into the room, closing the door behind them. He shifted a pile of yellowing parchments from a small pallet bed and cleared a space for Corbett to sit.

'You want some wine or a cup of water?'

'The water will be best, Brother.'

Brother Thomas nodded and splashed an earthenware bowl to the brim.

'You are wise, Hugh,' he said. 'Always remember what Galen said, though Hippocrates maintained different: "Wine before sunset is not to be recommended." You are well? And the Lady Maeve?'

For a while Corbett and the apothecary discussed gossip of mutual interest, acquaintances at Westminster, at the court, as well as the scandal of a certain physician now being investigated by the authorities at the Guildhall. The apothecary's face became serious.

'I know why you are here, Hugh,' he said sharply. 'Poison, the queen of murders. I am right, am I not?'

'You are right, Brother.'

'So what is the problem?'

'Could you sell me a poison, Brother? I mean, Belladonna or the juice of the Nightshade?'

The apothecary waved at the shelves around his room full of little phials and casks.

'They are yours for the asking, Hugh.'

'And they will kill?'

'In seconds. Ten or twenty heart-beats before the poison ices your heart and stops your breath.'

Corbett stood up and stretched.

'But poisons that would only kill if taken regularly over a long period of time, do they exist?'

The brother's eyes became even more sombre.

'Oh, yes, Hugh. Such potions do exist, but not here. They are of the Italian mode. Deadly concoctions.' He paused. 'For example, five hundred years ago an Arab produced a white, odourless powder, highly poisonous, from realger, an ore found in lead mining.' Brother Thomas shrugged. 'In small quantities, it may be medicinal, but given regularly will eventually cause death.'

'Could I buy it in London?'

The apothecary nodded.

'Of course.'

'Who from?'

'A Hell-hound not far from here. The first alleyway on Faltour's Lane off Holborn Street. Go down there and look for the apothecary's sign. He is a Spaniard, a Portuguese, a Moor...I don't know, but he may tell you more than I can. You see, Hugh, as I said, some poisons are medicinal. A little arsenic can cure disorders of the stomach, but given in regular small doses becomes a poison. I once heard the confession of a merchant from the Portsoken who wished absolution for killing his wife. For two years he fed the poor woman poison.' The apothecary turned and looked out of the window. 'You'd best go now, Hugh. The day is drawing on and this apothecary's shop is the very gateway to Hell. Or,' he grinned, 'as you manor lords would say: "Where the shit lies, the flies always gather."'

Hugh grinned, thanked him, and went back to the hospital gates where he warned Ranulf and Maltote to be on their guard. They followed a maze of alleyways which ran to the north of the city down to Holborn. Corbett realised that Brother Thomas was correct. The weak sun was setting and the area near the old city wall was one of musty decay. The stalls were battered, selling shabby geegaws. There were very few well-dressed citizens, most of the denizens of the alleyways being rogues and villains; tinkers, trying to sell without permission from the Guilds, professional beggars, and rat-faced slum dwellers looking for easy prey.

They found Faltour's Lane and turned into the dirty refuse-filled alleyway, the daylight almost blocked out by the overhanging gables of the houses which reared up on either side. Ranulf stopped his chatter and when Corbett drew his sword so did his companions as a blatant warning to the dark shapes which lurked in the half-open doorways. A beggar, smitten with white leprosy, one ear and half his nose eaten away, came out of the shadows, his hands extended, begging for alms. Corbett threw him a coin, raised his sword, and the beggar scuttled away.

The clerk was now uneasy. The alleyway was narrow, lined with darkened doorways; some had shadows deeper than the rest and Corbett knew he was being watched. Any sign of weakness or fear and the cutpurses lurking there would be on them like a pack of dogs. He stood beneath the apothecary's sign, dagger still drawn; two cats raced by, screeching and squabbling over the half-gnawed body of a rat. Corbett jumped, cursing his own nervousness. He sheathed his dagger, whispered to Ranulf and Maltote to wait at the top of the alleyway, and knocked gently on the shop door.

A young man opened it. Corbett was immediately struck by the fellow's swarthy good looks and elegant dress: dark purple hose, soft buskings on his feet, and an open-necked, spotless, white cambric shirt. The man smiled as if intrigued by Corbett, muttering a few words first in Portuguese and then in English. Corbett, acting his part, looked nervously back down the street and said he needed certain potions. The man smiled, his smooth dark face creasing in a grin, lips parted to reveal ivory white teeth as he gestured like a long-lost friend for Corbett to enter. Inside the shop was simple but clean; the stone floor had been recently scrubbed, the walls coated with lime to keep off flies. It was devoid of any furniture except a zodiac sign nailed to one wall, a small wooden table and two huge, high-backed chairs. The apothecary introduced himself.

'My name is Julio Cesar. Doctor, physician, formerly apothecary to his most Catholic Majesty, Sancho, King of Portugal. Now exiled from that country due to a,' the black eyes slid away, 'misunderstanding. And you, Sir?'

'Matthew Droxford,' Corbett lied.

The apothecary studied him, a faint smile on his full red lips as if he knew his visitor was lying.

'And you want some medicine?'

Cesar elegantly waved Corbett to a seat before disappearing into the small back room beyond, returning with two crystal goblets brimming with iced sherbet. He gave one to Corbett before sitting down opposite, sipping from his own cup as if he had all the time in the world. Corbett tasted the drink gingerly. He knew this man, not by name or reputation, but by smelling the rotten evil about him. Oh, he would be a doctor, an apothecary, but he was also a poisoner. Corbett could not prove that but he recognised the kind of man who could concoct cunning elixirs which could kill a man or woman and leave no trace.

Cesar put his own cup down on the floor.

'Come, Sir,' he said briskly. 'Your business? Why are you here?'

'You have been recommended to me,' Corbett answered brusquely. He half smiled, his eyes narrowed. 'You are a gentleman, Signor, you will understand if I give no names. I am married, and my wife has been unfaithful.' He saw the flicker of amusement in Cesar's face. 'Not for the first time,' Corbett continued hurriedly. 'I am a man of honour, Signor. I cannot divorce her nor can I proclaim myself a cuckold, to be a common joke amongst my tenants and fellows. I have not stinted in providing my wife with every luxury. I have begged for her fidelity.'

'But she does not keep her word?' The apothecary leaned closer, like a priest ready to listen to a confession. 'And now, Signor, you wish to carry out sentence?'

'Yes, I want a powder, a potion, one which will not kill immediately, but over a period of months, undetected by her or any physician.'

'Signor, that will be expensive.'

Corbett asked the price and stifled his amazement at the reply. It would take most of the silver he had on him and that would be just for half an ounce of what was needed. Nonetheless, he agreed; the apothecary rose and disappeared into the back room, emerging a few minutes later with a small leather bag. He offered it, smiling, to Corbett.

'You may taste it, Signor. It will not harm you. It's no more dangerous than chalk. But if you took it regularly...' He shrugged.

Corbett took the powder and counted out the silver. The price was worth it. The powder he would throw away but the information the poisoner had provided was invaluable.

ELEVEN

CORBETT LEFT THAT terrible shop without a word to Ranulf and Maltote, and walked out into the street off Faltour's Lane.

'Master!'

Corbett stopped and turned.

'What is it, Ranulf?'

'When you were in that apothecary's, I thought we were being watched. No, not just by some bully boy—someone else.'

Corbett looked around. They were back on the broad but darkened thoroughfare of Holborn. The stalls had disappeared, the shop fronts were boarded up. Some householders had even placed lantern horns outside their house, the weak flame of the candles fluttering in their protective iron grilles against the cool evening breeze. Two young urchins ran by, screaming and shouting. A bloody-mouthed mastiff tied by a chain to a lintel of a door snarled and barked. Somewhere in a room above them, a woman gently crooned the tune of a lullaby. Corbett could see nothing untoward.

'You are sure?' he said. 'Maltote, did you see anything?'

The serjeant-at-arms looked worried but shook his head.

'I did think we were being followed when we went to the apothecary's, but it was only a child.'

Two young urchins, their faces completely hidden by hoods, came hurrying by, kicking an inflated pig's bladder before them.

'There's nothing,' Corbett murmured. 'Nothing at all.'

They walked up Holborn, across the darkening common which stretched out before the old city walls, into the pestiferous area around Newgate and down towards Cheapside. Now and again they would stop and look around but there was no one following them. They reached Catte Street and Corbett decided they should stay in the tavern where they had stabled their horses.

'Tomorrow,' he announced, 'we go to Leighton.'

'And baby Hugh? I'd like to see him!' Ranulf angrily replied.

Corbett smiled.

'I'd not forgotten, Ranulf. However, as Scripture says, "Sufficient for the day is the evil thereof." Let's fill our bellies and try the ale.' Corbett looked slyly at Maltote. 'And, who knows, you may teach Ranulf the finer points of dicing!'

Laughing and joking, they pushed their way into the tavern's huge taproom, choosing a table near the great roaring fire. Corbett shouted for jacks of ale, demanding they be served the landlord's best.

'None of your watered stuff!' he shouted. 'Or I'll have the ale-masters down here!'

The landlord, a thin ashpole of a man, completely bald except for a stray lock of hair which constantly drooped over his eyes, wiped his greasy hands on a dirty apron, served them and scurried off. Corbett tasted the thick heady ale, pronounced himself satisfied and leaned forward.

'Thank God we are free of Godstowe,' he murmured.

'Do you know what happened, Master?' Ranulf asked anxiously. 'Which one of those well-fed bitches is the murderess?'

'It's more complex than that, Ranulf.' Corbett sipped from his blackjack. 'On Sunday the eighth of September, Lady Eleanor Belmont was murdered in her chamber. Her neck was broken without any sign of a struggle and there are no reports of any intruders. The good sisters,' he looked sardonically at Ranulf, 'whom you just referred to, were all in church. Lady Eleanor was seen alive when the Nuns of Syon were all in public view of each other, just before Compline.' Corbett paused. 'This includes all those who knew her well: the Lady Prioress, the two Sub-prioresses, and our comely Dame Agatha. They all sang their psalms and went to the refectory. Afterwards, the Prioress, anxious about Lady Eleanor, went to her chamber but found the woman murdered.' He threw a quizzical look at Ranulf. 'The corpse was then moved to the foot of the stairs to make it look like an accident.'

Ranulf swilled the beer around in his tankard.

'So, the murderer or murderess must have been an outsider?'

'Yes,' Corbett answered. 'Father Reynard was a suspect but I now know he was busy riding to Woodstock. Anyway, the poor man's dead and beyond suspicion.'

'Gaveston could have sent assassins.'

'True. But, as I have said, any outsider would have been noticed. The porter, drunk as he always is, would have raised the alarm. Anyway, why should Gaveston or the Prince do that? I have just discovered that Gaveston was probably poisoning the Lady Eleanor with a slow but subtle potion.' Corbett rubbed his chin against the palm of his hand. 'Yet that, too, raises problems. If Gaveston was sending these powders, killing the Lady Eleanor by degrees, surely the poison should eventually have worked? So if Gaveston was already trying to murder Lady Eleanor, why would he abruptly change his methods?'

'But,' Ranulf interrupted, 'if the Lady Eleanor was not murdered by any of the good sisters…if she was not murdered by Gaveston, if no one stole across the priory walls, what *did* happen?'

Corbett shook his head.

'I don't know. Riders were seen in the forest the day Eleanor Belmont died.' He shrugged. 'But I can see no connection between their presence and the lady's death.' He grinned at Maltote, who was staring at him open-mouthed. 'There are other mysteries,' he continued. 'What were the identities of the young man and woman killed near Godstowe some eighteen months ago?'

Ranulf smacked his lips and placed his tankard on the table.

'I can help you there,' he said. 'The tavern wench at The Bull told me how the landlord glimpsed the young lady and her companion riding through Godstowe.'

Corbett nodded.

'Yes, you told me that. Did he see anything else?'

'One further thing I have learnt from the wench. The landlord claimed a well-dressed young man also passed through the village about the same time. He walked his horse outside the tavern but left Godstowe just before the young woman and man were seen.'

'Didn't you learn anything more?' Corbett snapped. 'A description, further details?'

'Master, I went back time and again.' Ranulf shrugged. 'It was the same story, glimpses, nothing else.'

He looked at Corbett's troubled face.

'Master, let's go back to Lady Eleanor's death. If the murderer was not from Godstowe, and any normal outsider would have been noticed, perhaps there's a third possibility?'

'Such as?'

'A professional assassin who climbed the walls and murdered the woman without anyone catching sight of him.'

Corbett leaned back on the bench and stared up at the smoke-blackened beams. Ranulf was right. If all the nuns were in Compline, if no one was spotted stealing over the convent walls, then the only logical conclusion was a professional assassin. Was this the de Montfort murderer, killing Lady Eleanor to embarrass the English crown? Or was the assassin sent by the King, his son, Gaveston, or even the French?

Ranulf coughed.

'Of course, Master, there is one final explanation.'

'Which is?'

'That the Lady Amelia is a liar. She could have gone to Lady Eleanor, murdered her, and then moved the body downstairs.'

Corbett nodded. Ranulf's theory made sense. Lady Eleanor would have opened the door to her Prioress.

'Or,'' Ranulf grinned, 'perhaps the ancient ones, Dame Elizabeth and Dame Martha—maybe they are not as innocent as you think. The same could apply to one of the Sub-prioresses.'

Corbett smiled. Ranulf was correct. So many suspects, yet so few answers. He let the conversation drift.

Ranulf teased Maltote about his love life while Corbett ordered the evening meal: roasted capons stuffed with herbs, hare cooked in wine, and a dish of vegetables, leeks and onions smattered with garlic and thyme. They were half-way through their meal when the landlord appeared in the middle of the room, shouting: 'Master Corbett! Is there a Hugh Corbett here?'

The noise in the taproom stilled for a moment, even the farmers in the corner drunkenly arguing about the price of wheat; two harridans from the town shrieking at each other over an upturned barrel; and a group of young bloods, garishly dressed in costly silks, noisily roistering before a night out on the town. Corbett rose and beckoned the fellow over.

'There's a boy outside,' the landlord said. 'He has a message for you.'

'From whom?'

The fellow wiped his dripping nose on the back of his hand.

'By St. Paul's, I'm a taverner not a messenger! The urchin simply said he had a message which he must give only to you.'

'Then bring him in.'

'He says he's afeared.' The landlord turned and spat into the dirty rushes. 'For God's sake, man, he's just outside the door!'

Corbett shrugged, told Ranulf and Maltote to keep the flies off his food and went out. In the gathering dusk he saw the boy, his back to him, staring down the darkening street.

'What is it, lad?'

The boy turned. Corbett couldn't make his features out because of the hood pulled over his head. He saw the pig's bladder lying at the boy's feet, very similar to the one he had seen two children playing with on Holborn thoroughfare. The boy turned and Corbett suddenly sprang back. The long, thin stiletto missed his stomach by inches.

'Who are you?' Corbett whispered, backing away. 'What is it, boy?'

He was defenceless. He had left his sword belt and dagger in the tavern. He could hardly believe a young boy of no more than ten or eleven could be playing such a deadly game. The small, cowled figure shuffled towards him. Again the knife snaked out. Corbett caught the boy by the wrist and gasped in surprise at his strength. He shoved his would-be assassin away and, as he did so, the hood fell back and Corbett stood transfixed in fear. No boy but a manikin, a midget of a man. Corbett had never seen such evil in someone so small: black hair slicked back against the head like the ears of a wet rat; tiny, soulless eyes and a face as twisted and as sour as a rotten apple. To his left Corbett heard a slithering on the cobbles. He glanced over and his heart jumped into his throat. A second small figure now crept out of the darkness and started to edge towards him. Corbett glimpsed the arbalest in the midget's hand and, in the poor light, the shimmering sharpness of the lethal bolt waiting to be fired.

'Oh, Christ!' he murmured.

He heard a click and stepped back quickly as the bolt thudded into the wall of the derelict house behind him. Corbett lost his footing and went down, his flailing hands seeking something to grip. He touched a lump of rotting offal and, scooping it up, throwing it at the first assassin now tripping towards him. The handful of dirt caught the dwarf in the face, making him gag and drop his guard. He stopped to wipe away the excrement, which blinded his eyes and coated his lips. Corbett rose swift as an arrow.

'*Aidez moi!*' he shouted. 'Ranulf!'

And, using all his force, he ran and crashed into the second assassin, who was winching back the arbalest for another bolt. Both clerk and dwarf rolled and scrabbled in the mud. Corbett felt as if he was in a nightmare; the very smallness of the man made him a false opponent, almost cutting off Corbett's blood lust and desire to protect himself. The dwarf strained against him as they rolled and struggled in the mud. Corbett, determined the dwarf wouldn't reach the dagger in his belt, was trying to tighten his grip round his assailant's throat. He looked up desperately as he saw the other assassin now approach, his dagger raised, waiting to strike.

'Ranulf!' Corbett yelled.

The dagger began to descend. Corbett heard the whirr of a crossbow. Was there another attacker? But when he looked up, the dwarf above him was standing, arms limp like a ragged doll, staring dully down at the crossbow bolt buried in his stomach. Corbett regained his strength and scrambled to his feet, dragging the dwarf in his grasp with him as the latter's accomplice slumped wordlessly to his knees. He heard the patter of feet behind him and turned, his captive slid from his hands like an eel. The manikin threw a malevolent look at Corbett and fled into the darkness. Maltote came running up, Ranulf behind him. The manservant dropped to one knee, brought the crossbow up, again the death-bearing click, and the whirring crossbow bolt caught the second assassin just before he slipped into the darkness. It caught him full in the middle of his back, throwing him into the air before he crashed down on the cobbles.

Corbett went over and examined the bodies, wiping the sweat from his eyes as he turned each of the corpses over. He still felt strange, as if he was bending over the bodies of children, but one look at the dead faces calmed such scruples. They were almost identical in looks and equally steeped in depravity. Even in death their lips were curled in a snarl; their wizened faces and staring, blank eyes seemed to gloat over the evil they had planned. Professional assassins, Corbett thought. He recognised the type. They could come in many guises; a beautiful woman, a troubadour, a pedlar, even a priest or monk. Something stirred in his memory but he was too tired and disturbed to concentrate. Ranulf came up and expertly went through their wallets and pockets but there was nothing except a few coins.

'The mark of a true assassin,' Corbett observed drily. 'They carry nothing and wear nothing to identify them, where they come from or who sent them.'

'Except this, Master!'

Ranulf returned from the corpse of the second dwarf, some silver in his hands. He sifted through it with his fingers.

'Some English pennies,' he observed. 'But the silver's French.'

Corbett stared at the coins.

'De Craon!' he muttered. 'That bastard of a Frenchman sent them!'

He suddenly remembered Father Reynard's corpse and stooped down to examine the leather-heeled boots of the assassins.

'Well,' he said, 'at least I know how Father Reynard died. Remember the boot marks in the cemetery?'

'But there was only one set!'

Corbett rose and gulped the cool night air.

'But both these were there. Remember the angle of the crossbow bolt in the priest's body? An assassin's ruse: one would knock on the door, the other would be waiting in the darkness. It's an old trick played in many ways. Sometimes it's a beggar stretching out a hand for coins whilst the other conceals the knife. Or, in my case,' he added wearily, 'a dwarf pretending to be a boy. I almost walked on to the bastard's knife!'

Corbett looked back at the tavern doorway now thronged with onlookers. Doors were opening up and down the street, casement windows were flung wide and shouts were heard. A small portly figure swathed in robes waddled out of the darkness.

'My name's Arrowhead!' he bellowed. 'John Arrowhead, alderman of this ward.' He pointed a finger at Corbett. 'You, Sir, are under arrest until the watch arrive!'

Corbett leaned against the corner of the house, trying to stop the trembling in his legs.

'And you, Sir,' he retorted, 'are a pompous fool who acts before he thinks. My name is Hugh Corbett, I am senior clerk in the King's Chancery and his special emissary. The two corpses are Frenchmen. They were assassins. Now, if you still wish to arrest me, do so—but tomorrow I will be free and you will be in prison!'

Corbett dusted himself down, and with as much dignity as he could muster, walked back to the tavern.

They sat and finished their meal, Corbett chewing his food carefully and downing two cups of heady claret to calm his nerves. Ranulf was full of himself, rather peeved that his master did not thank him properly for his rescue, making sly references to his own archery.

'You took your time,' Corbett muttered ungraciously.

Maltote coughed and looked away.

'Master Corbett, he said, 'that was my fault. One of the customers heard the fight. We took the crossbow from the landlord. I shot a bolt.' He looked away and swallowed hard. 'It completely missed.' His eyes flickered nervously at Corbett. 'I just hope it didn't hit anyone else. Ranulf snatched it from me. You know the rest.'

Corbett stared at his bold-faced servant.

'How many times, Ranulf?'

'How many time what, Master?'

'How many times have you saved my life?'

Ranulf shrugged.

'It's my duty,' he replied so piously that Corbett leaned back and roared with laughter. He took his purse and emptied the coins on to the table.

'They are for you, Ranulf. My regards to your son. Maltote, you had better go with him.'

He put his hand over the young messenger's.

'Just promise me you'll never handle a crossbow whenever I am anywhere near you.'

Maltote smiled nervously and, led by Ranulf, left the tavern for a night of revelling.

Corbett sat muttering to himself, going over the questions which still vexed him. He realised that in his discussion with Ranulf he had not mentioned old Martha's death. Why did she die? What was so important about the phrase '*Sinistra non dextra*'. Corbett stared down at his hands gripping the table edge. He had thought of it before. Was the old nun referring to hands? But whose? What did she mean by the phrase? He shook his head.

'On the left, not the right!' he muttered.

The landlord, passing by the table, stopped and looked strangely at Corbett but the clerk smiled and shook his head so the fellow wandered off. Corbett remained sitting for hours following various trains of thought whilst Ranulf, having seen his son, was bouncing about on the broad, silk-canopied bed of Mistress Semplar. The young merchant's wife, her old husband away at a Guild meeting, had been delighted to see her amorous gallant. How pleased Ranulf was now finding out, whilst outside the front door a drunken Maltote kept watch.

A DAY LATER, Corbett sat on the edge of his own bed in Leighton Manor watching Maeve busy herself round the room. He had returned earlier in the day and Maeve was as ecstatic to see him as he had been hungry for her. A hollow-eyed Maltote had taken a strangely exhausted Ranulf off to their own lodgings so the clerk and his wife had dined by themselves in the small hall below and spent the rest of the time here in their bedchamber. As usual Maeve had been full of questions. Whom had he met? Where had he been? How long would they stay?

Corbett had tried to give her reasonable answers, deliberately omitting any reference to the attack in Catte Street or the murder of Father Reynard. Nevertheless, Maeve's sharp eyes had missed nothing; her husband looked exhausted, troubled, and now she felt agitated. Hugh had referred to de Craon and Maeve knew enough about the Frenchman to realise he meant nothing but ill for her husband. However, she had kept a brave face, telling him about the affairs of the manor, assuring him that the child growing in her belly was as well as could be expected. She kept her own bad news to the last.

'Hugh…' Maeve straightened up and pulled her shift around her. 'There's a letter for you. It came earlier this morning. It's from the King. He's coming south, he's at Bedford.'

'Bedford! He should be on the Scottish march. Maeve, the letter!'

His wife went over to a casket and took out a small roll of parchment.

'I broke the seal, Hugh.' She stared coolly at him. 'What concerns you, concerns me.'

He undid the scroll carefully. The King's message was sharp and cool: he was both sad and angry that his 'beloved clerk, Hugh Corbett, has failed to report any progress on our business at Godstowe'. The letter continued in a taunting, angry fashion, insults thinly veiled, about how the King's trust had not been repaid. The King was so concerned, the letter concluded, he had left his army under the command of others and was journeying south to resolve the matter himself. Corbett crumpled the parchment into a ball and threw it angrily at the wall. He glared at his wife.

'Hell's teeth, Maeve! St. Bernard was right. The Plantagenets come from the Devil, and to the Devil they will surely go! Is it my fault if the King has spoilt his son and made him a laughing stock in Europe? What does he know about bloody-mouthed dogs, silent assassins and…' His voice faltered off at the frightened look on Maeve's face.

'You didn't tell me!' she accused, and took her husband by the hand. 'But now you will.'

Corbett had no choice but told her from the beginning of the events at Godstowe. Maeve heard him out, quietly holding his hand.

'This Dame Agatha,' she asked pointedly, 'is she beautiful?'

'Yes, almost as beautiful as you.'

'Is she fair of face?'

'Yes.'

'Did you like her?'

Corbett knew Maeve would sense any lie and, when angry, his wife could be frightening.

'Yes, I did,' he replied slowly. 'But that does not matter. Everything I have seen, Maeve, is what I am supposed to see. It may be real but it is not the truth.'

'Do you have any suspicions?'

Corbett haltingly told her what he had discovered. Maeve agreed that the old nun had probably been referring to Lady Eleanor's hands.

'That's the key, Hugh,' she observed.

'What is?'

'The old nun's death. Tell me about it.'

Corbett shrugged.

'Dame Elizabeth came up and found the door unlocked. She went in behind the screen and discovered the old lady's body half immersed in a tub of water. There were no marks on the corpse. It could have been a seizure or the falling sickness.' He paused. 'There was also a trail of water on the floor, but would an assassin be so clumsy as to leave that?'

Maeve sat silent for a while.

'I don't know. Will you let the matter rest?'

'No.' Corbett patted her on the hand. 'Let me think for a while.'

He crossed the room, pulled back the arras on the far wall and went into his own secret chamber. He took a tinder, lit the candles on his desk and stared at the bundles of letters awaiting him. They had arrived during his absence and he had scanned them quickly. News from foreign courts, spies, envoys, merchants and other clerks. Only one of them concerned the business at Godstowe. A short note from a spy in Paris: Eudo Tailler's head had been fished from the Seine where it had been thrown in a sack.

'Christ have mercy on his soul,' Corbett whispered.

Tailler had sent his master the news about the mysterious de Montfort assassin. Had that cost him his life? If so, the price seemed too steep. Corbett had discovered no trace of any assassin active in England. He put the letter aside and took a fresh piece of parchment, smoothing it out and rubbing it clear with a pumice stone. He then began to itemise the problems and questions which confronted him. He worked for hours, taking each name and trying to draw up evidence to prove that person the murderer. Outside the dark woods and fields were silent as if waiting patiently for the approach of winter. Corbett dozed for a while and was suddenly awakened by a knocking on the chamber door. It swung open to reveal Maeve.

'The old nun, Hugh . . . isn't it strange?' She smiled. 'Remember I talk as a woman. Dame Martha wanted a bath and put a screen round the tub?'

Corbett rubbed his eyes and nodded.

'But if you go to the trouble of putting a screen round the tub, what else do you do?'

Corbett shook his head wearily.

'For God's sake, Hugh, any lady would do it! Your famous logic. She would lock the door!'

'So?'

'Oh, Hugh, think! You said the door was open.'

Corbett fell back in his chair and smiled.

'So, the old nun must have let her murderer in. She must have been in the bath, heard the knock and got out; the trail of water was not left by the murderer but the nun herself when she crossed to open the door.'

Corbett stared down at his piece of parchment. 'Thank you, Maeve,' he mumbled. But when he looked up, the door was closed and his wife had gone.

Corbett bathed his hands and face in the bowl of water standing on the lavarium. He reviewed his notes in the light of what Maeve had said, and began to follow it through. He forced his arguments on, jumping gaps, circumventing difficulties or problems. The cold hand of fear pinched his stomach. He knew the murderer! Was it possible? He scratched his tousled hair and went back again, taking in all the facts and like the lawyer he was, drawing up a summary bill of prosecution. He shook his head. A jury might not accept that he had proved his case, but they would agree there was a case to answer.

Corbett suddenly remembered his last meeting with the nuns at Godstowe and his heart began to pound. They were all in danger, every one of them! He got to his feet, threw his cloak round him and went down to rouse Ranulf and Maltote, dragging both of them, sleepy-eyed, into the dark kitchen. He gave them instructions: they were to break fast, saddle the swiftest horses from the stables and leave with him.

'We go to London first,' he declared. 'Then,' he grinned, 'visit every tavern along the Oxford road.'

Of course they protested, but Corbett was adamant. Within an hour he had kissed Maeve adieu and they were on the road south to Westminster. Corbett was determined to seek out the truth. He might not be able to stop murder at Godstowe, but at least he might trap the assassin who stalked the priory.

CORBETT WAS RIGHT in his dread premonition. At Godstowe Priory Dame Frances was only a few minutes away from death. The self-important Sub-prioress was both disturbed and fearful. She was troubled, distracted in meditation, and often found herself staring into the middle distance when the other sisters were chanting Divine Office. She had told her confidante but she had been no help, and how could she approach the Lady Amelia? No, she thought, that was out of the question. Dame Frances gazed round the small kitchen of the novitiate. Upstairs the young postulants were now retiring to bed in the long dormitory. Each knelt in her partitioned alcove, commending heart and soul to God and praying that Satan, who wandered around like a lion seeking his prey, did not harm their bodies or souls that night.

Dame Frances sat down on a stool, her face in her hands. What that dour clerk had announced must be connected with the death of Lady Eleanor, and, perhaps the death of old Martha. Dame Frances had seen that motto, '*Noli me tangere*' here, in Godstowe, but could not remember where or when. Should she flee the priory? Go to Westminster and seek an audience with Corbett or one of the King's Officers? But whom could she trust? Gaveston had his spies everywhere and the common jest was true, England had three kings; old Edward, his son and Gaveston. She stared dully at the logs crackling in the hearth. Perhaps she should wait, her mind was tired. A good night's sleep and tomorrow she would plot and plan.

Dame Frances rose, picked up the bucket and stopped, heart in mouth, at a sound outside. Was there someone watching her? Or was it just the wind rustling the leaves along the grass? Dame Frances walked towards the fire, muttering a short prayer that all would be well. She was still praying as she emptied the bucket over the logs. Her mumbles rose instantly to a terrifying scream as the flames jumped from the fire, ran along the hearth, and caught her robe. In a few seconds, Dame Frances was a blazing human torch.

Only a few miles away other actors in the macabre drama surrounding Lady Eleanor's death were taking up new roles and stances. In his velvet-lined chamber, Piers Gaveston lay under the great, silken canopy of his four-poster bed, chewing his lip and wondering what would happen next. He trusted his spy in London. Corbett had been snooping there and seized a juicy morsel, first visiting his old friend at St. Bartholomew's and then the poisoner in Faltour's Lane. Gaveston had ordered the apothecary to be killed. He knew too much, and besides Gaveston could not understand why Lady Eleanor had not died of those powders. The apothecary had assured him that anyone who took them would gradually weaken and die as if from natural causes. The apothecary had lied and Lady Eleanor had been murdered by other means. So what should he do next? Gaveston looked at the young page boy standing near him, a goblet of wine in his small white hands. The favourite sat up and grabbed the cup so hastily splashes of wine fell on his silken, multi-coloured hose. He rounded in anger, slapping the page across his sulky, girlish face.

'Get out!' he roared. 'Get out, until you learn how to serve a lord!'

The boy hurried away, rubbing his flaming cheek, as Gaveston sipped from the goblet. If only Corbett had kept his long nose out of this God-forsaken business! The royal favourite gazed moodily around the chamber. He would not forget Corbett, a man to be reckoned with. Should he make him a friend? Gaveston bit his lip. Perhaps, but that was for the future. The old King was now hurrying south and with him would come those grizzled warlords who followed like mastiffs at the royal heels. Gaveston knew how much they hated him. If only the old King would die! Gaveston would keep the Prince sweet until then. He would confess all, go on his knees, say he was the Prince's slave, buy him expensive presents . . . But when would the old King die?

Gaveston rose and went across to an old, ironbound chest, taking a ring of keys from a gold chain which hung around his neck. He undid the three locks and swung back the lid. He took out the waxen figure which also contained straw and fat from a hanged man. It wore a silver chaplet round its head. Then he removed a bowl of incense and a black inverted cross. Squatting down on the floor like a peasant, Gaveston began the dark satanic ritual learnt from his mother for the total destruction of his enemies.

In another chamber in the same palace Seigneur Amaury de Craon was also preparing to change tack. His assassins were dead, Philip would not be pleased by that; the dwarfs had carried out many an assassination on behalf of the French King and their skills and expertise would be sorely missed. De Craon pondered the choices facing him. If old Edward died, if he was murdered, what would the gossips say then? Would they hint at patricide? That the young Prince, or Gaveston, or both, not only murdered hapless ladies in convents but even the Lord's anointed?

De Craon shifted in his chair uneasily. He had searched for this assassin by silent threat and bribery but so far had discovered nothing. King Philip had sent him a name wrung from the captured spy Tailler, but de Craon could find no trace of such a man. De Craon smiled grimly to himself: Tailler had been brave and, to the very last, had told nothing but lies. Perhaps the assassin's fictitious name was Tailler's final joke. The envoy cursed quietly to himself. If only Corbett had been elsewhere. All might now depend on that interfering, extremely lucky, English clerk. Perhaps he might fail? Perhaps Philip's final plan, of finding and using the de Montfort assassin, could still succeed? Or should he, de Craon wondered, abandon this game, resume his official status and demand the betrothal of the Prince of Wales to the Princess Isabella?

TWELVE

THE RAIN WAS STILL FALLING as Corbett and his party reached London's Aldgate and made their way down through Poor Jewry, Mark Lane, and into Petty Wales near the Tower. They stabled their horses and hired a wherry at the Wool Quay. Maltote of course protested, but the two wizened boatmen only mocked his fears at having to go downriver.

'You only drown once!' they cried in unison, 'And it doesn't take long. If you fall in the water, just open your mouth and let the water gush in. You'll be amongst the angels within a few seconds!'

'Which is more than we could say for you!' Ranulf hotly declared, coming to the aid of the newfound victim of his dice games.

Corbett told them all to shut up. The boatmen cast off and rowed downriver past Billingsgate and Botolph's Wharf. The wherry shot under London Bridge where the water boiled between the closely built arches, the boatmen dipping their oars so the boats could squeeze by the starlings which protected them against the thick stone arches. Once they were through they all relaxed; the Thames was a cruel river but no more dangerous than in the seething caldron under London Bridge.

The wherryman now took their boat midstream, past Dowgate, Queenshithe and the Fleet. The stench there was dreadful. The city refuse, the corpses of dogs, cats, beggars, lepers and even unwanted babies, were dumped in the Fleet ditch, and, when the rains came, were washed down to the Thames. As they rounded the bend towards Westminster, Ranulf nudged Corbett and pointed to the near bank. Despite the thick refuse which bobbed and dipped on the river surface, water carriers were now filling their barrels full of Thames water to sell on the streets and alleyways of London. Corbett grinned wanly and nodded.

'Always drink wine or beer, Ranulf,' he murmured, then turned to the waterman. 'Is it true?' he asked.

'What?'

'That a sudden inrush of water will suffocate the breath immediately?'

'Oh, yes.' One of the boatmen grinned at a green-faced Maltote. 'Best way to die.'

Ranulf took up the argument as Corbett looked away and thought of old Dame Martha drowning in her bathwater.

At Westminster they disembarked at King's Steps, Corbett pulling the hood of his cloak over his head to avoid recognition by any of his colleagues in the Chancery or the Exchequer for he did not want to waste valuable time in idle chatter. He left Ranulf and Maltote to feed their faces in one of the many pie shops which stood just within the walls of the palace and pushed his way through the crowds, taking the path around the Great Hall to the buildings beyond. Here he crossed to one of the small outbuildings and, making his voice sound pompous, loudly demanded entrance in the King's name. A querulous voice told him to go and jump in the Thames so he knocked again and eventually the door swung open to reveal a tall, gaunt figure, dressed in a long robe of dyed brown fur. The man's face was pale, long and lined, his blue watery eyes squinted in the daylight. Corbett kept his hood up.

'Who are you?' the man demanded sharply.

Corbett pulled the hood back.

'Master Nigel Couville. I am a messenger from the King. He has decreed you are too old and senile for your post and I have been sent to replace you!'

The old man's gaunt face broke into a smile and his thin blue-veined hands clasped Corbett by the arms.

'You are as insulting as ever, Hugh,' he murmured. 'And as stupid! Come in. Unless you want us both soaked to the skin.'

Corbett entered the room. The light inside was dim and the air musty with the smell of candle grease, burnt charcoal, and the lingering odours of leather and parchment. There was a trestle table and a huge stool, the rest of the room being taken up with leather and wooden caskets of all sizes. Some were open to reveal rolls of parchment spilling out on to the floor. Around the walls were shelves which stretched up to the blackened ceiling, bearing more rolls of vellum. It all looked very disorganised but Corbett knew that Couville could select any document he wanted in an instant. This chamber was the muniment room of the Chancery and the Exchequer with records dating back centuries. If a document was issued or received it would be filed in the appropriate place in Nigel Couville's kingdom. Once the senior clerk in the Chancery, Nigel had been given this assignment as a benefice, a reward for long and faithful service to the Crown. Couville had been Corbett's master and mentor when Hugh first became a clerk and, despite the gap in years and experience, they had become and remained firm friends.

Couville searched around the room and brought a small stool forward.

'I can see you are going to be a nuisance,' he observed drily. 'Old habits never change.' He waited until Corbett sat down. 'Some wine?'

Corbett shook his head.

'Not if it's that watered vinegar you always serve!'

Couville went into a small recess and brought out an unstoppered jar and two pewter goblets.

'The best Bordeaux.' He filled a cup to the brim and handed it to Corbett. 'Now I know what Scripture means when it says: "Don't cast your pearls before swine".'

Corbett grinned as he sipped the rich red wine.

'Beautiful!' he murmured.

'Of course it is.' Couville sat opposite him, elbows on his knees, cradling the cup as if it was the Holy Grail. 'St. Thomas à Becket drank the same wine. Do you know, even when he became an ascetic and gave up the pomp of court, even when he fasted, The Blessed Thomas could not abstain from his cups of claret.' Couville smiled at the clerk. 'And you, Hugh, are you well? Maeve too?'

They exchanged banter and gossip about old friends, new acquaintances, and fresh scandals. At last Couville put his goblet down on the floor beside him.

'What is it you want, Hugh?'

Corbett took the faded leather dog's collar out of his wallet.

'There's a motto written on this—"*Noli me tangere*". I think it's from a family crest. Do you recognise it?'

Couville tapped his fingers together and narrowed his eyes.

'Somewhere,' he mused, 'I have heard that phrase.' He rose, scratching his head. 'But the question is, where?'

Corbett rested for an hour whilst his old friend, arms full of sheaves and rolls of parchment, searched the records of armorial bearings and heraldic designs. At first, Couville confidently announced, 'It will not take long, Hugh, believe me.'

But after an hour had elapsed, he stood in the centre of the room, shaking his head.

'Tell me, Hugh, why you want this?' He raised a hand. 'I know your secret business, Master Corbett. I know you despatch letters of which no copy is sent to me.' He sat down again on the stool opposite his former student. 'But why is this motto so important?'

Corbett closed his eyes and described the events at Godstowe: the death of Lady Eleanor Belmont, the subtle treachery of the French and Philip IV's evil intentions. He had almost finished when, as an afterthought, he mentioned the possibility of an assassin from the attainted de Montfort family being present in England. Couville's eyes lit up.

'I have been looking,' he said, 'through the noble families of England and Gascony as they are today. But what happens to a noble family when it is found guilty of high treason?'

'Of course!' Corbett cried. 'The insignia of such a house is destroyed, its titles removed and its lands seized by the Crown!'

Couville rose and went across to a long leaden tube. He undid the top and drew out a thick, yellowing roll of parchment. He laid it carefully out on the long table whilst waving Corbett over. The clerks studied the parchment curiously. It was divided into two; on one side were drawings of Coats of Arms. Corbett recognised a few: Percy de Bohun, Bigod, Mowbray. On the other side of the broad sheet of parchment were Coats of Arms with great black gashes through them.

'What are these?' he murmured.

'This is the Roll of Kenilworth,' Couville replied. 'Simon de Montfort rose in rebellion in 1258. As you know, Edward destroyed his forces amongst the apple orchards of Evesham in 1264. De Montfort was killed, his body hacked to bits and fed to the royal dogs. Some of his companions died with him, a few fled abroad, but most took refuge in Kenilworth Castle in Warwickshire. After a long siege the castle surrendered and de Montfort's rebellion was over.' Couville pointed to the parchment. 'On one side are the armorial bearings of those nobles who supported the King. These others with the black line drawn across their escutcheons belong to the leading supporters of de Montfort. Perhaps we can find your motto amongst them.'

Corbett walked away whilst Couville, muttering to himself, pored over the Roll of Kenilworth.

'Ah!' Couville looked up, face beaming with pleasure. '*Noli me tangere* belonged to the Deveril family.'

'What happened to them?'

Again Couville muttered to himself and wandered round his room checking other rolls and parchments and quartosized journals which contained an index of royal warrants and proclamations. He beckoned Corbett back to the table.

'The Deveril who fought with de Montfort died at Evesham.'

'And were there any heirs?'

Couville shook his head and pointed to the Deveril insignia.

'The clerk who drew this up added a note. Look!'

Corbett squinted down at the faded blue-green ink.

'*Nulli legitimiti haeredes*.'

'No legal issue,' Couville translated. 'According to this, the last of the Deverils died at Evesham.'

Corbett shook his head and picked up the faded leather dog collar.

'So why was this found round the neck of a little lap dog in the forest outside Godstowe?'

'I don't know,' Couville retorted. 'Be logical, Hugh. Just because it was found there doesn't mean it has anything to do with the crimes you are investigating.'

'But surely it must?' Corbett whispered.

Couville put a hand on his shoulder. 'Hugh, only God knows where that collar came from. After the defeat of de Montfort, the market stalls were swamped with the forfeited goods of rebels.'

Corbett wearily rubbed his face in his hands.

'Tell me, Nigel,' he began, 'a young woman and her male companion are found barbarously murdered in the glade of an Oxfordshire forest. Their corpses provide no clue as to their identity. No one comes forward to claim the bodies. No one makes petitions or starts a search for their whereabouts. They are brutally murdered yet their deaths provoke nothing but silence.'

Couville shrugged. 'Go out into the alleyways of London, Hugh. You will find the corpses of the poor, but no one gives a fig!'

'Ah!' Corbett replied. 'But these were well-fed, pampered people, used to luxury. Where did they come from?'

Couville grinned. 'They must have come from abroad.'

Corbett stared hard at his old mentor. Of course he thought. Father Reynard had described both of them as olive-skinned. So were they foreigners?

'If they were foreigners,' he said slowly, 'they must have obtained a royal licence to enter England. Would such a document be difficult to trace?'

Couville nodded.

'Of course. Hundreds enter England every month. Even if such a licence were issued, a copy may not be sent to me.'

Corbett scratched his head and grinned sheepishly.

'I have discovered something,' he said slowly, 'and yet it sheds no light.' Corbett picked up his cloak from the floor where he had tossed it. 'No jests, you know I am the keeper of the King's secrets. I admit you do not see the copies of the letters I send or the reports spies send me.' He fastened his cloak round his shoulders. 'Sometimes I am proud because I have the King's ear, but our royal master is a devious, sly man. He once told me that if his right hand knew what his left was doing, he would cut it off.'

'What is your question, Hugh?'

'I know all the King's spies and agents, whether they be working in the court of Castille or in the Papal Chambers in Rome. But is there anyone else?'

Couville spread his hands.

'You are proud, Hugh, and pride interferes with logic. You know there must be men who work directly for the King. The Earl of Surrey is one. There must be others.'

'Nigel, all royal accounts come to you. Have you ever discovered another name?'

Couville rounded his eyes in mock wonderment.

'Another Corbett? Of course not!' His face grew serious. 'I have seen one name. Payments made to a de Courcy.'

'Who is he?'

'I don't know. All I have seen is the occasional references, monies given *"pro secretis expensis in negotio regis".'*

'For secret expenses on the business of the King,' Corbett translated, and felt a flash of anger at his royal master's deviousness. He took his old friend's hand.

'Nigel, I thank you. One day you will come to Leighton?'

Couville grinned.

'To see Maeve, of course.'

Corbett found Ranulf and Maltote had moved from the pie shop to the nearest tavern. Both looked well pleased after hours of hard drinking and glowered at their sober master's harsh strictures to leave their ale and go back through the pouring rain to King's Steps and another unpleasant journey along the Thames. By the time they had reached London Bridge Maltote and Ranulf had vomited every drop they had drunk and had to spend the rest of the journey listening to the harsh witticisms of the grinning oarsmen.

They disembarked and stayed in a tavern near the Tower for the rest of the day. The next morning they began their gruelling journey up the ancient Roman road which ran from London's city wall into Oxfordshire. Ranulf and Maltote objected vociferously.

'Why this?' Ranulf shouted.

Maltote looked away, not daring to confront this dour but very important royal clerk.

'The reason, Ranulf,' Corbett announced softly, his face only a few inches from his servant's, 'is that I am trying to find out if, from some eighteen months ago, the ale-masters and tavern-keepers along this highway remember two foreigners, a young woman and her male companion. So,' he added sweetly, 'we shall stop at every tavern and ale house along the road. You will not drink anything but watered wine. You will not get drunk and you will help me in this business.'

'But I have told you,' Ranulf replied. 'The landlord at The Bull in Godstowe saw a young man and woman as well as a well-dressed stranger. What more do you want?'

Corbett gathered the reins in his hands.

'Ranulf, everything depends on this. I am searching for a pattern. First, did these two strangers suddenly appear in Oxfordshire or had they travelled from London? If the latter, they probably came from across the seas. Secondly, the young stranger who also passed through Godstowe at the same time—was it just a coincidence, or was he connected with the murder victims?'

Ranulf saw the seriousness in his master's face.

'In which case, Master, the sooner we begin, the sooner we finish!'

Ranulf was correct in his forebodings, the journey proved to be a nightmare. The rain fell incessantly until it seemed they travelled through sheets of water; the old cobbled road turned into a muddy mire, sometimes dangerous with potholes, where a man could plunge waist deep in water. Most of the time they led their horses as they moved from small ale houses and comfortable inns to huge spacious taverns. At first they had no joy and, on the evening of their first day out of London, went to bed so weary they could scarce speak to each other. On the following day, however, at a thatch-roofed tavern which stood on the outskirts of Stokenchurch village, the landlord listened to Corbett's questions and pursed his lips in self-importance.

'Oh, yes,' he declared. 'I remember the pair.'

'Describe them!'

The fellow made a face.

'It's a long time, Master Clerk.'

Corbett raised the silver piece between his fingers.

'But I remember them well,' the landlord continued hastily. 'Well-dressed and fed they were. She was comely, though dressed like a nun with rosary beads in her hand. Her companion,' the landlord shrugged, 'really nothing more than a boy. I thought he was her page.'

'Did they speak English?'

'Oh, no! The noble tongue—French. I asked them where they were going. She just shook her head and smiled but the boy said she was dedicated to God. I could scarcely understand him. They paid their silver and off they went!'

'Did anyone,' Corbett asked, keeping his excitement hidden, 'travel with them?'

The landlord shook his head.

'Did another stranger come here about the same time?'

'Oh, yes,' the tavern-keeper replied. 'A young, well-dressed fop, though armed. He carried a sword and dagger.'

'Did you see his face?'

'No. He arrived early in the morning to break fast just as the woman I mentioned earlier was leaving. He was cloaked and hooded. I thought that strange because the weather was fair.'

'So, how do you know he was well-dressed?'

'There were rings on his fingers. His jerkin was of red satin. As I said, he broke his fast and left within the hour.'

Corbett rose as if about to leave.

'The woman,' Ranulf broke in, 'did she have a lap dog?'

The fellow's rubicund face broke into a gap-toothed grin.

'Yes, she did, a little yappy thing wrapped up in her cloak. She fed it tidbits, morsels of bread soaked in milk. I remember it well. It whined every second it was here.'

Corbett left the tavern elated with what he had found out and they continued their journey to the outskirts of Oxford. Sometimes his questions only provoked blank glances, muttered oaths and shaken heads. But at two other taverns he elicited the same responses he had at Stokenchurch: a young woman and her male companion, both olive-skinned and quiet, with a less than perfect command of English. The boy, apparently a page, always did the talking. The woman seemed pious and withdrawn: indeed, one of the innkeepers actually described her as a nun. More ominously, the well-dressed young stranger always appeared at the tavern around the same time as the mysterious woman and her page were about to leave. At last, to his own satisfaction and Ranulf's apparent pleasure, Corbett decided they had found what they wanted and ordered them to turn back and travel south.

They reached Leighton Manor soaked and saddle-sore. Ranulf and Maltote disappeared like will-o'-the-wisps whilst Corbett received one of Maeve's lectures about the need to rest, as well as the dangers of charging about on the King's business in weather not fit for

the worst of sinners. Corbett heard her out, torn between his desire to sleep and excitement at what he had
discovered.

Once night had fallen and the manor was quiet, he
rose, took out his parchment and again began to fit the
puzzle together. He had the events at Godstowe in some
semblance of order. Now he concentrated on the mysterious murders in the forest. He believed the woman to
have been connected to the attainted Deveril family; the
motto on the dog collar could not be dismissed as coincidence. She was also a foreigner. The Roll of Kenilworth had indicated that there was no legitimate Deveril
issue so was she of some bastard line? If so, the Deverils were still proscribed so why had she been allowed to
enter England and, undoubtedly, to travel to Godstowe, a sensitive place where a former royal mistress
had been incarcerated. Who was the young page, and
the mysterious young fop who had trailed them? And
what happened in the forest outside Godstowe? Who
had murdered whom? It was logical to conclude the
young fop was the assassin but it could have been the
young page or, indeed, a complete stranger. And was
the mysterious woman the murder victim or was it
someone else? She had apparently been travelling to
Godstowe and must therefore have been expected. So
she must have arrived ...

Corbett threw the quill down in disgust. The priory
contained many nationalities and all the nuns, even
Lady Amelia and Dame Agatha, spoke in the Frenchified manner after the fashion of the court. That young
fop... Perhaps it had been the Prince or Gaveston?
Corbett went back to his notes about Lady Eleanor's
death, twisting and turning them. Daylight had long
broken when he reached the inevitable conclusion: he

was ready to confront the murderer. One final piece of
the puzzle remained. A protesting Maltote was roused
and ordered to ride as fast as he could to the royal camp
outside Bedford. Corbett entrusted him with a short
letter in which he asked the King to supply simple answers to what Corbett considered simple questions.
Nevertheless, the clerk was still uneasy: his theory was
well argued but there was little evidence and he wondered if the royal answer would come in time to pre-
vent another murder at Godstowe Priory.

THIRTEEN

AFTER MALTOTE HAD gone, Corbett paced the chambers and galleries of his manor, making himself a nuisance to both Maeve and his household. He found it difficult to sleep at night, anxious lest his delay might cause further tragedy at Godstowe. Should he leave, he wondered, take the swiftest horse in his stable and gallop into Oxfordshire? He dismissed the thought as nonsense. It would be like charging an unknown, hidden enemy. Maeve tried to calm him but Corbett remained uneasy. Early on the morning of the third day after his return, his worst fears were realised. A young groom, spattered from head to toe with mud, half-falling out of the saddle of an exhausted, blown horse, reached Leighton Manor. He gasped out his news even as Corbett, who had hurried down from his chamber, helped him out of the saddle.

'The Lady Prioress,' the fellow muttered. 'She sends greetings and asks you to come urgently!'

'Who's dead?' Corbett grasped the unfortunate messenger by the jerkin, forcing him to stand and look at him. 'Who's been killed?'

The man licked mud-caked lips, eyes half-closing in weariness. Corbett roughly shook him.

'The name?' he rasped.

'Hugh! Hugh!'

Maeve, a robe wrapped around her, came between them. She looked angrily at her husband.

'The poor man's half-dead with fatigue, Hugh!'

Corbett released the messenger whilst muttering his apologies and allowed Maeve and two of the servants to drag the fellow down the hallway to the buttery. Maeve ordered him to be stripped of his travel-stained jerkin and leggings. She forced a cup of watered wine between the fellow's lips whilst Corbett paced up and down.

'Master Clerk!' the fellow rasped hoarsely. 'The Prioress wants you now. Dame Frances is dead!'

'How?'

'A fire in the novice house. She died immediately. The rest of the nuns escaped.'

Corbett went and knelt beside the man.

'And who is the murderer?'

The man blinked red-rimmed eyes.

'Murderer?' he muttered. 'No murder, Master Corbett, an accident.'

Corbett snorted in disbelief.

'And any other news?'

'That's all,' the messenger murmured. 'Except you must go quickly.' And lolling back in the high chair, he promptly fell asleep.

Corbett would have packed his saddle bags immediately and left but Maeve was insistent he wait until the rain storm abated. She had her way and Corbett went back to his chamber, staring out through the window, glaring at the blue-black clouds gathering over Epping Forest.

In the end he was glad he had waited. Late that evening Maltote returned. Again Maeve intervened. She sensed Corbett's mood and insisted Maltote change out of his rain-drenched clothes and have something to eat before her husband began to interrogate him as if he was the King's Master Torturer in the Tower. After

Maltote was rested Corbett and Ranulf met him in the hall. They sat round a huge log fire, the flickering flames casting long shadows against the far wall.

Maltote was exhausted and had some difficulty remembering certain minor details, but, at last, a full account was given. Corbett, ignoring Ranulf's pleas and remonstrances, told them both to get a good night's sleep in preparation for the next morning. Even if the Devil himself was riding the wind which howled and sobbed outside, they would take the road back to Godstowe.

Corbett returned to his own chamber. Maeve sat crouched over a table using a pool of light from a huge candelabra to stab furiously with her needle at a piece of embroidery she had been working on for years. The clerk took a deep breath and hid his smile. Maeve hated needlework, detested it. So whenever she was busy sewing, Corbett always recognised it as a bad sign. This time was no different. His wife, red spots of anger high on her cheeks, gave him a pithy lecture on the rules of hospitality and gentility, so Corbett, like any good mariner facing a squall, decided he would run before the storm. Matters were not helped by Maeve occasionally pricking her finger with the needle, but at last she had had her say. One final thrust at the embroidery and she tossed it on the table with a muttered oath any of the King's soldiers would have admired.

She stood and came over to sit beside him on the bed. 'So you have your news? This nun who died, Sister...?'

'Frances,' Corbett answered.

'You expected her death, didn't you?'

Corbett nodded.

'I knew someone might die.'

'Do you blame yourself, Hugh?'

'Yes and no,' he replied evenly. 'There's murder in Godstowe, and tomorrow I will confront it.'

'And Maltote's errand?'

'He brought me the proof which confirmed my suspicions, but I don't know how to act. There are other pieces still missing.'

He turned and grinned at Maeve. 'If you haven't finished your embroidery,' he continued in mock solemnity, 'you can work at that. There are still matters ...'

Maeve dug her nails deep into the calf of his leg.

'I have had enough of needlework,' she whispered. 'Hugh, you will be gone tomorrow?'

'Yes, at first light.'

She rested her head against his shoulder.

'Be careful,' she murmured. 'I do fear for you.'

Corbett held her close and fought to hide his own deep unease.

CORBETT AND HIS PARTY reached Godstowe late the following evening. The drunken porter allowing them entrance after the usual altercation. Once inside the priory walls Corbett stayed near the gate, demanding the fellow go and bring Lady Amelia down to meet them.

The Prioress seemed to have aged since Corbett had last seen her. Even in the poor light of the flickering torches, Corbett could see how white and haggard her face had become. Her eyes were red-rimmed and circled with deep, dark shadows.

'Master Corbett.' She took both his hands in hers which felt ice cold and clammy to the touch. 'How was your journey?'

'Gruelling,' he replied. 'I am cold, wet—' he looked down at his boots, 'and caked in mud. The rains have turned everything into a morass.'

'Come with me.'

Corbett shook his head.

'I would prefer the guest house, My Lady. The fewer who know I have arrived, the better.'

The Lady Prioress stared back, as if lost in her own thoughts, then shook herself and quickly agreed.

The porter took care of their horses and Lady Amelia, walking like a ghost before them, led them across to the guest house. Dame Agatha was waiting there, her beautiful face pale, eyes concerned. Nevertheless, she greeted Corbett with pleasure.

'Hugh,' she whispered, grasping him by the arm, 'you have returned at last!'

He smiled and touched her gently on the shoulder.

'Dame Agatha, I need a few words alone with Lady Amelia.' He looked over his shoulder at his two servants. 'Ranulf and Maltote need food.' He grinned. 'If they don't eat, I swear they will feed on each other.'

He watched the young nun usher his two companions away and allowed Lady Amelia to take him into the small chamber, really no more than a cell with a table, stool and truckle bed. The Lady Prioress slumped wearily down on the stool as Corbett questioned her about Dame Frances' death. He heard her out in silence, asked a few questions, then went and stood over her.

'Lady Amelia?'

The Lady Prioress sat with arms crossed, staring down at the floor. Corbett crouched down beside her.

'Lady Amelia, tomorrow, in your chapter meeting after the morning Mass, tell your sisters that before

Vespers I will speak to them and explain all that has happened.' He touched her gently under the chin and made her look up. 'My Lady, you must do that.'

'Yes, of course,' she mumbled, her once proud face now crumpled in fatigue and worry. She smiled wanly at Corbett and, like a sleepwalker, rose and left him.

Corbett sat down on the truckle bed, lay back, and though he did not intend to, fell into a deep, dreamless sleep. The next morning he was roused early by the clanging of the priory bells. He felt cold, his arms and legs aching from the rough ride of the previous day. He went and roused a grumbling Ranulf and Maltote. Corbett then cleaned his boots, washed, changed his tunic and ravenously ate the bread and cheese brought up on a platter by an aged lay sister. He gave both Ranulf and Maltote careful instructions; he was going to inspect the burnt-out novice house. After a while they must follow him and be armed with dagger and sword.

'Ranulf, you bring a crossbow. Try not to be seen by anyone. Keep yourself hidden. But should you see anyone, threaten to attack. You are to shoot twice: once as a warning; the second time, make sure you kill whoever it is.'

Corbett repeated his instructions and, throwing his cloak about him, went downstairs. A thick sea mist had rolled in, obscuring most of the priory buildings. Corbett remembered the autumn sun during his previous visit and marvelled how quickly the weather had changed. Nevertheless, the mist helped his cause. He saw shadowy figures slip by him, their faces and footsteps muffled by the fog, as he made his way across to the blackened timber of the novice house. Corbett vaguely recalled the building as a pleasant two-storeyed affair: the fire must have caught the sun-dried timbers and turned it into this blackened mess. He picked his way carefully around the fire-scarred timbers of what was once the kitchen. Here the blaze had started, killing Dame Frances whilst the rest of the nuns, given some warning, had managed to jump out of the windows or find their way down the outside stairs.

Corbett could imagine the scene. The fire raging, greedily licking into the timbers and beams, while the sisters, the serenity of their lives shattered by the roaring flames, fled for safety. Against the far wall were the remains of the hearth. The stone here was so badly scorched the brick had turned to a blackened powder. Corbett stood before the hearth and looked around. Crouching down he dug his fingers into the now cold coal dust, picking it up, sniffing at it carefully. He glimpsed the twisted, molten remains of the metal water bucket: one of the sisters, hearing Dame Frances' screams, had hurried down, opened the scullery door, and had seen her companion, nothing more than a human torch, the iron water bucket lying at her feet.

'The poor woman,' Lady Amelia had told him, 'could do nothing to save Dame Frances, who was being consumed by a sheet of fire. The sister saw the bucket near Dame Frances' feet before she closed the door and ran to raise the alarm for help. Thank God,' Lady Amelia had murmured, 'otherwise more lives would have been lost!'

Corbett now examined the blackened remains of the water bucket. He already had a vague idea of how Dame Frances had been killed and, sniffing carefully at it, caught the foulsome stench of burnt animal fat. He threw the thing away, brushed his fingers and left the blackened ruin. Through the mist he could see the vague outlines of the priory church and followed its outline

round to the ruined oak stump where Lady Eleanor had
received her mysterious messages. He leaned against it,
staring across at the priory wall, shuddering when he
remembered how Gaveston's dogs had nearly tore him
to pieces. He heard a sound behind him. The snapping
of twigs as someone moved over the thick, soggy mass
of fallen leaves.

'I wondered when you would come?' he called, not
bothering to turn. 'I knew you would. Once the Lady
Prioress made her announcement. It's always the way
with assassins, they hate the light of day.'

Corbett spun round quickly and stared at the cowled
shadowy figure before him.

'Let me warn you,' he continued softly, 'my manservant is here somewhere in the mist. He has a crossbow
and his orders. So any knife you have in your hand had
better be put back in its sheath!'

The figure moved forward and one white hand came
up, clawing back both hood and wimple as Dame Agatha shook her lustrous blonde hair free. Corbett had
rarely seen such beauty. The mass of silver hair framed
a perfectly formed face, though the lips seemed thin-
ner, the eyes above the high cheek bones cold and un-
smiling.

'I knew it was you,' he said. 'It had to be. You killed
the Lady Eleanor. You then slew the old one, Dame
Martha, and finally Frances. But who are you?' he
whispered.

'My true name is Agatha de Courcy, so I always told
only half a lie!' She laughed, though her eyes never faltered in their steady gaze.

'And what happened to the real nun who left Gascony?'

'Oh, come, Master Corbett, don't be so coy! Let me see how much of the truth you really know.'

Corbett's hand went beneath his cloak, touching the hilt of the dagger he had hidden there. The young woman moved closer and Corbett realised her hands were still concealed. He took a deep breath and prayed that Ranulf was somewhere watching this small drama being played out.

'Let me see.' He leaned against the old oak tree. 'Eighteen months ago, Mistress Deveril, though she used another name, left Gascony and landed at Dover. She was an orphan of noble lineage with no immediate family. She was accompanied to England by a young page—his name does not concern us. Mistress Deveril took the road skirting London on to the old Roman highway bound for Oxford, Woodstock, and then Godstowe. You knew of her arrival and followed her discreetly. You joined them, probably after they left Godstowe village. You struck up an acquaintance, your offer to accompany them being gratefully accepted. I suspect you were disguised as a personable young man, a merry companion for the Gascons, after what must have been a long and gruelling journey. You were very clever, Agatha, your disguise was perfect. Only the landlord glimpsed you. He, like others, mentioned some young gallant who passed through the village about the same time. But, of course, he can help us no further, being torn to death by Gaveston's dogs. I am correct, am I not?'

The young woman pursed her lips and, for a few brief seconds, smiled sweetly, reminding Corbett of the pious, beautiful, young nun he once knew.

'How did I know?' she asked. 'Who lands at Dover and takes the road to Oxford?'

'Oh, I'll answer all that in due course. But for the rest? Well, you managed to persuade the young lady to leave the Godstowe road for a spot you had previously chosen. Perhaps take a noonday rest and sip some wine. She and her page boy probably dozed. Indeed,' Corbett stirred, staring behind the nun into the mist, 'they may have slept more deeply than they ever intended. The wine you proffered was probably drugged. Once asleep they were easy victims. You slit both their throats, stripped the corpses, changed your own robes and took Deveril's name as well as the letters of introduction. Your only mistake was that the small lap dog Deveril carried was either overlooked or ran away. The woman's belongings you kept for yourself. The rest, including your own clothes, now lie at the bottom of some deep, evil-smelling swamp. The horses?' Corbett shrugged. 'Naturally, you kept one, that and a sumpter pony. The other two were turned loose. A nice gift for some peasant farmer who would keep his mouth firmly shut. Then you come to Godstowe, armed with letters proclaiming you to be Deveril. You take your vows, you are personable, you ingratiate yourself both with Lady Amelia and Lady Eleanor. And who would suspect you?'

Agatha de Courcy nodded.

'Very good!' she murmured. 'Very good indeed!'

'The only person who did catch a glimmer of the truth was poor Dame Frances. You see, I found the collar of the lap dog and it still bore the Deveril's family motto: "*Noli me tangere*". Dame Frances, of course, remembered. She must have seen it on some of the murdered woman's belongings when you first entered the priory but she probably could not place it immediately. And who would she tell? None other but the ever patient, attentive Dame Agatha—so Dame Frances too had to die. A staid nun, with a set routine and customs; you would remember from your few weeks in the novitiate how careful Dame Frances was to douse the fire with water. She always insisted on doing it herself and that made it easy for you. Only the night she died, the bucket she used was full of oil, not water.' Corbett secretly marvelled at the cool composure of his opponent. 'The fire exploded, spilling out on to the hearth, licking at the few drops on the floor, and in seconds Dame Frances was a blazing torch and your secret was safe.'

Agatha joined her hands together, raising her fingers to her lips as if she was a teacher teasing a rather clever pupil.

'Master Corbett, you've told me how I am supposed to have killed this woman, but not the reason why.'

'Don't play games!' Corbett snapped. 'You know the reason. De Montfort was a rebel against the King, a Deveril was one of his generals. According to the records, after de Montfort's defeat, the Deveril line died out so the woman was probably the offspring of some illegitimate issue who fled to Gascony where she was raised to hate Edward of England.'

'And the King would allow a Deveril back into the country?'

'Only if she changed her name. As I have said, I suspect she was an orphan and, using a false name, wrote to Lady Amelia asking permission to join the Nuns of Syon and offering to pay the usual dowry fee. When her request was granted, she sought licence to enter England.' Corbett stared at Agatha. 'Oh, come, what name did she use?'

Agatha gazed coolly back.

'Let me try another tack,' Corbett continued. 'By what name were you called when you entered Godstowe Priory?'

Agatha giggled as if Corbett had posed some riddle.

'I took the religious name of Agatha, really my own, but if you ask the Lady Prioress, she will tell you I entered these walls as Marie Savigny.'

Corbett sighed.

'So it was Marie Savigny you killed in the forest outside Godstowe?'

Agatha chewed on her lip.

'Let us say you are correct, Corbett. How would I know this Marie Savigny was secretly a member of the de Montfort coven, who wanted to come to England to plot mischief, perhaps even murder? And how would I learn when she would come and what route she would take?'

'You know full well! The King himself told you. You're *his* assassin.'

'If Deveril changed her name, why did she carry the motto of her family with her?'

Corbett shrugged.

'Few would recognise it as belonging to a noble family disgraced some forty years earlier. How many nuns at Godstowe, never mind barons at the King's court, would recognise the Deveril motto?'

'But this Marie would speak fluent French.'

'As do you,' Corbett replied. 'As well as others in this benighted place.'

Agatha stepped closer, covering her head with her hood against the drops of rain which dripped from the overhanging branches of the oak tree.

'Oh, Hugh,' she whispered, 'the King was right. You may be squeamish but always so logical.'

'Perhaps I am not,' Corbett answered tartly. 'Marie Savigny or Deveril was murdered in the forest of Godstowe and you appeared in the priory at the same time. Perhaps I should have deduced something immediately from that coincidence. But, of course, Marie Savigny was awaited. She arrived and Godstowe expected no one else.' Corbett's voice trailed off.

'Oh, come, Hugh,' she murmured. 'Don't blame yourself. The woman was a foreigner, travelling under a false name, with no clue as to her real identity. Who would suspect that a pious nun like myself could be guilty of such an act?' She tossed her head. 'And if they did, who would care? Marie planned treason, whilst I enjoy the King's protection.' She smiled. 'I never intended to stay long enough for anything to threaten me. So there's no real mystery.'

'You are right. This is where the real mystery begins. You came here to watch the Lady Eleanor and make sure she did nothing foolish, such as escape or cause scandal at the English court. How alarmed you must have been to discover she was receiving secret messages from some mysterious adviser, who also promised he would arranged her escape from Godstowe! Now, on the Sunday she died, Lady Eleanor abruptly broke with custom, refusing to go to Compline, and someone as alert as you must have seen the secret preparations she had made.' Corbett's hand went back beneath his cloak to the dagger. 'So you went along the corridor to her room. The door was locked but the Lady Eleanor could trust Dame Agatha, who was ever solicitous for her happiness. She let you in, and the rest...' Corbett stared up, noting how the autumn sun was beginning to pierce the heavy mist. 'Like the professional assassin you undoubtedly are, you broke her neck. Quite simple, I understand, for a skilled murderer. A matter of touch, of knowing where to hold and quickly turn.'

The woman's hands suddenly appeared from beneath her cloak. Corbett steeled himself but Agatha only moved the wisps of blonde hair from her forehead. She cocked her head slightly to one side, staring at Corbett, a slight smile on her lips as if he was telling her some merry jest or interesting tale.

'You are a clever clerk,' she replied with an air of mock innocence. 'You really are. But you forget—I was in the sacristy preparing for Compline.'

'Oh, I am sure you were,' Corbett retorted brusquely.

'And remember,' she quipped, 'Dames Martha and Elizabeth recalled seeing Lady Eleanor walking in the grounds below their window just before Compline.' Agatha's eyes rounded in wonderment. 'So,' she murmured, 'how can a woman be dead and at the same time walking, waving her hands and talking?'

'They saw someone. They thought they saw the Lady Eleanor cloaked and hooded, but of course it was you. After you had slain the lady, you took one of her cloaks as well as the ring from her finger. Now suitably disguised, you went downstairs and into the grounds towards the priory church. Dame Martha indeed, as I suspect you were hoping she would, saw you and called out. You turned, shouted something back and waved your hand. Both Dames Elizabeth and Martha were deaf, so whatever you said or how you said it would not cause any alarm. Moreover, being old and poor-sighted, they could not distinguish you from Lady Eleanor. After all, you and the dead woman bore a passing resemblance, being young, fair-haired, and of course you wore her cloak and ring.' Corbett smiled. 'Remember, people see what they think they should see.'

'But what would have happened if someone had met me?'

'But who would dare approach the aloof Lady Eleanor? The Lady Prioress was in church, the other nuns preparing for Compline, and it was only a short walk. Once you reached the sacristy door at the back of the church, you took off and hid both robe and ring and entered the sacristy as Dame Agatha, the dutiful nun. You have established, at least in the eyes of the others who weren't watching precise times, that at the very moment you were in the church, the Lady Eleanor was still alive.

'Of course, you made another mistake, didn't you? You were hoping that Dame Martha, like everyone else, saw what you wanted them to see: a woman wearing Lady Eleanor's cloak and ring must *be* Lady Eleanor. But the old nun was sharp. When you waved your hand, the huge sapphire ring flashed in the sunlight. Poor-sighted as they were, they caught the brilliant light of the jewel, but you had mistakenly put it on your left hand, whereas Lady Eleanor always wore the ring on the right. The old nun remembered this, hence her constant little riddle: "*Sinistra non dextra*"—"on the left, not the right". She could not understand it.'

Agatha drew a little closer. Corbett noted she had lost some of her arrogance and was more watchful. She kept squarely in front of him, as if trying to block his view of what might be happening behind her.

'Let us say,' she replied quietly, 'that it happened as you described. I admit a cloak would not be missed, but a precious ring? Remember, the Lady Prioress found the corpse at the bottom of the stairs!'

'Of course you know that's a lie! The Lady Prioress, anxious about the whereabouts of the Lady Eleanor, left the refectory and went back to the darkened convent building. They found Lady Eleanor dead in her chamber and, concerned about the possible consequences, took her body to the foot of the stairs to make it look like an accident. It was dark, they were frightened, and would not notice the ring was missing. If anyone did, the logical explanation was that it had fallen off. Of course, they sent for you to help take the corpse back up to the chamber. That's when you thrust the ring back on to the dead woman's finger.' Corbett paused. 'Most subtle,' he added. 'You knew Lady Amelia would find the corpse and, for the good name of Godstowe, try to disguise Lady Eleanor's death as an accident. You, an assassin, cleverly used innocent nuns such as Lady Amelia and Dame Martha to protect yourself. Whether they liked it or not, they became your accomplices; Lady Eleanor's death was made so confusing, no one would ever discover the truth.'

Corbett, now concerned by the smiling malevolence which confronted him, pulled the dagger from its sheath.

'That,' he continued, 'would have been the end of the matter, but Dame Martha had to chatter and threaten to talk to the Lady Prioress. Did you understand her riddle?'

Agatha smiled.'

'You found killing her easy,' Corbett continued. 'Old Martha prepared a bath. She put up a screen and locked her chamber door. You, the ever caring sister, came along, probably with a bar of soap. The old nun gets out of the bath, leaving a trail of water on the floor as she unlocks the door. You give her the soap, chattering merrily as Dame Martha goes behind the screen back into the tub. She was an old lady, her death would have been quick. Perhaps you pulled her by the ankles, dragging her head beneath the water? Any sailor would tell you a swift inrush of water to the mouth and nose makes you speedily lose consciousness. You pick up the cake of soap and leave as quietly as you entered.'

Agatha nodded.

'Most logical,' she murmured. 'A concise, lucid description.' Her lips parted in a snarl. 'You should have taught at schools at Oxford.'

'And not come here,' Corbett added quickly. 'I upset your little plans, did I not? But, of course, others unwittingly protected you. Father Reynard, who sent messages to de Craon; Gaveston and his dogs; the Prince of Wales and his infatuation with his favourite. And, of course,' Corbett concluded bitterly, 'our most sovereign lord the King, with his penchant for mystery and secrecy.' Corbett walked towards her. 'I suppose,' he remarked drily, 'the only good deed you performed was to dissuade Lady Eleanor from taking the powders Gaveston sent her. The royal catamite must have been perplexed.'

Agatha smiled.

'Yes, I did. I watched Gaveston and his meddling tricks. On no account could Lady Eleanor die of poisoning. Such powders might be traced. If the good lady had to die, there had to be no link with the Prince. A nice, subtle mystery which would keep everyone guessing.' She shrugged. 'Naturally, I had to watch de Craon as well.'

'But the rest?' Corbett asked. 'And the deaths of two nuns? Surely the King ordered none of these?'

Dame Agatha opened her hand.

'No dagger, Hugh,' she whispered. 'For what I did *was* on the King's instructions.' She thrust the yellowing piece of parchment at him. 'Read it!'

Corbett unrolled the small sheet of vellum and quickly scanned the contents.

'Edward by the Grace of God, etc., to all Sheriffs, Bailiffs, etc. The bearer of this document, Agatha de Courcy, must be given every aid and assistance for what she has done has been done for the sake of the Crown and the good of our realm.'

Corbett looked at the faded, secret seal of his royal master.

'To quote Pilate, My Lady, what has been written has been written.' He looked squarely at her. 'But it does not make it right. The King would not have ordered Lady Eleanor's murder.'

'It was necessary!' Agatha snapped. 'She was going to flee. My orders were quite explicit. I was to stop the Deveril woman and proceed to Godstowe, do whatever was necessary to ensure Lady Eleanor did not embarrass the Crown or the English court.' She shook her head. 'Moreover, I was tired of this God-forsaken place. A whey-faced, pale-eyed, former mistress, and nuns more concerned with their own glory and bellies!'

'The Lady Prioress?' Corbett asked suddenly.

Agatha shook her head.

'She knows nothing.' She plucked the document deftly from Corbett's fingers. 'Now, Hugh, I must go.' She stood on tip-toe and kissed him gently on the cheek. 'Perhaps we will meet again. I hope so.' She smiled. 'Now you know the truth, the Lady Prioress is no longer needed and Ranulf must be getting as cold as I am.' She waved her hand, her fingers skimming his. 'Farewell!'

Corbett watched her disappear into the mist.

'Ranulf!' he shouted. 'Ranulf!'

But only a grey, mocking silence answered him. Corbett tugged his cloak around him and strode back towards the priory building, not caring whether he shattered the peace of a convent where so many dark deeds had been committed.

'Ranulf!' he bawled. 'For God's sake, man!' He had almost reached the guest house door. 'Ranulf!' he roared, and was greeted by the clatter of footsteps on the stairs.

His servant, followed by an even more wild-eyed Maltote, came tumbling down, carrying belts and cloaks.

'For God's sake, man!' Corbett shouted. 'You were supposed to follow me.'

Ranulf, sleepy-eyed, stared anxiously back.

'I meant to, Master. But Maltote fell asleep again. I tried to rouse him but I couldn't so I sat on the bed to pull my boots on and the next minute I, too, was asleep.'

Corbett closed his eyes.

'Ranulf, Ranulf,' he whispered.

'What, Master?'

'Nothing,' Corbett sighed. 'I just thank God Mistress Agatha did not know you were asleep. Look,' he continued, 'we must be gone soon. Break your fast and pack our bags. Make sure the horses are fed and settle what debts we owe. In an hour we will be back on the road again.'

And, ignoring his servant's muttered groans, Corbett went round to the priory church to Lady Amelia's lodgings. He found the Prioress alone in her chamber, the table before her strewn with manuscripts. She looked red-eyed and white-faced, slightly fearful and anxious. She rose as Corbett entered.

'Master Corbett,' she pleaded, 'I delivered your message.'

Corbett threw himself on to a bench beside the wall.

'Sit down, My Lady,' he said wearily. 'There will be no need for that. You have lost another member of your Order. Dame Agatha will be leaving, if she has not gone already. I suggest you let her go in peace. Do not mention her name again or send angry letters to the Bishop.'

'What are you saying?'

'Dame Agatha was no nun.' Corbett smiled thinly.

'She was here for Lady Eleanor?'

'Yes,' Corbett replied. 'She was here, like I am, because of the Lady Eleanor. Dame Agatha was the key to all the deaths here at Godstowe.' He raised his hand to still the Lady Prioress's intended outburst. 'The least you know the better, My Lady. Dame Agatha is guilty though you, too, are not blameless.'

The Lady Prioress squirmed in her chair.

'What do you mean?'

'You know full well,' Corbett retorted. 'The Lady Eleanor was murdered because she was planning to flee Godstowe. Secret messages were left in her room and in the ruined oak tree between the priory church and the wall. You know it well. You should do—you wrote the messages and left them there.'

'Why should I do that?'

'Oh, come, My Lady, you know full well. The King ordered Eleanor Belmont here and you hated it. It disturbed the harmony and peace of this little priory. It brought the unwanted attention of the Prince and Lord Gaveston as well as the unexpected intrusion of the French envoy, Monsieur de Craon, who could not be lightly turned away. Now, the Lady Eleanor was a young woman. She could have lived for years. In time she might even have threatened your own position. So you hired horsemen, God knows from where, though there are enough ex-soldiers around to do anything for silver.'

Corbett rose and filled a goblet of wine. He looked at the Lady Amelia questioningly but she shook her head. Corbett gulped the rich, red wine, relishing the way it warmed his stomach.

'You prepared the ground well—those messages hidden away in the old oak tree. At first I thought someone climbed the wall and put them there, but on the night I was chased by Gaveston's dogs, I found that was an impossible feat. The walls are sheer and any intruder would eventually be noticed, as he would if he came through the gate. I concluded the writer must be inside the priory.' Corbett paused. 'At first I thought it was Dame Agatha, but only you had the power and money to hire horsemen. Moreover, I could never understand why, on the very day horsemen were seen outside the priory, you permitted the Lady Eleanor not to attend Compline. On any other occasion you would have demanded her attendance. Moreover, you must have heard about or seen the horsemen hiding in the trees. Lady Eleanor's absence from Compline and the presence of these riders were no coincidence. You were hoping she would leave. The blame would fall on others and you and your priory would be well rid of her. But, of course, matters went terribly wrong. Lady Eleanor was killed and the riders left empty handed.'

The Prioress just stared back at him.

'You were frightened I might hear about these riders. That's why, the morning the porter took me down to the forest, you sent Dame Catherine after me to see where we were going. My Lady, I am correct?'

'Yes, Corbett,' she replied harshly. 'You are correct. I resented Lady Eleanor Belmont's presence here. We may not be the strictest Order in the realm but God-stowe is a nunnery not a refuge for former whores. Moreover, I disliked the Lady Eleanor intensely, with her sorrowful face and moping ways. I went to Oxford on business. You know the city well. Desperate men can be hired. They had their orders. On that Sunday evening Lady Eleanor was instructed to meet them outside the Galilee Gate. Of course, to achieve that I needed the former whore's co-operation so I secretly sent her the messages.' She shrugged. 'The rest you know.'

'What if she had left?' Corbett asked. 'I know suspicion would fall on the Prince, Lord Gaveston, the French, or even the King. But what was intended?'

The Lady Prioress smiled.

'Oh, nothing terrible. We have a sister house in Hainault just outside Dordrecht. Lady Eleanor would have been comfortable but securely kept, and I would have been happy.' She pulled a piece of parchment over to her. 'Now, Master Corbett, I am sure you must be as busy as I am.'

She stared blankly down at the desk and, when she looked up, the clerk had gone.

CONCLUSION

In the great hall of Westminster Palace, Edward of England sat on his throne beneath the great hammer-beamed roof. Huge scarlet and gold banners hung overhead and members of his household had covered the walls with silken tapestries and thick silver-and-gold-encrusted cloths. The floor in front of the dais had been swept clean and fresh rushes, cut from the river's edge, placed over the boards and sprinkled with herbs. Royal serjeant-at-arms in full steeled armour were ranged in serried ranks on either side of the throne, swords drawn, hilts point down. On each side of the King were the leading magnates and bishops of the realm and in front, seated along a trestle table covered in damask cloths, sat the senior clerks of the Chancery and Exchequer. Corbett was in the centre. The table in front of him had now been cleared of all parchments except one long document, freshly inscribed and sealed: the betrothal indenture affiancing Edward, Prince of Wales, heir apparent to the English throne, to Isabella, 'the sole and beloved daughter' of Philip IV of France.

Corbett watched de Craon approach and fix Philip IV's seal to the bottom of the document. The French envoy then went across and placed his hand on the huge copy of the gospels held between the gnarled fingers of Robert Winchelsea, Archbishop of Canterbury. De Craon, resplendent in robes of blue and white samite, proclaimed in clipped Norman French: 'How Philip, King of France, rejoiced that the betrothal had taken place which would be the basis of lasting peace and friendship between England and France.'

Corbett, his emotions masked by a diplomatic smile, watched de Craon call on God and his angels to witness how France intended a lasting peace. In any other circumstances the English clerk would have burst out laughing: de Craon, given any opportunity, would break or twist the treaty whenever it suited him or his devious master in the Louvre Palace. At last de Craon stopped speaking. On Edward's behalf, Corbett rose and replied with a similar tissue of official lies, and went round the table to exchange the kiss of peace with his arch-enemy. Behind him Edward of England sat watching through heavy-lidded eyes, though his mind was elsewhere, his body tense with fury that his son had chosen to remain at Woodstock with his catamite rather than attend this solemn betrothal ceremony. His son claimed he was unwell! The King ground his teeth together. By the time the week was over, he would give his son good cause to be unwell! The King leaned forward, watching Corbett and de Craon embrace and exchange the final kiss of peace. After the kiss, de Craon pulled his head back, a false smile on his face.

'One day, Corbett,' he hissed, 'I will kill you!'

Corbett bowed and muttered back, 'One day, Monsieur, as you have recently, you will try and fail!'

Again the false smiles, the perfunctory bows, the trumpets in the gallery braying out their silver din, and the ceremony was over. De Craon bowed towards the throne, snapped his fingers for his colleagues to follow and, turning on his heel, walked quickly out of the huge hall. Edward rose, unfastened his gold-encrusted cloak and tossed it to de Warenne.

'Thank God that mummery is over! De Warenne, I want to see Corbett now in my chamber. No one else to be present!'

'Of course, Your Grace.'

Edward's eyes narrowed.

'Less of the sarcasm, Surrey. And when you have done that, I want your fastest messenger to be on the road to Woodstock within the hour. He is to tell my sweet son that I wish words with him tomorrow—here.' The King jabbed a finger at the Earl. 'And a message for my Lord Gaveston as well. If he is in England by the end of the week, I will proclaim him wolfshead, an outlaw to be killed on sight!' Edward heartily clapped the Earl on the shoulder. 'And after that, we march north to give the Scots a lesson they'll never forget.'

Corbett found the King lounging in a window seat, a huge, deep-bowled goblet of wine in his hands.

'Ah, Hugh.'

Corbett's heart sank. Whenever the King played the bluff, hearty warrior, the clerk always smelt treachery.

'While you and de Craon were kissing each other's arses out there, I was thinking of your report about the business at Godstowe. You did well, Hugh.'

'Thank you, Your Grace.'

The King rose, poured a goblet of wine and thrust it into the clerk's hand.

'I am sorry I did not tell you about Mistress Agatha.'

'Your Grace, I have already protested. How can I gather information if there are people like her of whom I know nothing? Such men or women pose a threat. They need to be watched and guided.'

'Like the Lady Agatha?'

'Yes, Your Grace, like the Lady Agatha.'

The King looked slyly at Corbett.

'True, she acted beyond her orders, but if the Lady Eleanor had escaped . . .' He allowed his words to hang in the air.

'If the Lady Eleanor had escaped, Your Grace,' Corbett replied sharply, 'she would have been recaptured.'

'True! True!' the King murmured. 'But Agatha . . .' His voice trailed off.

Corbett slammed the wine cup down on the table.

'Mistress de Courcy may well have killed to protect Your Grace, but she also killed to protect herself. Three women died for no good cause, two of them nuns; women who died simply for being in the wrong place at the wrong time. Who will answer for their blood?'

'You are being sanctimonious, Corbett!' the King snapped.

'In Italy,' Corbett replied slowly, 'there is a new breed of man who maintains that whatever the Prince wishes has the force of law. Is that what they mean, Your Grace?'

'Perhaps.'

'So if Your Grace's mind changes and you wish my death . . . ?'

The King turned on him, lips parted in a snarl. He threw the wine cup down at Corbett's feet.

'Shut up, Clerk!'

'Three women,' Corbett continued evenly. 'Three innocent women died. Do you know what they call you in the halls of Oxford? The new Justinian of the West. The great law giver. They talk of your parliaments, of your famous speech about what affects all should be approved by all. I wonder what Dame Martha and Dame Frances would think of that? Agatha de Courcy is a murderess. She not only walks free, she flaunts your authority for doing as she did.'

The King kicked at the rushes.

'You'd best go, Corbett!' he said quickly. He looked up and smiled. 'Maeve is *enceinte*. If it's a boy, Corbett, I want him called Edward.' The King looked away. 'What you did at Godstowe I shall not forget. I understand you want Maltote in our household? You are welcome to him. Now, go! After Michaelmas you must return.'

Corbett bowed and walked towards the door.

'Hugh!'

Corbett turned.

'Yes, Your Grace?'

'Agatha de Courcy... leave her to me.'

Corbett bowed again and closed the door behind him.

Edward stood for a while, walked over to the window and reflected on what Corbett had said. In his heart Edward knew the clerk was right: de Courcy was an assassin. Edward had used her before. He called her his 'subtle device' against the deadly machinations of his enemies. Almost forty years ago, he had smashed the de Montforts but still they continued to harry him. Oh, he had heard about the Deveril woman, the illegitimate issue of one of the de Montfort's generals. Deveril's bastard son had fled abroad, gone to Bordeaux and married into a local noble family. His offspring had been Marie Deveril, a girl brought up to hate the King of England. He had watched her from afar: when she used a false name to apply for a license to travel to England and enter the Priory at Godstowe, he had suspected she was intent on stirring up trouble, to strike whenever opportune against Edward or his family. Perhaps Lady Eleanor had been her intended victim.

Or, Edward shivered, perhaps she had aimed higher, hoping that the Prince of Wales would visit the priory, or indeed himself. Edward had let Deveril come, wanting her out in the open, whilst he gave de Courcy her secret instructions. She was to follow and kill the Deveril woman, take her place, and go to Godstowe to keep the Lady Eleanor under close and careful watch.

Edward smiled bleakly to himself. And who would suspect? De Courcy always dressed as a man, acting the young Frenchified fop with rich clothes bought by the Treasury, and speaking in a drawling French accent which would be the envy of any courtier. De Courcy would kill Deveril, keep matters at Godstowe under view, report on the Prince's doings at Woodstock and search out the truth behind the idle rumour that the Prince had secretly married his former whore. No one would suspect Agatha had killed Deveril. Or, if they did, who would care? The Deverils were traitors and Edward had given de Courcy a written pledge he would defend her. Of course, he'd kept it quiet from Corbett: the clerk was an excellent master spy but his tender conscience might balk at the silent assassination of a woman and her page. All had gone well until Lady Eleanor's death and de Courcy's strange silence. Oh, de Courcey had informed him how she'd intended to tell the truth eventually, but how could he trust her? What authority did she have to decide who lived and died? Corbett was right. Only a Prince could do that. Edward peered out of the window. He saw Corbett in the courtyard below, smiling and laughing as he chatted to Ranulf and Maltote.

'If it's a boy, call him Edward,' the King murmured to himself. He felt a stab of envy at his clerk's good fortune. 'I have no son,' he whispered.

He leaned against the wall and watched Corbett and his party mount and leave the courtyard. The King went across to a small desk, picked up the quill from the writing tray and carefully wrote out a short message. He then took some heated wax, marking it with his secret seal before shouting for an attendant. A few minutes later John de Warenne, Earl of Surrey, sauntered in.

'Your Grace?'

Edward continued to stare out of the window.

'Your Grace, you sent for me?'

'There's a woman,' Edward began slowly. 'She lives in a house opposite The Swindlestock tavern near the church of St. Catherine's by the Tower. She is both a traitress and a murderess.'

'Her name?'

'Agatha de Courcy.' Edward cleared his throat. 'She must die. Her crimes are self-confessed but for reasons of state cannot be divulged. You will take care of it, de Warenne. Make sure it is fast. Let her suspect nothing.'

'Your Grace, on what authority do I do this?'

The King smiled to himself, and without turning proffered the piece of parchment he had just written upon. De Warenne took it and read the words carefully.

'What the bearer of this document has done,' it ran, 'he has done for the sake of the Crown and the good of the realm.'

De Warenne bowed and slipped silently from the room.

AUTHOR'S NOTE

In 1301 Edward I and his son did have a violent altercation: the reason for this dispute is not known though the Prince of Wales certainly had a mistress by whom he had an illegitimate son. In the light of Philip IV's negotiations to marry his daughter off to the Prince of Wales, the mistress may have been 'retired' to accommodate French wishes. A similar move against the Prince's friend, Gaveston, may also have figured in the row between King and Prince.

This betrothal and marriage had been imposed upon England by a Papacy very much in the pocket of Philip IV; Edward of England had to accept it or lose the beautiful, rich vineyards of Gascony in southwest France. The treaty was signed in 1298 and, for ten years, Edward of England squirmed like a snake trying to extricate himself from it. Philip of France, however, held fast. There are documents in both the Record Office, London, and the Bibliothèque Nationale, Paris, which demonstrates how Philip was going to use this marriage to make one grandson Duke of Gascony and another King of England. As in modern diplomacy, such ventures can backfire; Philip's three sons failed to beget an heir and Isabella's son, the great warrior King Edward III, immediately laid claim to the the throne of France and plunged that country into a hundred years of wasteful war.

Edward's infatuation with Piers Gaveston is well documented. Most historians concede that Edward was bisexual; the young prince openly declared that he loved his favourite 'more than life itself'. Gaveston was a Gascon upstart whose mother was burned as a witch and there were allegations that he, too, dabbled in the Black Arts. Eventually King Edward I exiled him but when his son became King, Gaveston was recalled and made Duke of Cornwall. The young king did marry Isabella but handed all of Philip IV's wedding gifts, including the bridal bed, over to Gaveston. The royal favourite also organised their coronation and made a complete nonsense of it; the food was cold, spectators were killed in the crush, and Gaveston upset the established nobles of England by his pre-eminence during the coronation ceremony. The young Gascon made matters worse by being handsome, an excellent jouster and very witty in choosing nicknames for Edward's nobles. He remained witty even unto death.

In 1312 the English barons captured him and led him to Blacklow Hill in Warwickshire. Gaveston turned to one of his captors, the Earl of Warwick, and said, 'My Lord, surely you will not spoil my looks by striking off my head?' Warwick happily obliged and struck Gaveston to the heart with his dagger. The young Edward was distraught. He had Gaveston's body embalmed and kept in his palace at Kings Langley until the Church forced him to carry out the funeral ceremony.

There is an interesting link between Edward II's favourites and the English Royal family in the last decade of the twentieth century. After Gaveston's death, Edward chose a new favourite, the very sinister but able Hugh de Spencer, whose tomb can still be seen in Tewkesbury Abbey, Gloucestershire. De Spencer's control over the young king led to civil war between Edward and his Isabella. The Queen was victorious. De

Spencer died a horrible death and, according to unpublished chronicle, the Commons took an oath never to allow a de Spencer to become King. The present marriage of Charles, Prince of Wales, to Diana Spencer, one of Hugh's descendants and mother of a future King, perhaps lifts the curse on one of England's most ancient families.

NO MARDI GRAS FOR THE DEAD

D. J. Donaldson

First Time in Paperback

An Andy Broussard/Kit Franklyn Mystery

NO BED OF ROSES...

Criminal psychologist Kit Franklyn has had experience with skeletons in the closet—but not in her own backyard. The discovery of a body's remains leads her boss, New Orleans chief medical examiner Andy Broussard, to some interesting facts: female, twenty-five, twenty years dead, a prostitute...and brutally murdered.

Two more violent deaths soon follow: an aquarium shark consumes the limbs of one individual; someone else takes a messy plunge at one of the city's classiest hotels. The trail leads back two decades to a night of violent passion in the French Quarter among a group of medical students...and to a present-day killer with more than just secrets buried in his own backyard.

"...keeps you coming back for more." —*Booklist*

Available in March at your favorite retail stores.

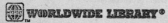

DEADSTICK
Terence Faherty

AN OWEN KEANE MYSTERY

Why would a millionaire in his sixties, with no accusers to answer to or social ambitions to protect, move to reopen a forty-year-old scandal?

That's what ex-seminarian Owen Keane, an introspective, introverted, often idiosyncratic law-firm researcher is being paid to find out.

The firm has been discreetly retained by Robert Carteret, seeking answers to the mystery surrounding the plane crash that killed his brother and socialite fiancée. Now the archives are buttoned up tight, and Owen has to fall back on the gossip.

Following a cold trail of the dead, he finds something alive and almost forgotten—and threatening—as he winds his way backward to the players in the mystery: the murderer, the victim and the crime.

"Plenty of intellectual guts."—*New York Times Book Review*

Available in May at your favorite retail stores.

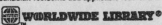

FIRST WIFE, TWICE REMOVED
CLARE CURZON

A THAMES VALLEY MYSTERY

First Time in Paperback

TOXIC LOVE

Two disturbing deaths have Superintendent Mike Yeadings's team spread out from the Thames Valley to Amsterdam, looking for answers.

The first victim, Penny Winter, a divorced mother of two, dies as a result of food poisoning. Someone sent her tainted pâté with intent to kill. The second victim, Anneke Vroom, was a young Dutch national found crammed into an antique mahogany chest. She was shot full of heroin—and pregnant.

As the investigation of the separate incidents develops in sinister parallel, the men and women of the Thames Valley Police Force will confront more untimely deaths before tangled skeins come together to create a diabolical tapestry of murder.

"Clever misdirection."   *—Kirkus Reviews*

Available in May at your favorite retail stores.

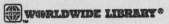